PRAISE FOR THE WORK OF PAULETTE KENNEDY

The Artist of Blackberry Grange

"Original, exceptional, and a fascinating read from start to finish, *The Artist of Blackberry Grange* by Paulette Kennedy is an extraordinary novel . . . Especially and unreservedly recommended."

—*Midwest Book Review*

"*The Artist of Blackberry Grange* is an utter gothic delight. [Paulette Kennedy's] signature use of an atmospheric Southern setting, evocative prose, and gothic suspense creates a winning combination. Kennedy keeps readers hooked until the very last page. Pitch-perfect pacing combined with very real—very human—characters make this a novel that will stick with you long after the final pages."

—Jess Armstrong, *USA Today* bestselling author of *The Curse of Penryth Hall*

"Paulette Kennedy has once again proven herself to be a true master of gothic fiction. *The Artist of Blackberry Grange* is unsettling, atmospheric, and deeply moving, a haunting and heartfelt exploration of love and letting go. Perfect for readers who appreciate both the beauty and darkness of the human experience."

—Molly Greeley, author of *Marvelous*

The Devil and Mrs. Davenport

"With a mystery that steadily builds, this gothic novel masterfully captures the horrors and sexism of 1950s suburbia. A bewitching page-turner with author Kennedy's signature: a strong heroine who cleverly navigates twist after twist."

—*Booklist*

"Paulette Kennedy is the modern Daphne du Maurier with her dazzling ability to usher readers into any point in history while making it feel vibrant and fresh with her magical, gothic touch. Her newest novel deftly captures both the simplicity and horrors of being a midcentury housewife in a patriarchal society. With gorgeous lyricism and a determined heroine, the story spellbinds from the first page until the harrowing end."

—Heather Levy, Anthony Award–nominated author of *Walking Through Needles*

"Mesmerizing from start to finish! Paulette Kennedy delivers suspense, empathy, compassion, resilience, and just a hint of the paranormal in a way that keeps the reader guessing until the last page."

—Mansi Shah, bestselling author of *The Direction of the Wind*

The Witch of Tin Mountain

"With LGBTQ representation, Kennedy's captivating second novel is perfect for historical fiction readers who enjoy a bit of witchcraft, folklore, and mystery."

—*Booklist*

"Kennedy weaves an achingly beautiful tale full of dark folklore, powerful women, and spine-tingling suspense. Deirdre's and Gracelynn's stories will grab you by the heart and stay with you long after the last page."

—Hester Fox, author of *A Lullaby for Witches*

"Brilliant and enthralling, *The Witch of Tin Mountain* left me breathless. Gracie and Deirdre are two unforgettable characters, and their stories twine in an intricate braid of complex beauty. Kennedy has secured her place as one of the very best in historical fiction."

—Olivia Hawker, bestselling author of *One for the Blackbird, One for the Crow*

Parting the Veil

"Well written, the novel admirably recalls Emily Brontë's *Wuthering Heights* and Henry James's *Portrait of a Lady*."

—Historical Novel Society (Editor's Choice)

"A beautiful, crumbling mansion in the English countryside; a charming but enigmatic viscount; ghosts; rumors; and a labyrinth of dark secrets, lies, twists, and well-executed turns . . . As if that wasn't enough, add rich atmosphere and an American-heiress heroine determined to settle her own future. Kennedy has crafted a delicious, romantic gothic mystery that will keep readers guessing even as they're feverishly turning the final pages."

—Megan Chance, author of *A Splendid Ruin*

"A darkly romantic old-school gothic novel with a gasp-inducing twist that's decidedly new school. In this lushly detailed page-turner, Paulette Kennedy piles on all the haunted-house tropes you could hope for, and then some. Read this one with the lights on."

—Kris Waldherr, author of *The Lost History of Dreams*

The TWO DEATHS *of* LILLIAN CARMICHAEL

OTHER TITLES BY PAULETTE KENNEDY

The Artist of Blackberry Grange

The Devil and Mrs. Davenport

The Witch of Tin Mountain

Parting the Veil

The Two Deaths of Lillian Carmichael

A Novel

PAULETTE KENNEDY

This is a work of fiction. Names, characters, organizations, places, events, and incidents are either products of the author's imagination or are used fictitiously.

Published by Lake Union Publishing, Seattle

www.apub.com

EU product safety contact:
Amazon Media EU S. à r.l.
38, avenue John F. Kennedy, L-1855 Luxembourg
amazonpublishing-gpsr@amazon.com

ISBN-13: 9781662531286 (paperback)
ISBN-13: 9781662531293 (digital)

Cover design by Kimberly Glyder
Cover image: © Lauren Rautenbach / ArcAngel Images; © Renphoto, © NSA Digital Archive / Getty

Printed in the United States of America

For those in the shadows, and those in the light

CONTENT NOTE

While most scenes are not graphic in nature, this novel contains references to murder, suicide, and death and descriptions of dead bodies, sexual abuse, child neglect and endangerment, racism, and chattel slavery.

ONE

Charleston, South Carolina

January 1853

These three things I know for certain: Arsenic has no taste, I did not kill my sister, and tomorrow, I will die.

I look through the barred window at the exercise yard two stories below, where Claudia Hamilton sits, her dingy, prison-issue skirts fanning out on the bench. A crow pecks at the ground near her feet. Claudia loves those birds. Talks to them. Sings to them in her high-pitched, reedy voice. Claudia also kicked me in the shins yesterday, for no good reason apart from boredom. Boredom is in ready supply here at the jail, but for me, the endless despair and monotony will soon be over. In the morning, I'll become the second woman ever to be hanged in South Carolina history. I wonder what my predecessor, Lavinia Fisher, thought about in her final hours. I wonder if she was truly as innocent as she claimed to be. As innocent as I am. The stories say she was a coldhearted seductress who lured travelers to her roadside inn, only to poison them so her husband might rob them. But how much is true? No one will ever know, for certain. The evidence used to convict Lavinia was circumstantial. Just like with me.

The door to my cell creaks open, and the matron, Mrs. Banks, trudges in, feet shuffling across the straw-covered floor. "Brought your breakfast."

I mouth the words silently as she says them. The same words, every morning, for the past two years. Mrs. Banks has only a handful of phrases, really, all of them said in a lilting Cockney accent:

Brought your breakfast.

Wash your bits.

Outside with you.

Lights out a'nine.

I sit at the narrow ledge that serves as my table. Mrs. Banks places a bowl of porridge in front of me, sprinkled with cinnamon (Cook must be feeling kind this morning), and a tin cup filled with bitter, tepid coffee.

"You can have whatever you like for dinner tonight. Anything at all." Mrs. Banks presses her thin lips together in something that might have resembled a smile in her younger years.

"My last meal?"

She grunts, her gray eyes sliding to the window. "I suppose it is. Think on it, dove. I'll be back in a bit."

After she goes, I run my spoon through the thin gruel, lifting it to my mouth with a trembling hand. Memories of the food from my life on the outside drift through my head, tempting me. Oyster roasts in the fall. Veal cutlets, apple fritters, syllabub. I don't miss much about the past, but I do miss the food. I often helped Mother decide our menus for banquets and holidays, deliberating over the enticing choices in our cook's repertoire. I was preparing to run a household of my own soon, after all. At twenty-one, I was betrothed to Second Lieutenant William Cameron—freshly commissioned from the Citadel and easy to look at as a June day. We were going to live on the East Battery, in his family's grand, three-story mansion, with wide windows overlooking the harbor.

But my sister stole William from me. Rebecca was ever stealing from me—whether it was a simple thing, like my best ribbon for her bouncing curls, or our mother's attention. She used her frail constitution to her benefit, begging indisposition when it suited her needs, only to emerge from her moribund state whenever an engraved invitation arrived bearing her name. She was the cleverest of thieves, a born charmer with bright-blue eyes, blooming cheeks, and fragile, doll-like beauty.

"She needs someone to take care of her, Lil. More than you do." That's what William told me, on that summer day he asked for his ring back, so he might give it to Rebecca instead. Spurned and shamed by his rejection, I decided to become a governess, only to be forced to abandon my studies at Miss Murden's Seminary School to help my mother care for Rebecca in her final illness. Two weeks later, my sister was dead.

Everyone believed I'd killed Rebecca out of jealousy. When I'd taken the stand to plead my innocence, even Mother's tearful eyes had accused me. But although my very life depended on it, I could not bring myself to tell the judge and jury the full truth. And now, because of my reluctant tongue, I will die.

It's not the thought of death that concerns me; it's the *getting* there I dread.

I saw a man die here once, by hanging. The drop from the gallows wasn't high enough to break his neck, so it took a long time. He made such sounds. He even soiled himself. I push the bowl of gruel away. No. I will eat no more food. What little dignity I have will remain once I'm dead. I take the cup of coffee and go back to the window. Claudia is gone. Only the crows remain, cawing and pecking at the ground. A breeze brushes my face, bringing with it the salt-tinged fragrance of an ocean I'll never see again. I close my eyes. For the first time in many years, I pray.

The priest comes just as dawn breaks. I didn't sleep last night, imagining the sensation of the noose tightening around my neck, the spectators jeering for my death like jackals, all the poor choices that led me here. The priest crosses the room and takes the chair next to my cot, his wrinkled cassock draped over his thin frame, the stole adorning his shoulders heavily embroidered with gold thread. He's young for his station and handsome in a bland, nondescript sort of way, but with a world-weary air that does little to alleviate my anxiety over my impending death. He must be the jail's new chaplain—the replacement for Father Mark, who died shortly after Christmas.

"God's peace be with you. I've come to hear your final confession and to bestow the sacraments, Miss Carmichael." An Irish brogue accents his words. I wonder if he's one of the many recently driven from their mother country by famine.

"I have nothing to confess, Father."

"Nothing? Are you certain, my child? Your sister . . ." he continues, clearing his throat.

"Is dead. But not by my hand."

He smiles patiently, as if he's heard this sort of pronouncement a thousand times before.

"I can see that you don't believe me," I say. "No one does."

"I'm only here to grant absolution. Not judgment. Let me offer you God's forgiveness before you depart this life." He beseeches me with watery blue eyes. At least there's kindness behind them.

I turn toward the window. Despite the roar of the unrelenting rain, I can hear the crowd gathering in the jail's courtyard. From the corner of the cell, I sense Rebecca's spirit watching me. I refuse to look at her. I've been seeing her more lately, as my own death approaches. She looks much the same as she did the week she died. Pale, with vacant eyes and those horrid bruises on her hands. Outward proof of the arsenic that had damned me. I wonder if my spirit will soon join hers, cursed to wander this world without rest.

"My soul . . ." I start. "What do you think will happen to it, Father? After?"

He's silent for a long moment. "If you die with unconfessed sin on your spirit, you may face purgatory."

Purgatory, then. Not hell. The heaviness in the room lifts, ever so slightly, but still—I'd much prefer heaven. I glance at the corner. Rebecca is gone. "I'm not guilty of murder," I say. "Only a lie."

"A lie?"

"Yes. A lie of omission." I pull in a slow breath and turn to look at the young priest, calculating. My secret sits ready on my tongue. If I were to speak it to him now, would he believe me? Would it be enough to grant me pardon even at this late hour?

"My child," he says gently, "if you have anything to confess, let it be now."

"It's only that I . . . saw things. I knew things. I can't be certain, but Rebecca might have died because of them." Even now, the memory of it all sickens me, tumbling like sharp glass in my empty gut.

"Yes?" the priest prods, his back straightening. "If you know anything about your sister's death . . . who killed her, it might be possible to plead your innocence to the governor. He's here, today, in the city."

It would be so easy to say the betraying words, to place this yoke of guilt on another's shoulders. But I cannot. Because I do not *know* for certain what killed Rebecca. They *said* it was the arsenic. Our doctor. The coroner. As to who killed my sister, I only know where my suspicions lie—where they always have—but that, too, is only conjecture.

Heavy footsteps sound from down the corridor. The warden. Panic flits across the young priest's face at the same time it races through my heart. "Miss Carmichael, I beg of you . . ."

I steel myself. I must speak, because Collingwood is on the way—horrid man—and I refuse to die without the sacraments. Only God above will ever know the full truth of Rebecca's demise. I must make peace with that. My confession, at least, will grant me absolution in death, even if it's a lie. "I did it," I say, in a rush. "I killed her. Poisoned her with arsenic. She stole my fiancé, right out from under my nose, and I hated her for it."

The priest regards me, his eyes narrowing warily. "You're absolutely certain this is your final confession? There isn't something else you'd like to tell me?"

"No. You asked for my confession, and there it is, Father. Please. The sacraments."

He stands and removes a small vial of anointing oil from the folds of his cassock. "Kneel before me."

I sink onto the floor, and he hurriedly completes his holy ministrations, fragrant oil dripping sloppily down my forehead, the Eucharist dissolving on my tongue. He makes the sign of the cross and offers his hand to help me rise. "May God's grace be with you, my child."

The ritual brings some measure of comfort to my spirit but does nothing to allay the heavy tug of dread in my gut. A key rattles in the cell door. I suddenly feel as if I might faint. I cling to the priest's arm to steady my spinning head. "What . . . what is your name, Father?"

"Donal."

"Please don't leave me until it's over, Father Donal."

He pats my hand. His palm is sweating, and I realize he's just as afraid as I am. "I promise I won't."

Collingwood enters my cell, his brows drawn together in a frown. Mrs. Banks trails him. She's been crying, poor bird. She's fond of me. I've always thought so, but I can see it plainly now. She served my meals before the others'. Brought me books to read, paper for letters. I've always been a good girl, after all. The eldest of four daughters. Biddable and eager to please. Prison didn't change that.

The warden roughly brings my hands behind my back and loops a length of scratchy rope around my wrists.

"Not too tightly, Mr. Collingwood, sir," Mrs. Banks says, her voice thick. "She's but a wee thing after all."

My mouth is a desert, my pulse a drum. "Are my parents here, Mrs. Banks?" I ask.

"Only your father, Miss."

Dear Papa. Of course he came. My heart sinks at Mother's absence, though I'm not surprised. "Might I have a word with him, before?"

Collingwood sighs. "We've already gone late."

Late to my own execution. How disappointing. I've never been late to anything in my life.

"I'll find your father after and tell him whatever you'd like, Miss Carmichael," Father Donal says, his voice gentle.

"I'd be grateful." My tongue is sluggish and thick in my mouth. "Tell him I love him. Mother, too."

Collingwood tugs on my bonds, leading me to the door. I spare one last glance at my cramped, narrow quarters. The hay-strewn floor. The slender cot bolted to the wall and the dented chamber pot beneath it. A single chair, now empty. Papa's money has afforded me, as a gently bred woman of the chivalry, a private cell on the upper ward. Most of the prisoners here aren't so fortunate—left to rot and fester in overcrowded communal cells on the lower floors, the tidewaters bringing in rats to bite and scurry at their feet, pestilence, and sickness. Few survive more than a year at City Jail. I've been here for two. After I'm gone, this room will be swept clean in readiness for the next unfortunate soul, with nary a mark to show I've ever been here.

Father Donal follows close behind as we pass into the cold, damp corridor. My gorge rises as the stench of human excrement and vomit accosts me. I've never grown used to it. The other prisoners peer through their barred windows as we pass, banging their breakfast spoons against the metal. "Godspeed, Miss Carmichael!" Claudia calls with a taunting lilt.

I ignore her, the sound of rain on the roof drowning out her cackling as we progress to the tower and down its spiraling steps. At the bottom of the stairwell, the strange sensation of being outside my body overtakes me. Gray light floods through the windows lining the passageway leading to the courtyard, where the gallows await. *The Long Walk.* The name given to it by the condemned.

I turn my head and glimpse Papa through the window, dressed in black mourning, his face mottled from the cold rain. His hair—white now—is plastered against his scalp. It was still a glowing copper the last time I saw him. William is there, too, at Papa's side, his face aged beyond its five-and-twenty years. He catches sight of me and his eyes skitter away, his lips tugging downward. He's here only for justice, then. Not for any lingering affection. Resentment curdles in my stomach.

Collingwood flings open the heavy wooden door. A blast of rain-chilled air drives into the vestibule. Water sluices across the floor, as it always does at high tide. Outside, the gallows stand, stark and grim. Six rickety steps lead up to the platform. All that remains is the muddy path ahead. The path to my death. At the sight of me, framed by the door, the crowd's murmuring grows louder. Their faces blur. I begin to tremble. My heart beats so fast and hard I fear it may burst.

"It's all right, dove," Mrs. Banks soothes.

But it's not. I don't want to die. I don't deserve to die. I didn't kill my sister. I didn't do anything wrong.

"Come on then," Collingwood urges, his impatience palpable. "If you don't move, I'll be forced to carry you."

Yes. Just like Lavinia Fisher, who had to be hauled up to the gallows to face her fate, only to bestow a volley of curses on the crowd gathered there. I channel some of Lavinia's famed defiance, her anger. William's disdain has piqued me. I'll not give him the pleasure of seeing my fear.

But no matter how much I will myself forward, my feet remain firmly planted on the threshold, as if encased in ice. I try to speak, to let the warden know that I cannot move, but I find my jaw is locked, too. My breath catches in my lungs. This is more than fear. More than shock. Something else is happening. Something that has happened only once before—the memory of it faint and hollow. Cold seeps up my body, through my toes, as if drawn from the wet floor beneath me. My vision narrows until the world fades from view, taking the light with it, until everything becomes the same dull shade of gray. I feel Father Donal's arms go around me as I fall, and then I feel nothing more.

TWO

Drip. Drip. Drip. My hearing comes back to me first, ears tuning themselves to the repetitive sound of water falling on stone. The rest of my body slowly awakens, my limbs stiff, cold. My eyelids unseam painfully, but only darkness meets my vision. At first, I think myself returned to my jail cell, but my fingers sink into soft velvet instead of my scratchy, lice-ridden cot. I'm on a bed—the nicest one I've slept on in years. I try to sit up, but my forehead collides with something solid. A dull, painful *thunk* reverberates through my skull. I press my hands upward, realization and panic flooding through me at the same time.

This is no bed. I'm inside a coffin.

I scream, my breath fogging the air. I kick and thrash, twisting as I try to fight my way out of this new prison. The last thing I remember is standing on the threshold of the jail, facing the gallows. Not being able to move. Falling backward into the young priest's arms. I obviously swooned, somehow escaped my own hanging, but they must have pronounced me dead all the same. If so, I certainly didn't stay that way. But if I don't escape this casket, I won't be alive for long. I've heard stories of people buried alive—have seen the coffin bells on the sides of gravestones. But the potter's field outside the jail has no such bells. Once buried there, you are forgotten, with no marker to proclaim you ever lived.

I've dreaded my execution, but this death would be far worse. Slow. Agonizing. Trapped beneath the swampy South Carolina soil and left to suffocate.

Despite my panic and confusion, my animal instinct to survive takes over. I draw whatever precious air might be left to me into my lungs and buck my hips like a bull gone mad, over and over, stopping only to claw madly—and futilely—at the lid of the casket with my fingernails. Memories flood my consciousness. Rebecca toddling through the garden, one of Mother's prized roses in her grubby hands. Papa lifting me in the air, the sun full on my face, my laughter bright and clear. My dearest friend, Eleanor, wearing the daisy crown I made for her, her rosy lips curving into a smile.

But my will to live is stronger than these dying memories. I turn on my side, the casket lid tight against my shoulders, and draw my knees up, much as I can, tensing my muscles and kicking explosively behind me. Once, and then again.

With a loud, splintering crack, the side of the casket splits, letting in the sparest sliver of light. I still . . . Light, instead of dirt. I must be aboveground, then. A momentary sense of relief spreads through me. I might still be in the jail's morgue, given the season—even with our mild winters, the ground was likely too stiff for the undertaker's shovel.

There's also a chance I might be in our family crypt. Papa was at the gallows. If he claimed my body, he'd have insisted on giving me a Christian burial. Thanks to Father Donal, I *died* in a state of grace, after all.

It seems folly, the chances slender as the crack I've made in the casket, but my hope rises all the same. I curl onto my side within the cramped space once more, tensing all my muscles, and kick. The crack in the side of the coffin widens, ever so slightly, letting in more light and the fragrance of stale lilies. I kick again, and again, until my muscles protest and my energy flags. I rest for a few moments and then change my tack, rocking back and forth, leveraging my weight. If I'm in the mausoleum, on a niche, and can make the coffin fall, it might break open on the marble floor, even if it's been screwed shut. I rock back and forth again, harder this time. The coffin scoots begrudgingly forward. Progress.

I pause for a deep breath (at least I have plenty of air, thanks be to heaven), sweat running into my eyes, then with a determined cry, I buck and kick out hard, using all my remaining strength. The coffin tilts with a groan and then falls, taking me with it. It shatters around me in splintered cherrywood planks, dead lilies showering the floor with brown petals. I free myself from the detritus, tears springing to my eyes. I'm unharmed but for a single scratch on my arm, below the draped sleeve of my finest ball gown. Mother's choice, no doubt. By the shriveled appearance of the lilies, I've been here for at least a few days, if not a week.

I stand on shaky legs. At the center back of the mausoleum, Rebecca's gilded coffin accosts me. Hers was the first to grace this place and, as such, given rest in the choicest niche below the crypt's rose window. "Well, sister, we're together again," I say aloud with a laugh. I half expect to see Rebecca's ghost leering at me with disdain, but she makes no effort to appear.

Mother argued with Papa over the cost of building a mausoleum at the new cemetery. She called it a vanity—the churchyard at Saint Mary's had been good enough for her people for generations. But when my twin sisters, Emma and Ruth, died of smallpox before their eighth birthday, Papa was devastated by the sight of their coffins being lowered into the ground. He commissioned the mausoleum as soon as the cemetery began selling plots. Papa's "vanity" is proving to be my salvation.

An ungodly thirst clenches my throat. I've never been so thirsty. I tilt my head upward, searching for the source of the dripping I heard inside the coffin. A thread of water beads down from the vaulted ceiling, seeping in through the stonework. I stand beneath the meager stream, stretching out my tongue, the water rolling down my parched throat one agonizing drop at a time. It does nothing to slake my thirst. In desperation, I sink to the floor and lap the water from the puddle gathering there, the marble cold against my tongue.

Once I've satisfied my thirst, I rise, stretching my protesting limbs. Moonlight slants through the vent above the door. A wave of dizziness washes over me as I cross to the mausoleum's anteroom and press my hand against the door. I push, gingerly. The door scrapes open a scant few inches before catching on the scrollwork gate, which is very much locked. I wriggle my hand through the opening, grasp the padlock, and tug downward, to no avail.

While the cemetery is upriver from town, in Charleston's Neck, someone passing by still might hear me if I scream or rattle the gate. A groundskeeper, perhaps. But even if someone did hear me and unlock the mausoleum, I'd surely be sent right back to jail. Back to the gallows.

Panic ties my stomach in a knot once more. I scan the space, frantically, for anything I might use to try to pick the lock. I played at such things as a child, with some success. I'd always wanted to see inside my mother's escritoire drawer, and one day, using a hatpin, I breached the lock. I discovered nothing of importance inside—only an envelope filled with receipts from our modiste and tepid letters from my aunt—but the sense of accomplishment was worth the effort all the same.

I pat my disheveled hair and find three hairpins tucked there, but they're much too flimsy to be of any use on their own. Finally, I see it. A small statue of Saint Peter perches on a shelf above Rebecca's casket. His shepherd's crook, fashioned of metal, looks just sturdy enough and solid enough to tackle the massive lock.

I stand on tiptoe on the edge of Rebecca's niche, using the casket's lid to brace myself as I lean forward—she's the whole reason I'm here, after all. I whisper a prayer of supplication to Saint Peter and give a tug to his metal crook, but Peter refuses to relinquish his hold. I extend my reach, my fingers brushing the porcelain saint's robes. I lean farther, poised on one toe, but just as I grasp the statue, I lose my balance, my slippered foot sliding off the marble ledge. The statue topples to the floor and lands with a sharp crack, Peter's head rolling to the corner, the rest of him in shards.

"Heavens. Forgive me," I say, cringing as I bend to extricate the shepherd's crook. "Please don't hold this against me when it really *is* my time to appear at your gates."

I rush to the door, my heart thudding against my rib cage. Hunger has supplanted my thirst, fierce and demanding. My body is fully awake now. Fully alive, with all its corporeal demands. I test the metal of the crook and find it pliable. I carefully bend the straight end into a square angle. Holding the padlock steady, I insert my hastily crafted pick through the keyhole, fishing around. I've always had sensitive fingers, and it takes me only a moment to discern the lock's inner mechanism—it's the sort meant to be opened with a skeleton key, which makes sense, given its purpose. Easy. I remove the crook and, bending it back and forth, break the metal to make a straight pick to work in tandem with the other.

After several failed attempts, and a few curse words that would shame my mother, the tumblers finally engage, and the padlock falls open. With a small cry of triumph, I gather my wits and slowly push the door open, peering out warily. The sky is a deep indigo gray, streaked with feathery clouds. A sliver of moon hangs low, shining dimly through the moss-veiled arms of the oaks. I can hear the quiet susurration of the river in the distance. There's not a soul about—only gravestones and the silent dead beneath them.

I slip outside, closing the iron door and its gate behind me. I secure the padlock once more and pull in a deep, greedy breath, filling my lungs with loamy air. I'm alive. I'm free. Two things I'll never take for granted again.

THREE

I stay near the banks of the Cooper, and follow it down to Charleston's old quarter, my ridiculous pink gown useless against the cold, its overlong hem snagging on cobblestones and tripping me without the layers of stiff crinolines I've always worn beneath it. The bells of the Huguenot church ring out twice. Anyone about at this hour will think I've just come from a ball, scandalously unchaperoned. I must find warmer, less conspicuous clothing soon. My toes, clad only in satin dancing slippers, have gone numb.

My luck improves behind a tidy yellow house on Queen Street, where a row of washing hangs stiffly from a line. I ease through the courtyard gate and pluck slender trousers and a linsey-woolsey shirt from the line, along with a pair of knitted socks. Thievery seems a smaller sin once one has been accused of murder, so I think nothing of stealing the clothing. Hidden behind the house, I shuck my silk gown, contorting myself at odd angles to unbutton the back. I remove the busk from my corset to give more freedom to my movements and gather my shift and single petticoat between my legs, wondering why Mother thought a corset necessary for my state of eternal rest, but not drawers. I tuck the tail of the petticoat into its waistband to serve as makeshift bloomers, then don the breeches and shirt. Once I'm dressed, I wedge my feet back into the slippers, thick socks and all. I can only imagine how ridiculous I look.

But I'm alive.

My stomach rumbles, reminding me of my hunger and that it's been days since I last ate. My refusal of Mrs. Banks's offered last meal seems foolish now. I worried more about my pride and dignity in death than my comfort. What people would think if I soiled myself. Meanwhile, they didn't care a whit about sending an innocent woman to the gallows.

In this, my newly resurrected life, I vow to be a little more selfish and unconcerned with the opinions of others.

I wad the gown into an untidy ball and shove it beneath the raised foundation of the house, then turn south toward Tradd Street. Toward home. I'll sneak into the back of the house, through the kitchen, gather food, jewelry to pawn, my cloak. In and out. But as I near Broad, my anxiety rises. It's been more than two years since I was last home. Since the day the City Guard came to arrest me. The memory of it all is still fresh. Two days had passed since Rebecca's funeral, and my aunt was still with us, visiting from Columbia. Everyone wore black—Aunt Tillie was in mourning for her husband, who'd died the year before, and Papa and my cousin Michael wore bands around their sleeves. My stiff crepe skirt whispered with every movement as we went about having tea in hushed voices.

It was raining when the knock came, just after three in the afternoon. Mother parted the heavy drapes in the parlor and looked outside. "The City Guard's come."

Realization fractured the numb fog of my grief as the sergeant read the warrant for my arrest, as his officers tore me from my mother's side. Though panic set me to trembling, I'd obeyed their brusque orders, done my best to go willingly, thinking it had to be a mistake. A misunderstanding that would sort itself out. Papa protested when they put me in irons, tried to reason with the sergeant, bless him, and sent counsel to the jail the next day. But my fate was sealed. Between Rebecca's friend Arabella Meade, who testified she heard me quarreling with Rebecca three days before her death, and our family doctor's assertion that he'd seen me place arsenic in her coughing tonic, there was enough circumstantial evidence to try me for murder. I will never forget my dear aunt Tillie's words to my mother as they led me away: "She's a good girl, Caroline. Shouldn't you say something?"

But she didn't. I'd excused her inaction as a symptom of her grief. Three children lost, in the span of a decade. It had surely taken a heavy toll.

I take a deep breath, pushing my memories of that day away. I will always carry the hurt and betrayal with me, but there is no changing the past. I must move forward now, into whatever new life awaits me.

As I near home, the tight slippers pinching my aching toes, I consider the possibility that Mother and Papa might have been forced to sell our town house and move elsewhere. We've faced hard times in recent years. Though he's always been circumspect in his dealings, rumors of Papa's secret efforts as an abolitionist have circulated all the same. We've slowly been ostracized by the upper echelons of Charleston society as a result, and Papa's earnings have suffered greatly. Rebecca's marriage to William was meant to ease our burden. Now, with my sister dead and my family cloaked in scandal, there will be no help from the Camerons, even with our shared sense of Scottish pride.

But even if Papa and Mother have managed to keep our home, another worry presses me. There will be consequences if I'm seen by them, or by our maid of all work, Siobhan, who has always been a light sleeper. I can only imagine their shock. Everyone believes I'm dead, after all.

Papa has a weak heart, and Siobhan is a notorious gossip. As for Mother? I can't even fathom how she would react. If they discover I'm still alive, they could be punished. Accused of harboring a fugitive.

Still, with no money, I haven't many choices. Either I steal from my family, steal from someone else, or starve. I've been given a second chance at life. But without money or food, my miraculous resurrection won't feel miraculous for long.

The night air is heavy with expectation as I square my shoulders and turn onto Longitude Lane. The familiar hipped roofline of our row house emerges through the gaslit fog. I'll have to be brave if I'm going to survive, so I might as well summon some gumption now. I stand in the alleyway outside our garden gate for a long time, peering through the ironwork. All the windows are dark, the dormant rosebushes cloaking the rear piazza in shadow. Siobhan always left a spare key beneath the pot of rosemary flanking the kitchen. Hopefully it will still be there. I lift the latch and push through the gate, which squeals in protest. I flinch, but no lights come on in our house, or those on either side.

I hurriedly cross the courtyard, keeping to the shadowed edges, and lift the rosemary pot. The key is right where I knew it would be. With trembling hands, I whisper a prayer before sliding it into the lock. It catches and turns, and in an instant, I'm in the kitchen, surrounded by warmth from the banked coals inside the hearth and all the familiar comforts I once took for granted.

Walter is there, sleeping on the rag rug before the fire. I try to creep past him, ignoring the sudden catch in my throat. But he hears me all the same, and wakes. He springs to his feet, tail wagging madly. He doesn't bark, thank heavens, only shoves his wet nose into my palm with a thin whine. I kneel and bury my face in his shaggy, gray coat. "I've missed you, too," I whisper, "but you must be very quiet, sweet. You mustn't wake Mother and Papa."

He looks at me with solemn eyes, as if he understands, then goes back to his spot on the rug, turning in a circle before lying down. I send him a lingering look and creep soundlessly up the servant stairs to the second floor.

Thanks to years of tremblers, the middle of our upstairs hall is uneven and rife with weak spots, so I keep close to the wall instead. A few of the sconces remain lit, their tallow candles burning low, but they provide more than enough light to see by. As I near my mother's bedroom, I can hear her snoring inside, her breath rising and falling with a shrill whistle. I wonder what the past two years have done to her. Has she kept her famed beauty, or faded as Papa has? She'd always hidden her feelings from me, her demeanor placid and calm even when they came to arrest me. Yet she cried all the same when I was sentenced to die. A brief pang of yearning courses through me—the temptation to go to her is strong, to wake her and let her know I've survived.

But I cannot. Knowledge of my existence would only endanger my parents. Make them culpable.

I hear the bells of Charleston's many churches ring out over the city and force myself away from her door. Three in the morning. Well paid as she is, Siobhan rises early. I must hurry. I rush to the end of the hall and the bedroom that Rebecca and I once shared.

The room is a shrine. Both beds are made, their coverlets taut and pristine. Our portraits hang above each of our respective headboards—Rebecca's wistful and romantic, her copper curls streaming over her bare white shoulders, pink lips softly parted. She'd seen Winterhalter's scandalous portrait of Queen Victoria in the papers and asked our portraitist to duplicate it.

My likeness, on the other hand, is somber and staid by comparison, my posture rigid, a book lying open on my lap, brown hair braided and looped below each ear, one arm propped on Papa's desk, my modest, high-necked dress draped with the Carmichael tartan. I've always been practical. Stoic and reserved. Rebecca was the vanguard. The charming rebel. Though she was frail of health, her beauty gave her an advantage in life, one she capitalized upon. Her name was always above mine on any invitation, her wardrobe steadily documented in the social papers. She had her first marriage proposal at fourteen, well before she was out. Were it not for Papa's insistence that I, as the eldest, be the first to marry, Mother would have likely entertained the thought. When William broke our betrothal, Papa did his best to comfort me.

Your mind is your greatest treasure, Lil. Beauty fades. But you are a keen and canny lass. It will serve you well.

I look up at our portraits again. Our likenesses reflect our opposing temperaments. If Rebecca was a wild rose, I am a thistle. Hardened by life. Bitter and sharp.

But thistles are strong. Resilient.

I cross to my wardrobe, where my gowns, underthings, and day dresses lay folded neatly on the shelves, my poke bonnets hanging from the hooks at the back. I find my carpetbag under the bed and hastily stuff it with my most practical clothing: shifts, drawers, woolen stockings, petticoats, and two of my favorite dresses. I sit on my bed and replace the satin slippers with my winter boots, my hands shaking as I lace them. I shove the ruined slippers beneath the wardrobe, toward the back, where Siobhan shouldn't find them, and smooth the coverlet.

I take most of my jewelry, including my jet mourning brooch, my gold locket with miniatures of the twins inside, which I fasten around my neck, and a sapphire ring Mother gave me for my debut. My pin money is still inside my dressing-table drawer: three dollars and some change. I pocket all of it. I briefly consider rifling through Rebecca's things—I could take some of her jewelry, too—but guilt stops me. My sister and I weren't always the best of friends, and we were often rivals, but I will not steal from her, even in death. I already have more than enough. As I pass her bed, a memory accosts me, sending another stab of guilt into my gut. I imagine I see Rebecca sitting there, fingers running idly through her long hair as she watches me, her eyes filled with unspoken hurt. I secure my traveling cloak over my shoulders and close the door softly behind me.

A familiar cough comes from downstairs. My muscles tense. Papa. I flatten myself against the wall and watch the soft glow of candlelight swell on the main stairs as he shuffles up the creaking steps. Thankfully, when he reaches the top, he turns right instead of left, toward his study. I remain hidden in the shadows until he enters the study, leaving the door open a crack. A cone of yellow light bleeds into the hall. Damn it. I'll have to pass his door to get back to the servant stairs.

I shoulder the carpetbag and pad silently forward—not easily done in my heavy boots. As I pass the study, I glimpse Papa's reflection in the mirror above the mantel. He's hunched over his desk, inspecting his ledger. I watch him for a moment—his soft jowls hanging above the collar of his nightshirt, his face lit with candlelight. He smiles at something he reads and lifts the book nearer to his eyes. It's not his ledger. He's looking at one of my old journals. I recognize the cover—a small, red book stamped with a gilded daisy. I thought myself a poet in my younger years and filled several little books with my childish scribbling.

He turns the page and chuckles. I wrestle my threatening tears into submission. I long to go to him, to sit at his side, as I so often did in the past, watching him as he wrote clandestine letters to senators and congressmen, pleading with his words and money to end the abomination of human slavery and the things he'd borne witness to.

I win the fight against my foolish heart and back away from the door. Downstairs, in the kitchen, I quickly gather half a loaf of bread, three tins of kippers, a jar of jam, and a good, sturdy knife—something I can use for protection, if need be. With another pat to Walter's head, I leave, closing the door soundlessly behind me. I replace the key beneath the rosemary pot and rush across the garden. In the lane, I turn and take one last look at the home where I was born. Papa's study window glows in the darkness. Comforting. Warm with his love.

I hold back my tears until I'm halfway down the block, then sink onto a stranger's tabby stoop and cry for everything I've lost and can never have again.

A VAMPIRE'S DIARY

Sally

A flash of coin and a smile. That's all it took with Sally. I'd been following her for weeks before I struck. I knew her habits, how she prowled the avenues south of Broad early in the morning. I watched as Charleston's finest young men had their way with her, their spirits high after twirling virtuous maidens over parquet floors. They used Sally instead, slaking their callow frustrations inside her eager body. And she was ever eager. Angel-voiced and graceful. In another time, another place, she might have become a famous courtesan or elevated herself to a king's mistress. Her beauty was singular. Splendid.

She beckoned me with a coy, knowing glance, pocketing my money and pressing herself against me as we kissed. Her mouth tasted of rum and cinnamon, her supple body yielding and warm. So warm. She invited me to follow her back to her rooms so we might take our time. She liked me. Wanted me.

But my needs were too urgent for a leisurely dalliance. I pulled her into a nearby churchyard, which amused her at first. When she realized what was happening, panic bloomed in her eyes before she fell into a swoon, which made my work easy. I waited until her heart stopped pumping, then covered her with my cloak and carried her back to the corner where I'd found her. I retreated into the shadows, Sally's essence with me, the rich treasure of her blood. Although she wasn't exalted in life, as she should have been, her death will make her immortal. Both of us were cut from the same cloth, after all. Used by the chivalry, only to be disregarded and forgotten about as soon as their needs are met. Well. Now I will use them as they have used me.

FOUR

Time slows to a trickle without a home. The days blur together. I measure the hours between waking and sleeping by the next meal. The next place to shelter for the night. The next drink of water.

Water. My parched tongue reminds me of my thirst as I uncurl from my cramped position beneath the deep eaves of the Huguenot church. I've sheltered here for the past three nights, out of the wind, but I'll need to move along soon, before someone notices and reports me for vagrancy. I stand and stretch. I finally abandoned my carpetbag yesterday, its weight too cumbersome to justify. I hadn't bothered to change into any of the clothing I took from home, anyway, apart from fresh underthings, preferring the freedom the stolen breeches give me. Much better than heavy, long skirts. With my slight frame, and my breasts hidden beneath the too-large shirt, I resemble a boy. I'm fine with the ruse. There's safety in it.

The sun is a faint, ash-gray glow below the horizon as I make my way to the public cistern. It hasn't rained for the past few days, so the water in the basin lies stagnant. I dip the ladle and bring it to my mouth, wincing at the stale taste. Thoughts of typhoid fever and cholera accost my mind, but I drink deeply all the same, trying not to gag.

If this is to be the rest of my life—survival in the shadows, with nothing more to look forward to than my next meal—I wonder at my wisdom in trying to live at all. Despair has taken hold of me more than once in the past, especially in prison, when the nights closed in and my regrets got the better of me. I contemplated ending my life many times. Many prisoners did, unable to bear the jail's unceasing torments. But for some reason, I held on.

Now I wonder why I've been given this second chance. Why I'm still here. I see the looks of disdain people give me. Or how they dismiss me outright, turning their heads. I've become invisible to them. A nuisance. Charitable souls are rare. In the past week, I've encountered only one—a fellow vagrant who offered me a crust of bread. I'd foolishly eaten through most of my pilfered supplies within the first three days.

It's time to pawn my jewelry and plan for my unsure future. I think of all the places I might go, with enough money in my pockets to buy passage on a steamer or a train. Savannah. New Orleans. Up north. I might disappear anywhere—but with Charleston's mild winters and familiar streets, I'm loath to leave. It's home. It always has been. Besides, Papa and Mother are here, their hearts forever tethered to my own with an invisible thread, even if they have no knowledge of my survival. A reunion is impossible, but leaving the city would mean abandoning them forever. I'm not ready to do that. Not yet.

Dawn is breaking when a scream pierces the air, near the corner of Market and King, halting me in my aimless amble. By the time I round the corner, a small crowd has gathered outside a shuttered storefront—a lamplighter, a City Guard officer, a woman in hysterics, and the bespectacled man doing his best to calm her. At their feet, a body lies prone on the cobblestones, covered with a woolen cloak, one white hand outstretched.

I approach cautiously, trying not to call attention to myself, and tuck into a closed storefront's recessed entryway, leaning forward to listen and catch glimpses of the scene.

"For god's sake, Cass. Pull yourself together." The gruff voice belongs to the bespectacled man. In response, the wailing woman snuffles, blows her nose.

"If I may, Mrs. Humphrey, was the young woman entertaining a gentleman last night?" The officer. His voice is cool. Detached.

"I assumed so. She went out around three, as she does. Sally's my best girl, you see. The prettiest of them. Catches the eye of fancy gents coming home after the balls. I run a fine establishment, sir. The best in the city."

"Did you know the fellow she was meeting?"

"No." Another sob. "She didn't tell me. But when I saw her, just an hour or so ago, she wasn't with a man. She was alone. Walking down by the docks."

I watch as the officer kneels next to the corpse, raises the cloak. I see a wan face. A tangle of copper hair. A shiver walks across my shoulders. "I'll need to fetch the coroner and the morgue wagon. All of you stay here until I've returned."

"I must see to the rest of the lanterns, sir," the lamplighter interrupts, lifting his snuffing pole. "Any wasted oil comes off my pay."

The officer stands, lowering his voice. I strain to hear. "I need someone trustworthy to keep an eye on those two, Sam. Make sure they stay here. I'll return soon." He dusts off his pin-straight trousers, frowns beneath his mustache, then departs at a brisk clip.

I slump onto the step, examining the ridges of my dirty fingernails. No more than a quarter hour later, the clatter of hooves rings out against the cobbles. The morgue wagon parts the morning fog and pulls along the curb, its pair of mules huffing steam. The coroner, a befuddled-looking man wearing a beaver hat, descends from the wagon, followed by the stern officer.

The madam's wailing crescendos as the coroner removes the cloak shrouding the body on the cobbles. I gasp. The woman is naked as a babe, her long, slender limbs a preternatural white. Her beauty, even in death, is undeniable, the rouge on her cheeks the only color present apart from the flaming red of her hair. An image of Rebecca on her deathbed flashes across my memory, her sunken eyes, the bluish-purple cast of her mouth. Sally looks like a graveyard angel by comparison. I draw my cape tightly around me to chase the chill from my skin.

The bespectacled man turns away from the sight. "Christ," he swears, his lip trembling. "Poor pet." The grief-stricken madam ducks her head and keens against his chest. My heart can't help but share in their pity. Over the past few days, I've contemplated my future enough to consider that I might be forced to sell my charms to strangers, just as this unfortunate young woman did. Women without means have few choices available in this world outside of marriage, and desperation often leads to peril and ruin. Workhouses and whoredom are common fates for those unfortunates born—or made—poor.

This Sally was once someone's beloved daughter. I wonder about her life and what led her to this sad end.

The coroner gives Sally a cursory examination. He pinches a fold of skin inside her elbow, listens for a heartbeat, then quickly covers her up again. "There's no evidence of lividity. I've never seen anything like this, Wesley."

"Nor have I, sir." The officer shakes his head.

"Exsanguination."

I've no idea what the word means, but the coroner's incredulous tone of voice conveys much. "Let's take her to the morgue," he says. "I'll conduct a more thorough examination there and determine the time of death."

Two young Negro men hop down from the morgue wagon, carrying a litter. They lift Sally and place her on it, then hurriedly cover her body with a length of white sheeting. The officer gingerly folds the cloak over his arm. I can hardly blame him for not wanting to wear it. He crosses to the madam and her male companion, mutters a few words I cannot hear. The couple walks away, arm in arm, the woman still bereft.

The scene holds the uncanniness of a dream. The horror is ephemeral and distant despite my proximity to it—like something on a theater stage. A tragic opera. I was sheltered from such things in my former life, but the past years in jail educated me in degradation. While I'm bothered by what I've just witnessed, prison has hardened me. After the morgue cart rolls away, my stomach clenches and growls. Unlike poor Sally, I'm still very much alive. Our bodies are carnal things. Demanding to be fed. To be satiated.

Lights in the shops down Market Street flicker on. Bleary-eyed proprietors emerge to sweep stoops and set out their wares to tempt passersby. I rise from the doorway I'm nested in and head for the pawnbroker.

❧

"How did you obtain these pieces?" The pawnbroker eyes me over his spectacles, one gray eyebrow lifted.

"They're family heirlooms," I say, pitching my voice low.

His gaze scrapes me up and down, taking in my disheveled appearance. He turns over the Whitby jet mourning brooch, inspecting its clasp and the maker's mark with his loupe. I'm eager to be rid of the brooch and the memories attached to it. I last wore it at Rebecca's funeral.

"This is a fine piece. But I'm afraid I won't be purchasing it. Nor any of the others." He gestures to the array of jewelry on the counter. "I run a reputable establishment, young man."

"And these are reputable pieces. I can assure you, sir, they are of the highest quality."

"I can see that for myself. But I cannot offer stolen goods to the very people they might have been taken from."

"Stolen?" I stammer. "These aren't stolen."

He shakes his head, his expression softening. "I'm being kinder than most would be. Only because you remind me of my son, god rest him." He gives me a sad smile, reaches under the counter, and produces a handful of coins. "I can hear your belly growling. There's enough here for you to purchase a week's worth of food from the market."

My long-buried pride bristles. Desperate though I may be, I make no move to accept his charity. "I thank you for your kindness, sir, but I'd rather sell you my goods, fairly and equitably."

The bell on the door jangles as another customer enters. The broker sweeps the jewelry and coins from the counter and deposits everything inside a velvet pouch, then shoves it into my hands. "You little fool. Take this to the east side. Or over to Mount Pleasant," he rasps. "You might have better luck there. Now, out with you."

I turn and rush toward the door, my face aflame. In my haste, I nearly collide with the well-dressed customer and her companion. My heart stutters. It's Arabella Meade—Rebecca's closest friend, daughter of Papa's merchant partner, and my chief accuser. Her doe-soft eyes widen in recognition as I brush past her. I duck my head, murmur an apology, and stalk out onto the street.

Panic threads through me. *Did* she recognize me? I glance at my reflection in a nearby shop window. I look nothing like I once did. My mangy hair sticks out at odd angles, my frame is thin and gaunt—I'm no longer the plump-cheeked young woman I was when Arabella saw me last. Besides, Arabella and everyone else thinks me dead . . . the best disguise of all. Surely she didn't recognize me. Surely not.

But all the same, I need to be more careful about avoiding people and shops. I catch my breath, shove the velvet pouch into my pocket, then trudge onward to face another day and night of hiding in the shadows.

I heed the pawnbroker's advice but have no luck pawning my jewelry along the eastside wharves. The shops there offer pennies on the dollar, well below worth, so I keep the jewelry and decide it's more expeditious to steal instead. I begin with low-hanging fruit. A drunken man stumbling out of an Elliott Street tavern, his wits whiskey-clouded. I follow him at a distance, observing his unsteady gait. When he stops to lean against a lamppost, heaving his guts onto the cobblestones, I seize my opportunity. I dart forward as he retches, my hand diving into his coat pocket, where I'm rewarded with three silver coins. He doesn't even notice me, deep in his business of being sick. As an afterthought, I snatch his fallen hat from the ground, and duck back into the shadows, shaking with nervousness.

But as the evening wears on and I bed down for the night in an alleyway off King Street, my guilt catches up to me. My theft of the clothes after I escaped the mausoleum was one thing. An act of necessity. This was too, arguably, but I took advantage of a man whose senses and judgment were compromised. A poor man, from the looks of him. It doesn't sit well with me. Going forward, I vow to steal from only the wealthy.

I try my luck on the Battery promenade the next evening. With the drunkard's Kossuth hat pulled low over my forehead, I sit alongside the Battery wall, slumped against a set of stairs—positioned perfectly to reach into a lady's carelessly open reticule or a gentleman's pocket as they ascend and descend the steps leading to the elevated seawall. Although I have no doubt there are people from my old life out taking the air, I keep still and quiet, lifting my head only high enough to glimpse a swishing skirt or a well-cut pair of trousers. No one pays me any mind. They're more interested in who is looking at *them* as they parade about in their fine clothes. When I go to sleep that night, I'm in possession of a small gold-and-enamel snuffbox and enough money to guarantee I'll eat well for a fortnight.

Emboldened by my success, I return to the Battery the next two nights. I need the practice—to become a master at my new trade. With my sensitive, fine-boned fingers and small hands, quick from years of piano practice, I'm an adept pickpocket. Though it goes against my law-abiding nature, stealing gives me a surprising sense of purpose. Hope. I enjoy the thrill—the rush of sheer pleasure each time I succeed.

All the same, I can't help but think Mother would be disappointed in how far I've fallen. She was ever worried about what people would think, so I was always a dutiful daughter—never wanting to stir the waters. Rebecca's persistent illnesses consumed our mother's attention. As a result, my days were scheduled from morning to night, filled with sewing and drawing and music lessons. My tutors and music master kept me occupied, broadened the horizons of my mind, but I was lonely, all the same. I longed for the tenderness and attention Mother lavished on Rebecca. But recognizing that Rebecca's needs were greater than mine, and that our mother was worn thin by caring for her, I suffered her neglect without complaint. It was Papa I went to when I needed attention and affection. He filled my life with books and conversation and nurtured my growing intellect with his gentle guidance.

Papa wouldn't be ashamed of me. He would see what I'm doing as a necessity. A means of survival, a way to keep my honor intact, without resorting to selling my body. I think of poor Sally, and shudder. I'll do whatever it takes to avoid a similar fate.

I'll never forget what Papa said to me at the jail, the morning after my arrest.

You're made of strong stuff, Lil. You're a Carmichael through and through. A daughter of Douglas, descended from kings and warriors. Hold fast, mo chridhe. You'll be free again. I know it like my very soul.

And he was right. I *was* free. Without a home, and with the future ahead of me filled with uncertainty. But free, all the same. Perhaps someday, I'd find a way to make him proud.

FIVE

They say that deaths come in threes. That tragedy, unlike lightning, strikes the same family over and over. The specter of mourning, once invited in, is loath to leave.

I've been on the streets of Charleston for less than a fortnight when I learn of Papa's death. The news comes to me in a shred of overheard conversation near the Exchange. A place Papa despised yet haunted tirelessly, bearing witness to the scourge of slavery. He'd written down the horrors he'd observed in essays and letters, all signed with his pseudonym, L. M. Pilco, and sent them to politicians and the northern presses alike. He insisted slavery would be our nation's downfall—a stain we would never scrub free. In doing so, he risked his life and made many enemies here among the wealthy planters of rice, indigo, and sea island cotton, who built their fortunes on the backs of enslaved men and women.

Gathered in the shadows, a raucous crowd stands on the north side of the imposing building, awaiting the arrival of the day's human chattel and the indoor auction to follow. I skim along their periphery, on the lookout for the rarefied moments of vulnerability the privileged usually enjoy without consequence. I feel no guilt taking advantage of them. No shame in stealing from these men I once danced and flirted with at cotillion, before Papa's crisis of conscience drove an irrevocable wedge between our family and polite society.

One of the younger Calhoun sons, Patrick, is talking in hushed tones to a man I recognize as one of the Draytons' overseers—a blight of a man. While his attention is diverted, I slink forward, fingers darting into Patrick's trouser pocket. I retrieve three gold coins and quickly secrete them into the velvet pouch the pawnbroker gave me.

Patrick slips a silver flask from his coat, offers it to the overseer. "Did you hear the news about old Carmichael?"

I freeze in place, stock still.

"Yes." The overseer laughs, then takes a drink. "Got his comeuppance, didn't he?"

"Indeed. I heard when they opened the crypt to bury him, his daughter's body was missing."

"The pretty one?"

"No. Lillian." Patrick chuckles. "She and her sister came all the way to Fort Hill for a ball once. Their mother kept shoving ol' Lil my way, but it was Rebecca who captured my fancy."

"She'd have been a fun toss, I warrant." The overseer smacks his lips. "Grave robbers get to Lil, do you suppose?"

Patrick hums. "Probably. Let them scatter her bones to the four winds, for all anyone cares. Good riddance to them all."

Suddenly, the air is too thin to breathe. I stand there, swaying slightly, disgust and disbelief running through me like cold water. As the doors to the Exchange open and the men eagerly rush forward, jockeying for position, I flee and crouch in an alleyway, back against the bricks, trying to catch my breath. Papa can't be dead. He can't be. I just saw him, not even two weeks ago, safe in his study.

Once I've gathered my wits, I lift myself from the alley's cobbles and start walking. By the time I reach the Neck, and the cemetery, a cold drizzle is falling. Our mausoleum crouches in the distance, its vaulted roof weeping with rain. I fight back the growing thrum of panic and set myself apart from my body, my emotions, as I approach the place where I was so recently entombed. I find the metal outer door, the portal through which I passed days ago, unlocked—an egregious oversight on the undertaker's part. Or is it? I remember the foul words I heard from the men outside the slave market. Our family is hated—despised by Charleston's elite. No one cares whether our graves are desecrated, our bodies stolen.

I hesitate before going inside, looking over my shoulder. There's not a soul about to witness my intrusion. I gingerly push through the mausoleum door, propping a rock in the threshold to prevent it from closing behind me. I've been buried alive once. Never again.

I blink, my eyes adjusting to the somber light inside the tomb.

A new casket sits where mine was, this one broad and long, its rosewood panels inlaid with gilt. Someone has cleaned the mausoleum. The remains of my broken casket are gone, the porcelain shards of Saint Peter's statue swept from the floor. Still, a slight stale odor lingers in the room—something animal and foul beneath the cloying sweetness of the lilies atop the new casket, reminding me that this isn't the church it was meant to resemble, but a place of death.

I pull in a shallow, steadying breath and rest my hand on the handsome casket. I now regret not going to Papa that night I returned home. My resurrection would have startled him, surely, and I would have needed to swear him to silence. But might it have saved him, if he knew that I yet lived? Grief weakened his heart after the twins' deaths, and Rebecca's ordeal took an even harsher toll. But I was his favorite. His grief over my loss may well have been the final blow to his great, loving heart.

Once again, remorse sidles close to me. If only I'd been honest about Rebecca, and what I witnessed. If I'd told the full truth, I might have saved her. Might have saved myself from rotting in a jail cell for two long years. Might have saved Papa from *this*.

I can feel her spirit nearby. Rebecca. Watching. I turn my head and see her faint outline, near her casket, long red-gold curls obscuring her face. Why won't she rest?

Grief and guilt wash over me then, cresting like stormwaters over the shore. I collapse onto the mausoleum floor, leaning my head against

Papa's casket as harsh sobs break free, racking my body. The urge to see him one last time, to prove to myself that he's truly gone, becomes a visceral need. Perhaps it's all a horrible lie. Perhaps he's faked his own death and left Charleston to begin anew. I could see him doing just that, going north, to Washington or Philadelphia, to better plead against slavery's blight. I imagine him in some vaulted chamber of government, his voice echoing over a crowd.

A slender, spare thread of hope brings me to my feet. I brace myself against the niche's arch, gazing down at Papa's casket. "Forgive me," I whisper, and before I can talk myself out of my folly, I pry open the lid.

I immediately wish I hadn't.

The smell of putrefaction assaults me. My father's corpse is a horror—his face a blackened purple, his fingers bloated and splitting apart, a foul ooze of liquid seeping from his flesh. The swollen bulwark of his body pushes against the edges of the coffin. Bile rises in my throat. I turn away and vomit, my senses overcome by the cruel due course of his death.

I drop the casket lid and rush from the mausoleum, fleeing my father's decimation. The putrid odor lingers on my skin, in my nostrils. I kneel on the ground, next to the grave of a child, my stomach purging itself again, until it heaves on emptiness. I wipe my mouth with my shirtsleeve, stilling at the sound of men's voices nearby.

I scramble to the back of our mausoleum and crouch among the yews planted there, listening as footsteps approach.

"I heard something, I know I did. Someone wailing." The man's voice is deep, sonorous, flavored with a thick Irish brogue.

I clench my teeth and fists. He must have heard me crying. If he goes into the mausoleum, he'll see evidence of my presence—my vomit on the floor, the fallen flowers from Papa's casket, the stone propping open the door. I should have mastered myself. Should have never opened that casket or come here at all. The not-knowing was far better. I squeeze my eyes shut, the image of my father's ruined body stamped forever on my mind.

"Carmichael. Isn't this the grave that was robbed?" another voice says. It's familiar, though I can't quite place where I've heard it before.

"Yes, sir," the Irishman says. "That's what folks are saying. But I watch this cemetery, day and night, and I've never seen any sign of grave robbers. The anatomists go to the public cemetery for bodies." The mausoleum's metal door whines. "Funny thing, though. This door was closed this morning, when I got here. Someone's been inside."

"Could have been animals. We'll have a look and then I'll be on my way."

"Not an animal, Officer. Look here. Someone placed a rock, to keep the inner door open."

It dawns on me, then, where I've heard the officer's voice. He's the same one who attended to the dead woman—Sally—on Market Street. I recognize his clipped cadence. I will myself to remain still as they go inside. I consider running. But with the dry grass and leaves, they'll surely hear my footsteps. My ears strain to make out their muffled conversation, though I can only discern a word or two. "Vomit" is one of them. I've always had a bilious stomach.

A few moments later, they come out again. "Probably just a drunken vagrant," the constable declares, sniffing. "It's been cold the last few nights."

"Gads, how could anyone stand the stench in there?" The Irishman coughs and spits, nearly gagging.

"Explains the vomit, sure enough. But there's no sign of anything suspicious, Billy."

"Maybe not now. But you should have seen that other casket, sir. Shattered, like it was hit by a mortar. I've never seen the like of it."

"What are you getting at?"

"That woman. His daughter—Miss Carmichael. Something weren't right about all that business. I saw her body in the receiving tomb, before they buried her. She looked too good for three days dead. Her skin still had color to it." The man scrapes his foot against the gravel. "I've heard things, too."

"What?"

"People have seen her. In town, like. Wandering the streets in the same dress she was buried in."

I swear beneath my breath. I was so careful that night, taking the back alleys in the wee hours of the morning after my escape. But Charleston, and especially the Peninsula, is at its heart a small town. All it would take is one person seeing me out their window to start the chain of gossip.

"Are you saying Miss Carmichael isn't really dead?"

Billy barks a dry laugh. "It's whether she *stayed* dead. Your mother ever tell you any stories, growing up?"

"I suppose so, yes. Fairy tales and the like."

"Well. *My* mam's stories would make your skin crawl. About monsters. Old horrors. Things like the Abhartach and the Dearg-Due, a beautiful woman risen from the grave, who hungers for the blood of men."

"I've heard those old tales." The officer chuckles. "Meant to scare children and keep them in their beds. Surely you're not implying that's what's happening here?"

"I saw the papers. Read about that dead prossie they found. Heard she didn't have a drop of blood left in her body."

The constable clears his throat. "We're still investigating that. Try to put superstitions and gossip aside, Billy."

"Fair enough, sir. But mark my words. If it's a Dearg-Due, that prossie won't be the last body to turn up. Just watch. Any woman that'd kill her own sister . . . she might have it in her to kill again, wouldn't she? The lads were talking about it at the Hibernian meeting, just last week. Some of 'em used to work for the family. The Carmichaels. Won't own slaves, so they hire our sort for work. The Scots think themselves a cut above us, you know."

A chill runs up my back, from far more than the cold marble crypt behind me. It took only one person seeing me on the street to start the rumor that I still live. And despite the constable's warning, I have a feeling Irish Billy won't stay quiet.

How long will it take for word to spread that I'm a blood-drinking, undead murderess, risen from her grave? It seems ridiculous. But the Lowcountry is a place that lives and breathes superstition.

I wait for the men to depart, until I can no longer discern their voices, and flee through one of the cemetery's side gates. I've no real idea of where I should go next, or where I might hide. My disguise has been successful thus far, but how much longer will it work? I think of Arabella—that flare of recognition in her eyes when I stumbled into her at the pawnshop. I must assume she recognized me. It will no longer benefit me to believe otherwise.

My image will have been all over the papers, with news of my "death" on my way to the gallows. Something that sensational wouldn't easily fade from the public's consciousness. It's only a matter of time before someone else recognizes me, even if Arabella didn't. I need to leave the city.

I stay close to the river on my way back to town, my mind awhirl as I comb through my limited options. I can't chance the steam ferry to Mount Pleasant—too crowded. But with the money I've stolen, I have more than enough to buy food and charter a skiff across the Cooper. I'll take refuge in the salt marshes for now, on one of the many barrier islands along the coast.

By the time I reach town, I'm wedded to my choice. I buy a crust of bread from a vendor in the market, just as he's closing for the day, and fill my new leather water flask at the artesian well. After midnight, once the streets have emptied, I walk to the eastside wharves, staying in the shadows. Exhaustion tugs at my limbs, the sorrows of the day taking their toll. I'll find a place to sleep, close to the wharves, then hire a skiff at dawn. I'm nearly to the docks when someone whistles, high and loud. I freeze in place, ducking into a doorway.

"You there. Boy!" The voice is authoritative and loud. One of the dock officers on patrol, no doubt. "I see you there, hiding. Come out. I only want a word with you."

I slow my ragged breathing and unfold from the doorway. A young, clean-shaven guardsman stands there, in the guttering light from a streetlamp. He nods at me and smiles tightly. "A bit late to be on the streets, isn't it, lad?"

I don't answer, my mind combing over the reasons why a boy might be out this late on a weeknight.

"How old are you?" he prods, taking a step toward me.

I dip my chin. "Four . . . fourteen, sir." I'm quietly grateful that I've always looked younger than my age.

"Does your mother know you're out here alone?"

I could almost laugh at the irony of his question. "I don't have a mother anymore, sir. I live with my aunt."

"I see," he says, giving me a calculating look. "Why are you out so late?"

"My cat. She's been lost these three nights past, and I thought I heard her crying." The lie is so quick and clever I can't help but be proud of it.

"Well, best hurry home. There's only trouble to be found this late. There was a murder just a few streets away."

"Tonight?" I feel my skin blanch. "A . . . a murder?" Another one?

"Yes. Now hurry along. And don't let me see you out here again."

"Yes, sir." I stand there awkwardly, not knowing what to do. I must be deferential and walk on, and look as if I'm going home, lest the officer follow me and ask more questions I don't want to answer. But if I truly did have a cat, I'd still be worried about her. "What about my cat, sir?"

The officer's lips purse. He shifts his weight from side to side impatiently. "What does she look like, and where do you live? If I find her during my patrol, I'll bring her home to you."

"She's a ginger cat," I lie. "And I live there." I wave my hand in the general vicinity of Guignard Street.

He gives me a curious look. "Well, run along now."

I turn and walk away briskly, with purpose, as if I've somewhere to go. When I'm nearly to the corner, I turn to look. The guardsman has gone back to his patrol, pacing the riverfront with steady, long strides.

I sigh, my shoulders wilting. Another murder. Probably a lady of the night, like Sally, close as I am to Elliott Street's brothels and taverns. I'm doing the right thing, leaving. These streets no longer feel safe. For many reasons.

I tuck into an unlocked stall in the market and rejoice at the sight of a shriveled orange the dock rats have yet to find. After eating its stringy, tough pulp, I collapse into myself, my grief over Papa and my fears of the future taking hold. When sleep finally claims me, I dream of Rebecca.

In the dream, we're both young, and it is Christmastide. Mother sits in the background with her tatting as Rebecca and I play by the fire with new porcelain dollies. But something isn't right. Rebecca's doll looks just like her. But my doll has no eyes, no face. Her neatly parted brown hair is her only defining feature.

"What will you name her?" Rebecca asks. Her eyes are bright, and her color high—the perpetual roses in her cheeks even more florid, as if she's feverish.

"I don't know," I answer. "What would *you* name her?" I stroke my doll's soft hair.

"Prudence . . . or perhaps Temperance."

"She has good Christian values, does she?" I ask, slyly.

"It's more that she's plain. Like you. Those are good names for a plain girl."

I bite my lip and turn to study the flames flickering in the grate. Tears bristle in my eyes. Rebecca doesn't mean to be cruel. She's only parroting the things Mother says: that she's the pretty one, and I'm the clever one. Never mind how that makes the two of us feel. I ignore the hurt coursing through me, and smile at her. "What's your doll's name?"

"Caroline, like Mama." She admires the doll's long-lashed blue eyes, her red-gold locks. "Someday, she'll marry a prince and have a kingdom full of riches."

"That's a lovely thought."

Rebecca turns her head and coughs. It's soft, at first, and then it overtakes her completely, shaking her slender frame. Her face reddens, her eyes bulging as she fights for each wheezing breath. Mother rushes over, lifts Rebecca by the elbow. "To bed now, Becca. I'll fetch your syrup."

Irritation floods through me. It's always the same routine. Rebecca has a fit of coughing. Mother comes with the syrup. And no one ever investigates *why* the coughing happens in the first place. "This always happens in the winter. When there's a fire," I say. "And again, in the spring. Could it be the oak leaves?"

"What?" Mother asks, frowning.

"The leaves from the oak tree. Siobhan uses them for kindling."

"Your sister has a delicate constitution, Lillian."

"Yes, but . . ."

"You've tired her out, playing too long, that's all. You should know better. She needs her rest."

Rebecca coughs harder, her eyes running with tears. Mama pulls her away, the pretty redheaded doll forgotten by the hearth. I pick up the doll, study her perfect features. The urge to toss her into the fire overtakes me. My anger and resentment at my mother's favoritism and coddling simmer beneath the surface. Instead, I lay the doll carefully on Papa's chair near the hearth and steal three cookies from the tray Siobhan left on the sideboard. There are benefits to being invisible.

A VAMPIRE'S DIARY

Denise

I watched them discover her last night, slumped like a rag doll in a heap of silk brocade, her lovely face frozen in the same expression of shock she wore when I first stepped out of the shadows. My second conquest. Denise.

The coroner arrived after the officers, that great artifact of a doctor. I smiled in amusement as he lifted her limp wrist, as he checked for a pulse that ceased beating hours ago. He only shook his head, covered her with a shroud, and whispered his concerns to Sergeant Wesley. Wesley was excited, though he hid it behind his stoic expression.

I've given him something new, beyond chasing slaves after curfew and corralling belligerent drunks. Something novel. And I've only just begun.

Sally was an easier conquest than Denise, by comparison, but Denise's naivete made her fertile ground for my manipulations. Most gently bred girls are innocent, sheltered as they are from the world's wickedness. I'd been priming her for months, plying her with my impeccable manners, with flattery and sincere compliments. She was an accomplished pianist with a lovely alto voice. We spoke often of our favorite composers. She admired my knowledge of music and grew to trust me—enough to confess her deepest secret: She had a lover. A young man her family would never approve of. A grocer's son. With some coaxing, I learned his name. I offered to pass her letters to him, and his to her. The rest was pitiably easy. I sent a note to her, copying his untidy scrawl. Bade her meet him near his home on Judith Street. A young woman's romantic fantasies are an apt playground for seduction. She was most surprised to see me there, instead, but her trust in me was implicit. All it took was a lie. He'd fallen ill, and could not meet her, but I would carry whatever message she wished to his sickbed. She embraced me in gratitude, and this was when I pulled her into the shadows to complete my grim, but necessary, task.

Soon, all my work, my patience, will be rewarded. I already have my next conquest planned. Young, sweet Marjorie, whose husband recently expired from dropsy. She's in need of a listening ear. Gentle company. Yes, Marjorie will be next. But I will give it the time it requires. These things must be planned. Must be carefully designed.

SIX

I wake to a cacophony of voices, my eyes snapping open, the remnants of my dream fading like fog. The sun accosts my eyes, too bright. I spring to my feet, just as the owner of the fruit stall arrives. He swats at me with his meaty hands, landing a glancing blow on my right ear. "Out with you, boy! You'll steal naught from me!"

I flee, hiding my face from the crowds queuing in front of the stalls. I ignore the pangs of hunger that the freshly caught fish and hearty boules of bread stir as I rush from the market. I've slept much too late. The wharves are swarming with sailors from every far-flung corner of the globe, humming with languages both foreign and familiar. They pay me no mind as they go about their work, but at this late hour, finding a solitary skiff to take me to the marshes will prove challenging.

I'm nearly to Fitzsimon's Wharf when I hear a shred of conversation that stops me in place. A longshoreman, with skin as dark as a storm and the kind of broad shoulders his work imparts, holds court like a king, leaning against a stanchion with several young men gathered around him. "They found another girl last night," he says. "Over on Judith. Not a drop of blood in her body. A wealthy one this time. My Minnie is scared. But it seems he's going after white women, and you all know what that means." The longshoreman shakes his head. "Sergeant Wesley was asking all sorts of questions this morning. If you're a free man, make sure you have your papers on you. Stay quiet and keep your head down. After your work is done, go straight home, well before the curfew bells ring. If you're a slave, be even more mindful."

A murmur ripples through the crowd of Negroes, their voices low. Papa told me how often the finger of blame lands on men just like these—whether free or enslaved—whose every move is scrutinized, cataloged, and viewed with suspicion, simply because of the color of their skin. The sense of vigilant wariness I feel now is something these men deal with every single day.

Two murders. In less than a fortnight. Both bodies drained of blood. This is no coincidence. It's a pattern. For once, I'm not thinking of being captured, or of going back to jail. I'm thinking about the predator haunting these streets. A killer who might be anyone. Anywhere.

I pat my pockets, reassured by the weight of the coins there. I have money. My jewelry. The knife tied to my thigh, beneath my breeches. After buying a bottle of ale, some dried venison, and apples from the market, I find a dock with skiffs bobbing hopefully in the water and a sign tacked to the wooden post: **Boats for Hire**, with various landings and their tolls listed below. I approach an ancient man leaning against the railing, his sun-bronzed forearms knotted with muscle. "Hello, are you for hire? Can you take me across the river?"

"Yep." He gestures wordlessly at one of the skiffs, and I lower myself into the shallow-berthed boat. He unties the skiff and joins me, taking up his oars. "Where to?"

"Hog Island, please."

He raises an eyebrow. "Ain't nothing there, boy."

"I know."

He merely grunts and shoves off, sweeping the oars steadily against the current. I'm grateful he doesn't ask me questions for which I don't have answers.

The crossing is choppy and tedious with a single oarsman. Mid-channel, a miserable, spitting rain kicks up. It frightens me, being out on the water in such a small boat. I've never learned how to swim. My mind goes dire with a thousand tragic fantasies. It would be the ultimate irony for me to survive my own execution and premature burial only to drown in the Cooper. I huddle in the bow of the boat and cover my head with my cloak, convincing myself that the constant rocking is a comfort rather than something to be frightened of.

We make portage on a sand spit spiked with spartina, and after running the skiff aground, the boatman helps me out. I'm still shaking as my boots sink into the pluff mud. I pay him generously for his trouble and help him to shove off again.

And then I am alone.

I turn slowly, taking in the marsh's unfettered wildness. The wind cuts across the desolate scrap of beach, frigid on my skin. Over the river, I can see the city's many steeples and, farther out, the shallow profile of Fort Sumter, which brings William to mind. I wonder whether he's there, patrolling its battlements. Whether he was disappointed that he didn't get to see me hanged. He loved Rebecca fiercely. Everyone did. And who could blame them? She was beautiful. Charming. Everything I was not. Arabella had been right about one thing: I *was* jealous. Were it not for Rebecca, I'd be a married woman—an officer's wife—with children of my own. And if she hadn't died, even if she married William, at least I'd be a governess by now, teaching wealthy children how to read.

It's futile to think about what might have been. I push aside my resentment and trudge across the beach, shells crunching underfoot, and make my way to solid ground, where a stand of sycamore and pine promises shelter from the rain. I shiver beneath my cloak, hunger clawing at my belly. Once I reach the copse of trees, I sit on a fallen log and eat an apple, savoring its sweetness on my tongue. I chew down to the core and toss it into the underbrush. My provisions won't last long, even with rationing. I'll have to learn how to hunt out here. How to forage and fish. My life has become a game of survival, my existence now at the mercy of this desolate place and whatever sustenance nature provides. Once more, I'm struck by everything I've lost.

My life was easy, before prison. And while my time in jail hardened me, and made me resilient, it did not equip me for a life in the wilderness. I'm ill-prepared. Afraid of what might be lurking in the shadows. The streets of the city were at least familiar to me.

As if taunting me, the distant bells of Saint Philip's ring out the hour—nine o'clock—and the other church bells follow, the wind carrying their chorus to me. Mother will be rising about now. Has her routine changed at all, since Papa's passing? Will she dress in her mourning clothes and entertain callers? Before Papa's antislavery sentiments were discovered, she was one of the most celebrated hostesses in the city. Now Mother is an outcast among them. Their ostracism was her punishment for being a fallen daughter of the planter aristocracy. The wife of an abolitionist. I wonder, briefly, if she'll go back to buying slaves to prove herself worthy of the chivalry's good graces. I wouldn't be surprised. She and Papa were at odds over the matter of slavery, and she resented him for giving her lifelong lady's maid her freedom papers. Mother was ever doing her best to maintain the status quo.

I take a swig of ale and curl up with my back against the fallen log, listening to the sounds of the swamp. At first, everything is quiet, as if the marsh is holding its breath at my intrusion. But then I hear the call of a heron. A bittern's throaty warble. Life is everywhere here, apart from man's bustle and hum. Prison acclimated me to loneliness, to solitude. Though the openness of the marsh is unsettling, I could manage to be happy out here, I think, with the sky as my ceiling and the trees my shelter.

I finish my ale, then drift off to sleep.

When I wake, the sun hangs low, a wash of pink swathing the sky. I rise and stretch with a satisfied groan. A twig snaps, behind me. I whirl, widening my stance defensively, my eyes scanning the tangled underbrush. It's probably only a wild creature—a raccoon, or a deer, grazing at dusk. But if it's one of the wild hogs the island is named for, or worse yet, the murderer—

There's another snap, and a rustle. A flash through the trees, so fast I nearly miss it. Panic floods my limbs with cold fire. I slide my hand beneath my waistband, fingers curling around the kitchen knife tied to my outer thigh. "Who's there? Is someone there?" The air stills, and a shiver of anticipation runs up my back. My heartbeat drums in my ears, but I strain to listen over its frantic rhythm. There's nothing. Only the distant coo of a mourning dove. The gentle swoop of a pelican coasting overhead. Several minutes pass. Although I hear nothing more, the sense of being watched lingers. I sit again, my posture rigid against the rotting log.

I'm not alone out here. And though, for a moment, I convince myself I imagined it, I know what I saw. Eyes. And a glimpse of a white shirtsleeve.

SEVEN

Days pass without another sign of my mysterious visitor. I keep my knife close at hand and sleep lightly, sitting against the rotting log like a sentry on watch. But if they intend me any sort of ill will, it has yet to manifest. And so I do my best to get on with my new life in the marsh. At dead low tide, I cross Hog Creek to make camp farther inland, close enough to walk to Mount Pleasant to gather fresh water and steal, should I need to, but removed enough from civilization that I'll be safe from curious eyes. In a clearing sheltered by sycamore and silver maples, I begin gathering materials to build a structure. I pile fallen limbs and sticks beneath a sturdy young tree and cut spartina with my kitchen knife to serve as thatch for the roof. At the end of the day, my hands are raw from the sharp edges of the winter-tough cordgrass, and I'm out of breath from my exertions. My hunger and thirst demand attention, so I sit to eat an apple and chew on a piece of venison before sleep claims me.

The next morning, invigorated with purpose, I attempt to make a three-sided shelter out of the sticks and spartina. I stack the limbs, alternating directions, and nestle them at right angles to each other. I observed a group of slaves building a log cabin on Daniel Island once, and they used a similar method. By midafternoon, the structure reaches the level of my hips—high enough for me to crawl inside to sleep, but low enough to remain stable in the wind. Now I just need a roof. But when I place the first limb across the stacked logs, I underestimate the angle. And my clumsiness. It knocks against the left wall. The entire structure collapses as I watch, helpless to prevent it, all my hard work now reduced to the same pile of sticks I started with.

I curse in frustration, tugging at my hair. A fitful wind starts up from the north, cold and wet with rain. I huddle beneath my cloak under the tree and wait for the storm to pass, thinking over the flaws in my construction. Then it comes to me. I need mud. Mud will hold the limbs together, will stabilize them. Once the rains have ceased, I go out to where the pluff mud meets the sand. Careful not to get stuck in the mud's sucking softness, I use a large scallop shell I find on the beach to scoop up some of the foul-smelling stuff. I take the mud back to my campsite and use it to cement two sticks together. It works. Encouraged, I scour the woods for anything I might use to carry more mud and find a half-round scrap of tree bark to serve as a means of conveyance. It's slow going, and by evening, my legs are aching, but I continue to work by the light of the moon until exhaustion pulls me under and I sleep.

I finish the walls the next day. Before adding the roof, I allow the mud to dry. This time, when I lay the limbs across the top, cementing them to the walls with more pluff mud, the structure holds. I let out a whoop of triumph, pleased with my progress. I finish the following day, thatching the roof with mud-dredged spartina and gathering pine needles for the floor. That night, I sleep inside my little hermitage for the first time, and though the air is brisk, with my warm cloak, I manage to stay cozy and dry.

Though I soon run out of the dried venison, finding food proves less of a challenge than I imagined. Oysters are plentiful, and at low tide there are always a few black drum or redfish left flopping about on the shoals. I get over my initial squeamishness at eating raw fish very quickly. It's too risky to start a fire, even if I had the means to do so. The smoke would only alert people to my presence—defying my entire reason for coming here. While I'd much rather have steamed oysters, or chowder, the jail's dismal fare made me appreciate the sustenance *any* food might bring. Besides, raw fish is rather tasty—as flavorful as it is fresh from the briny, brackish water.

I find a few wild persimmons still clinging to their branches, wrinkled and dry, but with a lingering sweetness all the same. There are beautyberries and purslane. A spare bounty, but enough to add variety to my diet. Spring will come to the Lowcountry sooner than it does elsewhere, bringing with it a cornucopia of blessings. I need only be patient. There are far worse places one could be stranded.

It's empowering, my survival in solitude. I think of the sheltered, cosseted girl I once was. I never had to worry about my next meal, or whether I'd have clean clothing to wear. Siobhan changed my bed linens weekly and emptied my chamber pot every morning. My only tasks each day consisted of music lessons, needlework, or reading. Prison broke me of all my soft ways. I was forced to do hard labor—if I wanted a clean cell, I had to scrub the floors and my chamber pot myself. Kitchen duty was particularly brutal, and I still bear scars from Cook's mean lash when I failed to stoke the fires before her arrival one winter morning.

But out here, in the marsh, I've discovered a way of life I'd never considered. At first, I found the openness unsettling, accustomed as I am to confinement. But now . . . now my perceptions have altered. No one cares about my plain looks out here. My manners. My mode of dress or my family's name. Among the birds and creatures of land and sea, I am one with them. I'm free, with the horizon as my only threshold. Arabella Meade and others like her can have their gilded salons and their wide piazzas. The marsh is my palace, and it holds beauty beyond measure.

My reverie doesn't last long. February comes in like a lion, with miserable, drenching rains that soak through my hastily built shelter. I shore things up as best I can with pine needles and waxy magnolia leaves, cementing them to the roof with pluff mud. But I can do nothing to stop the seepage from the ground. My clothes become caked with silty mud, and I spend the days between squalls trying to dry them. The creek overflows and transforms to a lake, inching perilously closer to my campsite at high tide. It's rare for this much rain to come to the Lowcountry outside of hurricane season, but it doesn't relent until my patch of dry land is an island in the tidal surge.

Most interestingly, despite the rising water, my visitor has returned, which means they must be in possession of a boat. I caught a glimpse of them last night, furtive eyes in the shadows, a dark face surrounded by a halo of frizzled hair. A girl, if I had to guess. Perhaps a Gullah girl, wondering at the strange, pale haint of a creature squatting on her land. Or perhaps she's a maroon, escaped from her master. The Lowcountry marshes are a haven for fugitive slaves and a waypoint to freedom, where fishing boats and whalers from the North sometimes secrete fugitives in their holds on their way back up the coast.

That evening, the storms finally break, and I decide to leave my visitor an offering—to let her know I pose no threat. I comb through the jewelry in my pochette and select the sapphire ring, which I place on a stump near the edge of my camp, where the woods still provide cover. Once the sun sets, I eat the final, mealy apple I brought here from town, taking small, deliberate bites down to the core. Then I lie down and listen.

Sure enough, after an hour or so, I hear the sound of oars cutting through water, then the telltale rustle of footsteps through the brush. I slowly turn, watching through the gaps of my hermitage. My visitor cautiously tiptoes out of the woods, her head on a swivel. She's dressed in a simple white frock with a wide blue sash around her waist, her dainty feet bare beneath the hem, her hair curling about her face. She's young—no older than fourteen or fifteen—and pretty, with a sylphlike grace. She snatches the ring from the stump, looks right and left, and then disappears into the undergrowth once more. I smile and roll onto my back, drifting off to sleep.

The next morning, on the stump, I find a paper packet with benne wafers inside and something even more precious—fishing hooks and a length of twine.

Another week passes without a sign of my visitor. But thanks to her generosity, my belly enjoys as much redfish and tarpon as I could desire. I spend my days fishing and foraging, and at night I lie awake, restless, considering my future, and how I hope to spend it. Though I am safe and content for now, the days are beginning to bleed together. The marsh has welcomed me, and I've developed an affinity for the solitude it affords, but the thought of spending my life like this, alone and isolated, stirs my ennui. I need to seek out some semblance of civilization, even if I must remain on its fringes. And so, after the floodwaters recede, I decide to chance a trip into Mount Pleasant to see whether there's any news from town . . . and to steal, should opportunity present itself. I wait for the cover of darkness and make my way south, using only the moonlight as my guide. My senses have adapted to outdoor life. My eyesight is keener. My sense of smell sharper.

Mount Pleasant has grown since I last visited, some four years ago. New, handsome mansions line the outskirts of the small town. Though my fingers itch to break into any number of them, and raid their larders, I restrain myself. It isn't worth the risk. On the boulevard along Shem Creek, I have a run of luck. A shop window, left carelessly open. I peek inside, giddy with delight. It's a bakery. I hesitate for a moment, my conscience pricked. Apart from the drunken man, I've only ever stolen from the wealthy. But my survival—and my hunger—demands that I must put aside my reservations in this case. I push the sash up and climb through. While the kitchen is mostly bare, I spot two loaves of rye bread above the hearth, crusts brown and inviting. My mouth waters. I tuck one of the loaves under my arm and scan the small kitchen for anything else of use, but with no way to cook, flour and yeast will do me little good, although I grab a tin of salt to try my hand at curing fish. I climb back out the window and lower the sash to its original position. I tear off a chunk of the bread with my teeth, the taste exploding on my tongue. After weeks of nothing but fish, oysters, foraged berries, and bracken, the bread is an ecstasy.

I meander along the docks, admiring the high-masted ships and fishing boats, remembering the stories Grandmama told me. George Washington boarded the barge that took him to Charleston here on Shem Creek. She attended the lavish ball welcoming the president to the city when she was a girl of nineteen, something she spoke about with great fondness until her dying day. She wore a blue silk gown and a fashionable French wig, decorated with an ostrich-feather cockade. Washington danced the minuet with her and called her the most beautiful woman he'd ever seen. She claimed they enjoyed an evening of bliss together, and she even had a lock of hair she swore was his, although Grandmama's stories often bore too much shine to be fully believed.

I've nearly reached the middle of town, where I fill my water flask at a public well, when I see it. Tacked to a brick wall, alongside posters demanding the return of fugitive slaves, my own image stares back at me. It's the drawing the artist made of me in the courtroom, my eyes hollow, my cheeks gaunt, lips scowling. Unlike my grandmother, I've never been much to look at, but this likeness is decidedly ungenerous.

WANTED

LILLIAN CARMICHAEL

CONVICTED MURDERER AND FUGITIVE FROM JUSTICE

ANY PERSON WITH KNOWLEDGE OF MISS CARMICHAEL'S WHEREABOUTS

LEADING TO HER CAPTURE WILL RECEIVE AN AWARD

IN THE AMOUNT OF $400

DO NOT ATTEMPT TO APPREHEND THIS DANGEROUS FUGITIVE

An involuntary trembling starts in my legs and travels up my body. Just as I predicted, the gossip has spread, likely by Arabella. I'm certain now that she recognized me that day in the pawnshop. And although there's no mention of the recent murders, they're looking for me all the same. They know I'm alive. That I avoided my execution and escaped my grave. I was wise to flee the city. But even here, in this much smaller town, I'm not safe. If they capture me, if I'm seen and reported, it will mean certain death.

I wrap my cloak tightly around me, tuck the remaining bread into its folds, and walk at a fast clip with my head down, startling at every small sound. When I reach my hermitage, I crawl inside, where my trembling turns to full-body sobs. The next morning, after a fitful, restless night, I find more benne wafers and a small sweetgrass basket filled with cooked rice, red peas, and sausage. At least there's one person in this world who cares that I live. But can I trust her? Four hundred dollars is a lot of money. Enough to tempt anyone. But as I eat my friend's offering, the warm food nourishing my hunger, I feel ashamed. It's a hard way of life, to suspect every kind gesture as something sinister. My friend has just as much to lose as I do. She must. And so I place my Whitby jet brooch inside the sweetgrass basket after I'm finished eating and set it on the stump, to let her know her generosity is returned.

EIGHT

I'm out fishing in the marsh one mid-February morning when it happens. With the tide coming in, sluicing around my feet, I don't see the boar trap until it's too late. I only hear the snap of its jaws closing around my shin. A cry of pain tears through me as I tumble into the pluff mud. I will myself to remain calm, to breathe through the bright, sharp agony as I attempt to pry the teeth of the trap open with my hands. My exertions yield nothing but more pain, lancing up my leg with even the tiniest movement. A cold, familiar clamminess washes over me, and I vomit, heaving up my meager breakfast. The sun beats down on my face, reflecting off the estuary waters as the tide creeps higher. A new kind of panic washes over me. I'll be trapped here as the waters rise, pulled under by the thick, sucking mud. If I don't move soon, I'll drown.

Even through the pain, I have the sense to tear the fishing hook and twine from the branch I've been using for a fishing pole. I pocket them, then grasp the trap and pull it loose from the mud. I struggle to my feet, fighting the tug of the water around my shins. Blood streams into the water as I drag myself free, taking the trap with me. The teeth bite deeper into my flesh with every step. My head swims, stars sparking in my vision. I scan the landscape, trying to find my bearings through the fog of my agony, and trudge toward the trees, where the shelter of my campsite and dry land await. I've no mind what I will do once I achieve this smallest of victories. How I'll remove the trap. How I'll manage out here, alone, with a mangled leg. This could very well prove to be the end of me.

Once I reach the shore of my tiny island, I collapse, dragging myself on hands and knees toward my hermitage. My vision flickers before I make it inside, and I fall into a delirium of pain, the distant throb of my heartbeat the only sound in my ears.

When I come to my senses, two people are kneeling next to me on the ground, staring at me through the dim. I blink, my vision adjusting to the darkness. It's my friend, and she's brought someone with her. A man.

"We can't," he says, his voice low and sonorous. "You know that."

"She'll die if we leave her out here like this." The girl is sweetly voiced, but firm in her resolve. She's watched me long enough to know I'm not the boy I pretend to be.

They turn from me, continuing their conversation in hushed tones. Though I can't make out their words, I can tell they're arguing, and I can gather why. Two Negroes—whether free or not—found with an injured white woman means a death sentence. I'm a threat to their safety, even if there is a bounty on my head.

Their footfalls brush closer, and the girl squats next to me. I smile at her through the throbbing pain. She's wearing my sapphire ring on her thumb. "Daddy says we can take you up to Angel's Rest."

Before I can protest, before I can ask what Angel's Rest is, strong arms scoop me from the ground, lifting me. I cry out as the trap tightens around my shin, cutting into my flesh anew.

"Hush, girl. Be quiet now," the man scolds.

I wrap my arms around his neck and do my best to soundlessly breathe through the pain as he carries me to the water with long strides. A shallow canoe sits moored in the spartina. The girl boards first, one foot in the water, the other steadying the boat as her father loads me into the hull, pillowing me against a bundle of fishing nets. He takes up his oars, and we shove off into the current. It's a clear, star-filled night, lit by a fingernail sliver of moon.

Sometime later, I can't determine how long, the canoe slows, and comes to a stop, sand scraping against its berth. I lift my head. Lights stream across the marsh, reflecting in the shallow water. In the near distance, I see a house—a large one—silhouetted against the sky, lights blazing from its mullioned windows and its wide, lantern-lit piazza. A plantation house.

"Run and tell him what's happened," the man says. "I'll bring her."

"Yes, sir." The girl steps out of the canoe, bare feet splashing in the shallow water.

"Where are we?" I ask drowsily, my consciousness flickering. Everything feels like a dream.

The man sighs. "Angel's Rest."

Without another word, he heaves me over his shoulder like a sack of grain. I throttle the yelp of pain that tries to leap from my throat. The man steadies the trap with his other hand as best he can as he carries me. I can't see the house as we approach it, only the tabby path below us, winding through a corridor of mossy oaks and resurrection ferns.

"Good heavens, Noah. Bring her to the kitchen house." Another man's voice cuts through my flickering consciousness, crisp and luxuriously accented. An Englishman. Amid the jostling, I can make out a pair of long legs in well-cut trousers. Polished shoes. The scent of camphor and something vaguely herbal accosts my senses as he strides past us, leading the way. We go through a doorway, and light blooms all around me. "There, put her on the table."

Noah lays me gently down on a rough-hewn table and steps back. I turn my head and see a cast iron cookstove, shelves stocked with dry goods and spices, a deep soapstone sink. My friend stands just beyond the halo of lantern light on the table. She wears her hair wound up in a yellow turban tonight, the jet brooch I gave her pinned to the front. The style is becoming and makes her look older. She sees me looking at her and drops her eyes to the dirt floor.

"We'll have to get this trap off before we can do anything else," the Englishman says. "I'll put some water on to boil." I hear the door to the stove creak open. The clatter of crockery, followed by the smell of burning firewood. The Englishman floats into view again and gazes down at me with deep-blue eyes, ringed by a fringe of heavy black lashes. His dark hair grazes his collar in a tumult of waves, but he's clean shaven—a deviation from the current fashion for full beards. His cool hand brushes my forehead, sending a shiver through me. "She's already feverish. Could you help me, please, Noah? Hold her leg straight. I'll do the rest. These traps are nasty things." I feel Noah's firm grip close around my knee and bite my lip to keep from crying out as he straightens my leg.

The doctor—for he must be that—goes to the foot of the table and leans forward, his hair obscuring the lean planes of his face. "Now. Be very still, young miss," he admonishes me. "This is going to hurt. A lot. But then it will be over."

Just when I think I've reached the upper limits of pain, a white-hot knife's blade slices through me, followed by a wave of nausea as the doctor presses all his weight onto the leaves of the trap. It springs open with a groan, freeing my leg. "There we are!" he exclaims.

Suddenly, I feel hot and cold all at once. I begin to shake, from head to toe. My vision narrows to a pinprick. An ocean roars in my ears.

"She's falling into shock," I hear the doctor say. "That's to be expected, poor thing. I'll clean her wounds, stitch her up, and ready a room."

The last thing I see is the girl as she rushes to my side. And then the world goes dark.

NINE

The next few hours, or days, or weeks go by in feverish confusion. I fade in and out of consciousness. The doctor and sometimes the girl visit me. She presses warm cups of beef broth to my lips and bids me drink. I learn her name is Ruby. Ruby with the sapphire ring. The doctor changes my dressings once a day, with quick, gentle motions, dabbing a foul-smelling paste on my sutures before wrapping fresh linen around my leg again. I know the scent of him. Camphor. Lemon. Something earthy and warm I can't mark, but it's pleasant, all the same.

Through the fog of my fever, I can see that my accommodations are lovely, if a little shabby. The room they've placed me in must be on the second story of the house, with a gentle breeze that comes through the French doors in the evening, stirring the cobwebs in the corners. The walls are papered with a motif of bluebirds and cherry trees. Sometimes, when my fever is at its highest and the doctor covers my sweating body with cold, wet sheets, the wallpaper bluebirds flutter their wings and cock their smooth heads to study me with beady eyes.

In my delirium, I see Rebecca. She sits at my bedside and strokes my hair. Sometimes she sings to me, with a voice like spun honey. Once, she bids me follow her, beckoning me toward an open door, but I refuse. This is how I know I'm dying.

But I don't die. By some miracle, my fever finally breaks. With the doctor's assistance, I can sit up in bed for short periods of time and even lower myself onto a chamber pot. He turns his back, like a gentleman, but I feel no embarrassment. He's a doctor. The human body is far from a mystery to him, and prison destroyed all traces of my modesty.

Even though his caring nature is disarming, I'm wary. A man like him would be well read. Canny. He'll begin asking questions. Eventually, if I stay here long enough, he'll figure out who I am. As soon as I'm recovered, I need to leave. To find a new campsite. Or use the rest of my money to leave the Carolinas entirely, though the thought pains me and frightens me almost as much as staying.

One evening, he lingers in my room after bringing me dinner, and sits across from my bed, folding his long, lean body into a chair. I've progressed to soup, from broth, and it's delicious, with bits of carrot and potato. I steal glances of him as I eat. He's more beautiful than handsome. With his long-lashed eyes and finely sculpted jaw, he reminds me of an angel in a fresco. The plantation is appropriately named.

After I've finished eating, he rises to take the tray. He places it on the floor, then presses a cool hand against my forehead. "You've not run a fever for two days."

"That's good, isn't it?"

He smiles. "Yes, very. I think you're recovering."

"Thanks to you. You've saved my life."

He shakes his head. "No. Ruby did. And Noah. By bringing you here."

"Yes. All of you, then." I run a hand over my untidy, cropped hair, suddenly self-conscious of my appearance. "I must look a fright."

"May I brush your hair?"

"I'd like that," I say.

He crosses to the vanity and retrieves a silver hairbrush and comb, then returns, sitting on the edge of the bed behind me. He begins working the tangles free from my shorn locks. His ministrations are as gentle as always. "Why did you cut your hair?" he asks. "You were dressed like a young boy when you came here."

Just as I feared, he's curious about me. Too curious. And I'm unprepared for his questions. "I . . . I'm a vagrant. I found it safer to resemble a boy on the streets."

"I see," he says archly. "What is your name?"

My fever-addled mind skitters like a frightened mouse. In all my days of being alone, in concocting this ruse, I didn't consider my name. I need a new one. And quickly. "Mary," I spout. "Mary Jones." What a common name. My former cleverness has apparently departed along with the fever. I pray he can't see the flame of my face.

"Well then, Miss Jones, I'm pleased to meet you. I'm Alexander Mayhew."

Alexander. It suits him. Dr. Alexander Mayhew.

"Likewise, Dr. Mayhew."

He chuckles under his breath. "Oh, I'm no doctor. My father was, though. I helped him occasionally. Assisted with surgeries, once I was older. I was good with suturing." The brush stills. He rests a hand on my shoulder, and a quiver of something delightfully unexpected runs through me at his touch. "There we are. Would you like a mirror?"

I shake my head. I don't relish the thought of looking at my reflection in this state.

"Very well. I'll leave you to your rest. I can bring you some books from the library if you'd like."

"Oh, I would like that. Thank you, Dr. . . . Mr. Mayhew."

"Alex, please." He smiles at me. "There's no need for formalities here."

"When . . . when do you think I'll be well enough to leave?" I ask.

"Not for a while. You've just recovered from blood poisoning, and the effects of the infection could linger for months. The trap tore through your calf muscles, when you dragged it. It will take weeks for your leg to fully heal. You won't be able to walk unassisted for a while."

"That long?"

"I'm afraid so." That arch look again. "Surely, as a vagrant, you're grateful for a clean bed and a roof over your head, Miss Jones. I'm pleased to host you until you're well."

"I'm grateful, sir." For what else can I say?

He takes the tray and leaves me. I collapse back against the soft pillows. I've survived my own execution, live burial, a run-in with a boar trap, and blood poisoning. And all that brought me here. Surely there is a purpose yet, for my life. I'll just have to be patient with my recovery. And I'll need to be cautious about how much I share with Alex, despite his disarming nature.

Within another week, I'm back on my feet, but to walk, I need to lean on Alex, his arm firm around my waist as I make slow, trudging steps across the bedroom floor to sit by my window. The exercises make my leg seize and ache, but the menthol and camphor salve Alex massages into my muscles afterward helps. I've never been touched in such an intimate way by a man. And even though I know he's just using his skills to help me heal, the flutter in my belly is revealing.

A few days later, he removes my sutures, and I have my first proper bath in years, in a copper tub that Alex hauls to my room and places next to the fireplace. The clean, warm water sprinkled with fragrant medicinal herbs soothes my aching muscles. While I soak behind a screen, he brings me ladies' clothes—a calico day dress and undergarments.

Though my leg is still healing, and Alex tells me it will always bear scars, the deep puncture wounds from the trap have scabbed over and the infection is gone. In another week, I can manage to walk on my own for short distances, and Alex gives me a cursory tour of the second floor, including the library, which is filled to the rafters with books. Angel's Rest is a handsome house, like many built in the last century, tinged with an air of genteel decay. But although this house is beautiful, I can't help but wonder how many enslaved people worked here, how many gave their lives for its construction and toiled in thankless labor on the land surrounding it.

"Is this your family home?" I ask, running a hand along a row of gilded leather spines.

Alex shakes his head. "No, not at all, although I inherited it. I took one of my father's patients under my care after he died. A planter's widow. Lucrezia Phillips. She suffered from a chronic inflammation of the joints, and I agreed to become her live-in caretaker. She had no children and no relatives here—she was born in Italy. Milan. When she died, she left Angel's Rest to me."

I ponder this—a young, handsome, educated man giving up his life to care for an elderly and infirm woman. Surely a rare thing. "It was kind of you, to do that."

"Some say so," he says. "Some say it was greed. That I took advantage of her and an unfortunate situation. The truth of the matter is, Lucrezia and I fell in love. She died before we could marry."

"Was she young, then?"

"Only a few years older than I."

"That's terribly romantic. And sad." I look down at the dress I'm wearing and wonder if it belonged to her. "I'm very sorry."

"Thank you. The heart never heals from such a loss, but it's been nearly a decade since her passing. Please," Alex says, leading me through the library doors and down the hall. "You'll want to take in the view from the upper piazza."

He swings open the French doors leading to the wide balcony, and I go out to the railing, my breath catching in my throat. Beyond the moss-shrouded oaks, the salt marsh spreads out in all its languid beauty, its channels and inlets curving and curling through the spartina like golden ribbons in the setting sun. A falcon cries out, its chittering call echoing in the soft, briny air.

"Beautiful, isn't it?"

"Yes."

"The view from the widow's walk on the roof is even more spectacular. You can see all the way to Sumter and beyond from up there. But it's not safe. The railing is rusted. The weather, you know."

I turn my head and look south, where rows of leggy, untidy indigo grow. "Is Angel's Rest still a working plantation?" I ask lightly, with no judgment in my tone. As the daughter of an abolitionist, these sorts of questions are rife with inherent danger, but I aim to learn the measure of the man next to me . . . and whether Ruby and Noah are as free as they seem to be, or enslaved.

"No. Lucrezia was just as appalled by slavery as I. After her husband died, she released her slaves and gave them their freedom papers. Indigo sales were declining at that point, and she had more than enough money to live the rest of her days in comfort. Some of them stayed on in the marsh and took up with the free Gullah. Most took advantage of their freedom and went north."

"Are Ruby and Noah . . ."

"No," Alex says. "They're from another plantation. Up the Wando. They escaped and came to the marsh last year."

"I see."

"You've seen Ruby." Alex clears his throat. "I reckon you can gather why her father is so protective."

"Yes." With her youthful beauty, Ruby would be considered a "fancy girl." A house slave who would likely be subjected to her master's unwanted attentions. "It's good that they have you looking out for them."

He laughs. "They don't need me. They know these marshes better than I do. They bring me fish once a week. I pay them. It's enough to form an accord. They've grown to trust me. I don't take that lightly."

A beat of silence passes between us, one in which I consider telling Alex about Papa and his work. But it would be too revealing. Even though this man has shown me nothing but kindness, I must remember why I fled Charleston—to escape my past. I don't yet know Alex well enough to trust him. I'm still a fugitive—one with a healthy bounty on my head. The less he knows about me, the better. Still, my time of isolation in the marsh showed me I crave human companionship. A purpose, apart from merely surviving. Perhaps, if I can fully become someone else, there might be a future here for me, at Angel's Rest, if I prove myself useful. Even in my current state of infirmity, I might find ways to be helpful to those who have shown me kindness.

"Do you think . . ." I say, considering. "Do you think Ruby has been educated? That she knows how to read?"

"It's highly illegal for a Negro to learn to read, Miss Jones."

"I know that. But she's very clever. And she's already a fugitive. Knowing how to read will hardly endanger her more. Do you think she would *like* to learn how to read?"

Alex turns to me, his lips curling into a wide smile. "I think she would. Very much."

With Noah's reluctant permission, Ruby's reading lessons begin the following week. Alex builds a fire in the hearth and arranges a comfortable set of chairs at the long table in the library. I greet Ruby there. She's nervous, her arms clenched tightly at her waist as her eyes take in the shelves of books and come to rest on the writing slate and chalk pencil Alex procured for us.

"Please, Ruby. Sit," I say motioning to one of the high-backed chairs. "Don't be nervous."

We start with the alphabet. Ruby is a fast learner. By midafternoon, she's forming letters just as gamely and easily as I. We go through the alphabet twice more, and by the third time, Ruby has memorized it. We pause to enjoy the tea and lemon cakes Alex brings us (I've learned he does all the cookery himself—quite rare for a man) and then resume our lessons. I can tell Ruby is invigorated. As the afternoon advances and we begin sounding out simple words, her face glows with pride and her posture relaxes. She even laughs once, a sweet sound that makes me beam. She's beginning to trust me. I realize how much of a gift her trust is. It's unlikely I will ever have children, but teaching Ruby gives me a motherly sense of pride, even though what we are doing is highly illegal.

But at this point, what does it matter? Having faced my own execution makes me bold and reckless in ways I never would have been before.

When Noah comes to fetch Ruby that evening, she nearly skips to meet him. Although Noah is wary of me, he nods at me once from the library's threshold, his hat in his hands. When they depart, I can hear Ruby's excited chatter filtering from the hall. "I learned how to spell 'cat' today, Daddy!"

I go to the shelves and begin choosing books for our next lessons. I find a New England primer from the last century, proof that children once lived in this house, and a well-loved volume containing Washington Irving's *The Legend of Sleepy Hollow*. Alex comes in as I'm perusing his collection.

"You must be tired," he says. "You've been at this since morning."

I turn to him, smiling. "On the contrary. I've not felt so well in a long time."

"It seems you've found your calling." His eyes linger on mine, and I feel my cheeks redden. "I've never seen Ruby so giddy. Even Noah smiled to see her joy. A rarity."

"He *is* very stoic, isn't he?"

"He has reason for it. He's told me enough about his life to understand why."

"I can't imagine."

"Neither of us can, Miss Jones. Supper will be ready soon. We can eat in here, if you'd like. Together."

"I . . . I would like that." My blush deepens. I clutch the books in my hands. I'm becoming besotted with him. And is it any wonder? He's kind, handsome, and generous. My bitterness over William's betrayal has faded, with each day I've spent in this house. My attraction to Alex makes my courtship with William seem childish and shallow by comparison. Though I enjoyed our walks through the garden and about town, William never inspired desire in me. Only the familiar comforts of friendship. But now . . . something new is stirring within me. And perhaps the chance is there, slight though it may be, that Alex might feel the same bloom of longing as I. At the very least, he enjoys my company.

"I should go wash up before supper," I say, placing the books on the table, next to Ruby's slate.

"I brought a fresh ewer of water to your room. And another dress. I hemmed it this morning. It should fit." He grasps the back of his neck, as if nervous, gazing at me through his long lashes. "I believe the color will enhance the color of your eyes."

"I'm eager to see it," I say, pondering his ability to sew. Like his skills in the kitchen, it's another rarity among men, but he stitched up my leg remarkably well. Papa often had modistes and seamstresses for customers, who came in to choose fabrics with the ladies who hired them, but there was also the occasional tailor. Perhaps a man knowing how to sew wasn't so far-fetched.

Alex excuses himself to see to our supper. On my way to my room, I imagine I see Rebecca's form in front of the window, lit by the setting sun, her eyes hard and accusing. I brush aside the chill her presence engenders. Perhaps my senses are only deceiving me.

TEN

The dress Alex chose fits as if it were made for me. Its graceful neckline sweeps across my shoulders, exposing their freckled tops before falling into subtle ruffles that cover my upper arms. The fabric is embroidered with vines along the edges of the Basque waist and layered, bell-shaped skirt. I recall seeing samples of this fabric in one of Papa's swatch books. Chinese silk taffeta, in a rare shade of periwinkle blue. Fine and very, very expensive. This dress must have been Lucrezia's. One her modiste made from the same fabric I helped Papa choose years ago, when I was but a girl. Even though Rebecca was the fashionable one, Papa always trusted my instincts when choosing our inventory for his mercantile. How strange for my old life to intersect with my new one. I take it as a sign. A hopeful one. I think Papa would approve of Alex. Perhaps, in some small way, this is his way of guiding my future, and giving me his blessing, from beyond the grave.

I glance at myself in the mirror above my dressing table, pinching my cheeks. The color of the fabric enhances the violet tone of my eyes, and livens my sallow skin. I step into the hall. Candlelight streams through the open library doors, beckoning me. Inside, Alex has laid the table with china and crystal, sparkling in the light of a multiarmed candelabra, fitted with sperm oil candles. No smoking tallow at Angel's Rest. A roast sits on the table, surrounded by carrots and potatoes. The smell is so delicious it makes my head spin.

"Miss Jones," Alex says, rising as I enter. He looks even more handsome than usual, dressed in formal dinner clothes, a silk cravat tied at his throat. His dark waves gleam. The candlelight etches shadows beneath his high cheekbones, accenting the lift of his smile. "I see the dress fits."

"It's beautiful," I say, gesturing to the layered skirt. "This fabric. My fa—" I bite my tongue, cursing myself for my near, careless slip. I've decided to tell Alex my father was a soldier, not a merchant, if he ever asks about my family. I long to be truthful with him about my former life, but I cannot. The stakes are much too high. "The dress is very fine. Thank you."

"Well, it seems a shame to let it go unworn. Beautiful things deserve to be enjoyed. Please, will you join me?"

I sit next to him, and he pours wine into the crystal goblet nearest me. I raise it to my lips and drink. It's rich and dark, with an underlying peppery tone.

"Zinfandel," Alex says with a smile. "A newer wine variety. Have you ever tasted anything like it?"

"I can't say that I have." It's been so many years since I've enjoyed a proper, seated dinner, much less wine. Papa preferred ale and cider with supper, although Mother would insist upon French wine for formal occasions. "It's delightful."

Alex carves the roast and serves it to me, ladling sauce over the meat. I dredge the meat in the sauce and lift my fork to my mouth. A moan of pleasure escapes my lips. It's so tender it melts on my tongue. After years of near starvation in prison and in the marsh, and nothing but broth and soup during my recovery, this meal feels worthy of a queen. It makes me curious about Alex's financial standing, and how he can afford such sumptuous food.

"Is it good?" he asks, his eyes sparkling.

"Heavens, yes," I say, laughing. I carve another piece with my knife, savoring the taste more slowly this time.

"Perhaps in a day or so, we might try the stairs, and have supper together in the dining room," Alex says. "I'm pleased with how your recovery is progressing, but you still need to build your strength."

I thrill at the thought of more dinners with Alex. Not just because of the decadent food, but his company. "Meals like this will certainly help, I think. I already feel quite restored."

He takes a drink of his wine, the liquid staining his lips berry dark. I imagine the feel of those lips against my throat, and press a hand against my face to cool it.

"I think it might be best for you to remain here, after your recovery, Miss Jones. Have you heard any news from Charleston?"

I still. Lift my wineglass again, my mind going in a thousand directions at once. "No, I haven't," I lie.

"Two young women have been found murdered in the city. Very unusual circumstances. *Exsanguination.*"

"I don't know what that means." I compose my face and concentrate on carving my roast into orderly squares.

"It means their bodies were drained completely of blood. It's extraordinary."

"How terribly gruesome."

"Yes. It is. The first was a prostitute. The other a planter's daughter, a young woman out on an evening walk alone." Alex leans forward in his chair, studying me. "I think it's very unsafe for a woman to be alone, don't you?"

"It seems so."

"I'm glad Ruby brought you here, Mary. Brought you to me. There are far too many monsters in this world."

Alex's fingers brush my hand. I shiver, a tingle of delicious longing trembling through me at the sound of my new Christian name on his lips. If he believes me to have any part in these murders, it doesn't show. There's only concern, and a disarming warmth in his eyes. I take a deep breath, my other hand unclenching beneath the table. "I'm glad of it, too."

After we finish our meal, Alex escorts me to my room and turns down my bed. "Tomorrow, after your lessons with Ruby, let's walk the upstairs hall to build your endurance. And the day after, we'll try the stairs."

"I'd like that," I say. "Thank you."

"Good night, Mary. Sleep well."

After he leaves, I undress down to my shift, folding the beautiful dress and placing it in one of the bureau drawers. A faint hint of Lucrezia's perfume lingers in the fabric. Something earthy and exotic, like incense from the Orient. I wonder what she looked like. What made Alex fall in love with her. Whatever it could have been, I hope that in some small way, I might inspire the same affection, given enough time. If tonight's conversation is any indication, Alex wants me to stay here, with him, at Angel's Rest. Perhaps, as Mary Jones the orphaned young governess, I might have a new chance at life—and love—yet.

A VAMPIRE'S DIARY

Marjorie

Marjorie was nearly my undoing. She fought me. Quite unexpectedly. Her town house was a horror, afterward. I detest gore. It offends my refined sensibilities, but it couldn't be helped, I'm afraid. My seductions began pleasantly enough. Her tearful confession to me in the weeks before my conquest—that she had never loved her husband, that his death had been a blessing—was her tacit invitation. I lavished her with attention, with praise, with flowers, and sent her ardent letters, declaring my desire to court her. She demurred at first, but I quickly overcame her initial reticence with my charm.

On the appointed evening, Marjorie dismissed her servants before my arrival, as I'd instructed, and served me a sublime dinner before leading me to her boudoir. I'd taken my time undressing her, savoring her little gasps and moans of pleasure. She'd been ready for me. Pliant and submissive. When she realized my desire transcended the sexual, she panicked, just as I've come to expect. But the excitement of the moment provoked an excess of energy—and she fought so heartily she nearly escaped through her window. My task was not easily completed. I must consider an alternative method for my next conquest. I've become too cavalier. Brash. My successes with Sally and Denise emboldened me. But all my work could be for naught if someone heard Marjorie's screams or saw me arrive earlier in the evening. Thank God I had the foresight to take all the letters I sent to her and burn them.

I must be cautious until the fervor is forgotten and the chivalry grows complacent once more, as they always do. But Marjorie's blood, her rich, sweet blood flavored with precious fear, is my greatest prize yet.

ELEVEN

The next day, Ruby arrives for her lessons at noon, eager to learn. We go over the alphabet again, which she recites to me twice, without hesitation. I carefully open the primer, its binding worn from years of use. The illustrations are puritanical, and the language antiquated, but they'll serve our purpose all the same.

"In Adam's fall, we sinned all," I recite, and Ruby follows, tracing her finger over the words. Everything is going well, until we get to the letter *F*.

"The idle fool is whipt at school."

Ruby glances at me, then at the book. She pulls her lower lip inward. Her posture stiffens.

"What's the matter, Ruby?" I ask.

"I can't . . . I can't say that, ma'am." Her voice is soft, tremulous. She looks at me, her eyes wide. "You ever been whipped before?"

I have been. By the cook, at jail. I still remember the painful welts from her lash. "Yes. Once."

Ruby grunts. "Well."

"Let's move on, shall we?"

But things don't improve. The dismal alphabet is full of recrimination and punitive rhymes. Ruby goes silent after "*J* for Job," her hands folded on her lap. Job's story of suffering is certainly a somber one, but there seems to be something else going on beneath the surface of Ruby's reticence. I close the primer and set it aside.

"Ruby, what's the matter? We were doing so well."

"I'm just tired. That's all."

But there's something deeper behind her eyes. An old hurt I can't fathom.

"If there's something bothering you, Ruby, you can talk to me. You can trust me."

She sucks in a quick breath, draws her lower lip into her mouth. "They use Bible stories and verses . . ." she says, her words trailing away. "The masters. They use them to make us think our suffering is some kind of glory. To keep us down. Their preaching ain't no kind of blessing." She looks at me, her eyes narrowing. "Their god is mean."

A wave of shame washes over me. I've witnessed what prison does to the enslaved. How the warden forces them to labor. How they are sent to the jail by their masters, to be punished. I should have considered Ruby's past when I chose the materials to teach her. I was rash. I push the book away. "I'm so sorry, Ruby. We'll choose something else to learn with. No more Bible verses or stories. No moralizing."

"I . . . I do want to learn to read, Miss Mary. I do."

"I know. But there are other books you might learn from. How about I read a story to you, instead?"

I open the other book to *The Legend of Sleepy Hollow* and begin to read, running my finger along the sentences while Ruby looks on. Eventually, her shoulders lower and her demeanor softens, drawn in by this charming story about a bachelor schoolmaster sent to the haunted countryside. Although I worry when we get to the passages about Mr. Crane's classroom discipline, Ruby seems unbothered, given the context of the words and the schoolmaster's apparent favor for the meek over the strong.

"I like this, much better," she says after a while. "Can I try?"

I place the book in front of her and point to a sentence. "You've seen this word several times, Ruby. What is it?"

"'All.' *A-L-L*."

"Yes! Very good."

She smiles. I point to the next word. "This one is longer, but you've seen a similar word as well."

"'The'?" she asks.

"Yes. Now, put an *s* on the end of it and extend the *e* sound. It's called a long *e*."

"Thes . . . these." Her eyes brighten. "All these!"

"Yes!"

She progresses through the phrase with focused deliberation, until she's nearly read the entire thing: *All these, however, were mere terrors of the night, phantoms of the mind that walk in darkness . . .*

We talk about commas and semicolons, and then I close the book to mark our place, noting Ruby's yawn and my own aching legs and back, stiff from hours of sitting. "Why don't you lie down on the davenport, Ruby, and take a nap, until your father comes to fetch you. We've done a lot today, and a young mind needs rest. You're safe here, I promise."

"Maybe I will, just for a little while. To rest my eyes. I won't be able to come tomorrow. We've got to empty the crab traps. It takes all day."

"All the more reason for you to rest."

She nestles onto the leather-covered sofa in front of the crackling hearth. I cover her with a woolen blanket and leave her, closing the library door behind me.

I find Alex on the upper piazza, looking out over the marsh. He turns at the sound of my step on the boards, greeting me with a smile. "I heard you and Ruby laughing. Things are going well, I take it?"

I join him at the railing, basking in the warm glow of the lowering sun. "Yes, she's a quick and clever study." I consider telling him about Ruby's response to the primer but decide not to. I've apologized to Ruby and will be more careful in the future. I don't want to give Alex any reason to question my abilities or cause undue concern.

"I'm not surprised she's catching on quickly. She's a bright girl." Alex clears his throat. "I've been wondering about you, Mary. How did you come to be all alone out here? An educated young woman, who can read and write . . . quite rare for a vagrant."

I school my face into a neutral expression. "I hoped to be a governess, but I was orphaned at a young age and was forced to leave my education behind. My father was a soldier. He died in the Mexican War."

"I'm sorry to hear that."

The lie about Papa is smooth, impressive, and believable, just as I hoped it would be. Now I just need the right sort of lie for Mother. "My mother passed when I was just a few days old—of puerperal fever. After Papa died, I was on my own."

"Ah." Alex turns to me, a smile twitching at the corner of his mouth. "Yet your posture and manners are those of a gently bred woman. A lady. I watched you, last night, when we dined together. Absolutely impeccable, wiping your mouth before every sip of wine."

I stumble over my words, trying to recover my wits. "Papa was an officer. He could afford a governess. She taught me proper etiquette. Dancing."

"So, an officer who could afford a governess for his daughter, but died without leaving her either a pension or a guardian? You're hardly the street urchin you've made yourself out to be, Miss Jones."

I freeze, taken aback by his return to formality. "What do you mean?"

"Who *are* you? Really?"

Panic steals my breath, my tongue suddenly dry and useless in my mouth. "I . . . I'm not—"

"Are you married? Is that it? Ill-used by your husband?"

"No. Not—"

"Is it the law, then? Have you done something wrong? People don't take to the marshes unless they're desperate, or on the run."

I grip the railing, my breath coming faster. This is what I feared. Why I isolated myself. To avoid these kinds of questions. "No. I . . ."

He fixes me with his steady, keen gaze, one dark eyebrow arching upward. "I see. You don't trust me. How old are you? At least be honest with me about that."

"Four and twenty."

"And your real name?"

"Mary. I swear it."

He smirks. In the distance, Fort Moultrie's cannons ring out, as they always do at sunset, an apt counterpoint to Alex's volley of questions.

"I'm not feeling very well, Mr. Mayhew," I say. "I'm going to go lie down." My head is woozy, a tumble of nausea running through my gut. I turn to go back to my room, leaving Alex on the piazza. As I pass the library, I see that Ruby is already gone. Once in my chambers, I splash cold water onto my face to calm my flushed skin, and turn down my bed, drawing the covers over me. I'll need to leave soon. Abandon this place of fragile respite. But I don't *want* to. I've grown accustomed to the comforts of Angel's Rest. The purpose I've found with teaching Ruby. The pleasure of Alex's company and the thoughtful way he looks at me. Against my better judgment, I'm smitten. My misplaced affection could cost me everything. Still, I consider what might happen if I told him everything. Perhaps, if I were honest, he'd understand. Ruby and Noah trusted him with their secret, after all, and they have just as much at stake as I do.

Instead of sleeping, I war with myself as the hours grow long. Alex brings food and leaves it at my bedside. I pretend to be asleep. After the house goes completely silent, and the moon glows through the windows, I rise and pace the floorboards in my room, my thoughts disjointed. I go back and forth with myself, arguing in hushed tones. I could tell Alex the truth. All of it. Or I could sneak out, tonight, and find another haven. Some remote hummock of an island where I can disappear. But how long will it be until the past catches up to me again?

I wonder about the murderer, and whether he still stalks the streets of the Peninsula. Whether there's still a bounty on my head. It's been over a month since I fled to the marshes. Ignorant of the news as I am, out here in the hinterlands, I've no knowledge of the wider world.

A sound interrupts my harried deductions. I still, listening. Footsteps, coming down the hall, then descending the staircase just outside my room, followed by the creak of the entry hall door. I rush to the window, parting the drapes ever so slightly. A woman descends the front steps, long blond hair streaming loose down her back. She wears a low-cut ball gown, her slippered feet quick on the tabby path. She glances furtively over her shoulder, her rouged lips pursing, and then disappears between the oaks.

I step back from the window, surprise and jealousy stealing my breath. So, he has a woman, then. Paid company, from the looks of her. My hands clench and unclench. I imagine them together, Alex's mouth tracing kisses down her slender white neck. I might have known. A man's loneliness craves succor. Bachelor though he may be, Alex is no celibate. My jealousy is fierce, radiating through my body and stealing any chance of sleep.

As the sun rises, I dress, buttoning my borrowed calico bodice with trembling fingers. I don't wait for Alex to bring my breakfast. I swing open the door to my room and head decisively for the stairs. Though my leg protests, my spite helps me manage the descent. I find him in the front parlor, reading the newspaper. He lowers it and looks up at me.

"You should have waited for me," he says steadily. "You may have gotten down the steps on your own, but your leg hasn't healed well enough to climb them again."

I glare at him, my breath heavy from my exertions. "Then I suppose I'll stay downstairs, won't I?"

"You're upset about something, Mary. It's all over your face." He folds the paper and lays it aside. "Have I offended you in some way?"

"I saw you had company last night," I say.

I note the brief look of surprise that flits across his countenance.

"So. You saw Varina." He clears his throat. Crosses his right leg over his left knee.

"Who is she?"

"A friend."

"I see." I say nothing more. I merely stare out the lace-curtained window over his shoulder and blink rapidly against the tears threatening to spill over. As much as I want to lash out, I hold my tongue. He's already suspicious of me. I have no right to feel jealous. I'm a guest in this house, here by his grace. He could turn me out in an instant.

"You've no reason to be concerned, Miss Jones. Varina comes to see me for tonics. Medications. That's all. A lot of the local women do. Sometimes they come to me by night because it's safer for them to do so. Especially if they're in some sort of trouble." He sighs, and stands, stretching languidly. "I have a great deal of sympathy for a woman in trouble. Don't you think it's time you told me the truth? I had the feeling you've been lying to me. Now I have proof of it."

A high-pitched whine starts up in my ears. "I don't know what you're talking about."

"Don't you, *Lillian*?"

All the air goes out of the room.

He takes the newspaper from the table next to his chair, and hands it to me. Above the fold, my courtroom portrait glares in black and white—my dour expression, my severely parted hair. The headline beneath declares: Lillian Carmichael Suspected in String of Uncanny Murders. Reward Offered.

"That's you, isn't it? A terribly unjust likeness, but it *is* you."

"No. My . . . my cousin," I stammer. "Lillian is my cousin. We look alike."

He advances on me, backing me toward the staircase, until I can retreat no farther and the newel post presses against my shoulder blades. The newspaper drops to the floor. My heart is a wild, panicked bird trapped in the cage of my ribs. He traces a finger up my cheek. Pauses on the mole next to my right eye.

"Cousins don't usually have the same birthmark. Twins sometimes do, but even that is rare." His eyes search mine. He's so close I can feel the heat from his body. I draw in a shallow breath.

"You haven't read the article yet," he continues, "but it's full of ridiculous conjecture. They're saying you're undead. That you're some sort of craven creature, risen from the grave with a hunger for blood.

But I can see your pulse, through your skin. Hear your breath. I also know you were here when the most recent murder happened."

"There's been another?"

"Yes. Three nights ago. Which makes me *your* alibi, Lillian. I can help you, if you'll let me. If you'll trust me."

"How?"

"Your ruse is lacking in confidence. You have far too many . . . tells, my dear." His finger traces my jawline. "Your eyes widen when caught off guard. You stumble over your words." He smiles wickedly, and my belly swoops. He's read me like an open book. "Yes. Every one of your cards is showing. And from the shadows beneath those pretty eyes, I gather you didn't get a wink of sleep last night, because of our conversation on the piazza, or your assumptions about Varina. So now, I'm going to help you back to bed. When you wake, we'll talk about the future, and the nature of our relationship." He grips my chin, his thumb pressing against my lower lip, and I nearly swoon at the hunger in his eyes. "Do you trust me?"

"I don't know. I . . . I don't trust anyone."

"Given your situation, I don't think you have much of a choice." Without hesitation, he sweeps me off my feet and carries me up the stairs, like some helpless damsel in a fairy tale. But in this story, I don't know whether I've met my charming prince, or the wolf.

TWELVE

When I wake, the blond woman I saw from the window last night sits at my bedside. Varina. I startle, sitting up. She smiles at me, one hand idly stroking her long locks. Up close, she's undeniably beautiful, with wide, blown-out pupils rimmed with blue. There's something familiar about her face, though I can't mark what it is. "There you are, love," she says in a lilting voice. "Alex sent me to check on you. You've slept most of the day."

"I . . ." I glance around, trying to get my bearings. Warm sunlight streams through the windows. This feels like a dream. "What are you doing here? Where is Alex?"

"Alex is occupied with other matters." She bites her lip and smiles at me coquettishly. "Aren't you a dainty thing. Like a pretty doll."

I blush and look away. I've always been self-conscious of my petite frame, and dislike when people comment on it.

"I didn't intend to insult you," she says.

"You haven't," I say defensively. I decide I don't like this woman. At all. For more reasons than my jealousy. I want her to leave.

"You've no reason to be jealous of me. Alex is quite taken with you."

My blush grows more furious. I don't know what to say, so I don't say anything.

Varina rises, the cheap, rose-colored satin of her skirts whispering softly. "Come along, I've something to show you."

"What is it?"

"You'll see. It's a surprise."

I stay in bed, eyeing her warily as she walks toward the door. She glances over her shoulder, gives me that same flirtatious look. And god help me, my curiosity gets the best of me. I stand, shoving my feet into my slippers. "You're very convincing."

She laughs and opens the door. "I know."

I trail her down the hall, to a room near the end. She grasps my hand and pulls me inside, her eyes luminous in the half-light pouring through the heavy drapes. "Do you trust me, Lillian?" she asks. Only her voice has changed. The lilting tone is gone. Alex's crisp British tenor has replaced it.

Before I can gather my wits, the curtains open, sending a blinding wash of yellow light into the room. I gasp, blinking. Alex stands before me, in Varina's rose-colored gown, a blond wig in his hands, his dark hair wild about his face. He gives me an impish smile with his rouged lips, and gestures around the room, which is filled with racks of costumes and gowns. Wigs of every imaginable color and style sit on wire forms.

"As I told you, I'm not a doctor. Nor am I the charming Varina," he says, his accent shifting once more, to one touched with a hint of Carolina hill country. "I'm all of them. And none of them. I'm an actress, Miss Carmichael. A rather good one, if I do say so. And my real name is Kate O'Malley."

I stand there, stunned, for at least a full minute. "How did you . . ." I whisper.

Kate/Alex/Varina smiles at me and closes the distance between us. "You're not angry, are you? Perhaps I went too far with my dramatic reveal."

"I don't know what to think. To say." I sink down on a nearby divan, flummoxed.

"You were going to find out eventually, you know. Alex is just an invention to keep outsiders from prying too closely into my life. It's much easier to navigate this world as a man. You know that. It's why you were pretending to be a boy."

"I suppose you're right." I find I can't look this person in the eyes—this person I was fully convinced was a man. One I've all too quickly become infatuated with.

"I know you're disappointed. You had an idea of who I was, and now I've shattered that. But Alexander Mayhew *is* me. All of my characters are me, my dear, whether male or female. And if you truly want to fool people into thinking you're Mary Jones, or whoever else you'd like to be, you need to inhabit her completely, just as I do with Alex and Varina. Because what you're doing now . . . it isn't deceiving anyone, I'm afraid."

I sit there, still in shock. I've been tricked. Played for a fool. I can't quite parse how I should feel about it. But I was a liar, too. Pretending to be someone I was not.

"You need to know everything about Mary Jones," Kate continues. "Who she loves. Her favorite color. What she eats for breakfast each day. Just as if you've *been* her your entire life. That's how you sell your act. Whether you're performing for an audience of one or a thousand."

The next words pour from me, without thought. "Did your Lucrezia know? That you're really a woman?"

"Yes. And Lucrezia taught me almost everything about acting. She was once an opera singer. A prima donna. That's where her husband met her—at the theater. It scandalized Charleston when he brought her home as his wife. A wealthy planter marrying a foreign actress? Unheard of."

"You said you were in love . . ."

"We were." Kate's blue eyes crinkle at the corners. "Now you're well and truly scandalized." She clears her throat. "Not only is she *not* a man, ladies and gentlemen, she's a follower of Sappho." Kate gives a crisp bow, and I can't help the smile that jumps to my lips. "I can go back to being Alex," she says. "If it makes you more comfortable. Your dashing British gent."

I look at Kate and consider my words carefully before I say them aloud. How many times have I pretended to be someone I'm not, even before now, wearing the mask others expected? To gain acceptance and love, I've spent my whole life appeasing. Placating. My fawning nature nearly destroyed me. How on earth can I ask the same of this person I've only just met, merely to continue my girlish infatuation? It would be selfish. Wrong.

"No. I don't think that would be fair of me, would it? I'm very pleased to meet you, Kate," I say, offering my hand.

"Likewise, Lillian." She takes my hand and quickly releases it. "Now, let's find you a proper costume. I need to go to town tonight to perform as Varina, and I don't want you doing anything foolish while I'm gone. You're coming with me."

Three hours later, we're strolling slowly along the Battery, arm in arm, two well-dressed ladies out for an evening constitutional. The first hints of springtime are in the air, and the days are getting longer. Even at six o'clock, the sun's muted glow still casts soft light over the harbor.

I catch a glimpse of myself in a window—I'm adorned in green shot silk of middling quality, my shorn hair covered with bouncing auburn curls. The wig itches terribly, though Kate told me I will grow used to it. I don't recognize myself. I doubt my own mother would.

Every few feet, my leg reminds me of my injury, my calf muscles pinching as we turn the corner and walk up a small incline. Though my range of motion is improving every day, and I can manage long, flat distances with relative ease now, any sort of rise is still a challenge. Kate slows, allowing me to rest. "The teahouse where I read fortunes is just ahead," she says. "You can find a table and sit to rest your leg. If you order a cup of tea, Mabel won't mind if you stay there all night."

"That's how you make money, then? Reading fortunes?"

"Yes. I read tea leaves and then perform. I provide the odd tincture and tonic to the locals out in the marsh, but this work is my real bread and butter. I play in the occasional operetta at the theater, too, and entertain at private parties. Those pay the best."

"I see." It explains her array of costumes and wigs . . . and makes me wonder just how many characters live underneath Kate's skin.

"You're judging me, aren't you?" she says, her chin tilting up. "You think my work tawdry."

"No . . . not at all. Besides, I'm hardly in a position to judge anyone."

"You're right about that," she says rather smugly. "Be mindful, tonight. Most of Miss Mabel's patrons are ladies, and polite gentlemen, but there's the occasional blackguard with wandering hands who likes to try his luck."

"I'll do my best to avoid attention."

She nods and pulls me toward a café, its flagstone patio lit with oil lamps. With bow windows trimmed with blue sashes, it has a vaguely Parisian feel (although I've never been to Paris, so I can't say for certain). A sign hangs above the door, etched with gilded blossoms: **Mabel's Tearoom.** I walked these streets countless times in my free years and never noticed it, tucked away in this little alley off Gibbes.

Some of the ladies sitting at the outdoor tables wave at Kate as we cross the patio. Regulars, then. One of them tugs her aside—a pretty, portly young woman wearing a cheerful, striped dress. "Varina, you must know," she rasps conspiratorially. "You were right about the sister. She isn't really his sister. Not at all."

"I'm dreadfully sorry to hear that, Millicent," Kate says, slipping effortlessly into Varina's soft, lilting accent. "I don't relish being right. But the leaves never lie."

Millicent shakes her head with a sigh. "Well, it's better I find out now than after taking my vows. Can you imagine?"

"You deserve better, Millie."

"I do, don't I?" With a satisfied nod, the young woman turns back to her companion.

"Did you really see that in her tea leaves?" I ask.

"No," Kate whispers. "But her suspicions were well founded. Her fiancé came here with her once. He cornered me in the back and propositioned me. She already knew he was a cad. I just provided confirmation." She smiles. "The *sister* was his mistress. I found out about *that* from one of the other actresses at the theater. I read people much better than I read tea leaves, my dear. Just like I read you."

Inside the cozy café, which smells of freshly baked goods and coffee, an older woman with a warm smile approaches us, an apron tied around her waist. "Ah, Varina. There you are!" she exclaims. "You've already had two customers looking for you."

"I'm sorry I was delayed, ma'am," Kate says. "They haven't left, I hope?"

"No. They're waiting in your alcove."

"I'll get to it, then." Kate glances at me. "This is my friend, Miss Jones. Miss Jones, this is Miss Mabel Cahill, the proprietress of this fine establishment. Could you please find her a table and a cup of tea, Mabel? Take it off my evening pay."

"Certainly. Follow me, Miss Jones."

Kate weaves through the tables toward the back of the room, then disappears into a candlelit alcove draped with deep-blue velvet. I'm nervous without her at my side, but follow Mabel into the main dining area. It's been years since I've been to any sort of restaurant. My eyes skate around the room, but I'm careful not to let my gaze linger on anyone for too long. I pray my costume is successful enough to disguise my identity. After my brief encounter with Arabella, I'm wary of public establishments.

"How long have you known Varina?" Mabel asks. She sits me at a table next to a small stage in the front corner, near the windows. "She's never brought a friend with her before."

"Oh, only a few weeks," I say.

"Well, you're welcome to come any evening she works." Mabel smiles. "What sort of tea do you like, dear? We've just gotten a new shipment of oolong. It's lovely, bright and fresh. Or we have coffee, if you prefer."

"The oolong sounds delightful."

"Milk and sugar?"

"Yes, please."

While I wait, I try not to look too closely at the other patrons, many of them middle-aged matrons. It's the sort of bourgeois café my mother and her friends would frequent. A place to see and be seen. Being seen is the last thing I want, so I lower my gaze and turn slightly toward the window. I'm relieved when Mabel brings my tea, along with two warm scones. I thank her and tuck in, the tea's crisp bouquet a perfect counterpoint to the sugar-encrusted scones, which remind me of the ones Siobhan used to make. Teatime was Papa's favorite part of the day, and he'd always break his work to enjoy a full complement of pastries, jams, and biscuits and regale us with stories. From the time he was a pup, Walter remained close at hand, eagerly awaiting any morsel we might drop. It's the simple, everyday things like this that I miss the most about my old life and my family.

I lift my teacup and drink to quell the pinch at the back of my throat and drown the nostalgic memories threatening to overtake me. Now that survival isn't my driving force, at least not as keenly, my mind has slowly been excavating my grief—examining it in my sleep. My dreams are haunted by Rebecca. By Papa. Even by my little sisters, long dead.

A few minutes later, Mabel seats a pair of ladies at a table near mine. I flinch. One of them is Arabella Meade—I recognize her hairstyle immediately, with its high topknot and cascading side curls. I dip my chin, my wig swinging forward to hide my face. She's so close I can smell her perfume, a heady tuberose scent. Thankfully, from this angle, she'd have to look over her shoulder to see me, but her companion has a full view of me, and I her, though I don't recognize the young woman, who's dressed in mourning clothes that match her solemn expression.

After they've settled in and ordered their tea, I hear Arabella ask how the young woman has been getting on. The temptation to eavesdrop is much too strong to resist, so I crane my neck forward, ever so slightly.

"Well enough. Considering." The young lady's lip quivers. Her voice is choked with emotion.

Arabella reaches out, places a hand over her companion's. "These things take time."

"I keep expecting her to come home. As if she'll walk through the door at any moment. It's like some horrible dream I can't wake from."

"I remember feeling that way about Eleanor. It isn't right, is it?" Arabella sighs. "It's terrible to lose a sister. Especially in the way you did."

"The coroner said she didn't suffer . . . but how can they know that for sure?"

"Try not to think like that, dear. Remember what a blessing she was to you in life, instead of thinking about her death," says Arabella.

Arabella was always smooth and well spoken, knowing just the right things to say in any situation. Her unruffled manner made her courtroom lies about me all the more believable. Oh, how she hated me. And I never gathered quite why, apart from resenting my friendship with her sister, Eleanor. But my dear friend tried to warn me, didn't she? Years before she died. *Be careful of my little sister, Lil. She despises you behind her smile.*

Arabella makes cooing sounds, patting the young woman's arm as her face crumples and she sobs softly into her handkerchief. "Denise was always so proud of you. Your brothers, too."

My ears perk. Denise. Might Arabella be talking about Denise George? She was one of Rebecca's friends as well. If so, Arabella's companion must be Denise's younger sister, Alice, who was still a child the last time I saw her. I recall the conversation I heard on the wharf the day I left for the marshes—the longshoreman admonishing his cohort to be cautious. The well-to-do victim he spoke about might well have been poor Denise. I pray Arabella's penchant for gossip continues, my curiosity piqued.

"Did you see the papers this morning? The *Daily Courier*?" Arabella continues, just as I hoped.

"No, I didn't," says Alice. "I've been avoiding the news."

"Well, they think the murderer is Lillian Carmichael." At the sound of my name on Arabella's tongue, I flinch, goose bumps prickling up my arms.

"How can that be?" Alice asks. "She's dead."

"Supposedly. But her grave was disturbed. The undertaker claims he heard strange sounds coming from their family mausoleum. And I saw her. Here in town. I *know* it was her, even though she was dressed like a street urchin. People *are* buried alive sometimes. I went to the City Guard and told them I saw her. There's a reward, you know. Lillian is capable of anything."

Arabella's voice becomes a shrill, distant whine in my ears. Suddenly, the intimate café is too close. The air too warm. I do my best to keep my panic from registering on my face. Though my inclination is to flee, I must stay and listen to this conversation. I need to know how much Arabella *knows*.

"I remember Lillian and Rebecca," Alice says. "Mama used to attend a sewing circle with their mother."

"Our families were close for many years. I've never gotten over Becca's death." Arabella sighs, shifts in her chair. "Lillian was always jealous of Rebecca. And I'll never forgive her for leading my sister astray. It still sickens me."

What on earth is she talking about? I never led Eleanor astray, in anything.

"Were you very well acquainted with Marjorie Blanchard?" Alice asks.

I still. Why is she asking about Marjorie now?

"We met, a time or two," Arabella says. "I found her rather blasé, but she was pleasant enough. She wasn't happy in her marriage. That much was obvious." There's a certain air of morbid glee in Arabella's tone. I'd forgotten just *how* much she relishes hearing about other people's misfortunes. It's one of her least flattering traits.

"Well, we were in cotillion together, before she met her husband." Alice looks from side to side and lowers her voice. "I heard that when they found her, her throat was torn to shreds, as if some wild beast had gotten to her. That's why they can't have a proper wake. It's a blessing she had no children yet, at least."

"Heavens." Arabella raises her teacup. "That's three now, including your poor sister. I'm frightened. Mama no longer wants me out after dark, even with a companion." She glances out the window at the dusky sky, purple as a bruise.

"I don't like the thought myself. It's getting late. We'd better head home, hadn't we?" Alice says. "Walk with me, as far as the park?"

"Of course, darling."

They hastily finish their tea and leave, Arabella's tailored merino skirt brushing my own as she passes. She doesn't spare me a glance. I contemplate their conversation. At least it's no longer a mystery whether Arabella recognized me and reported the sighting, although her comment about Eleanor is puzzling. What was she implying? I must be very careful to avoid running into Arabella going forward. My boyish disguise didn't fool her. The best way to blend in with Charleston's gentry is to be a part of Charleston's gentry. Kate is right. Mary Jones must become so completely enmeshed with me that she doesn't stand out and no one can distinguish us.

And poor Marjorie. Younger than me but already widowed and now dead. Her father was a minor politician with a small rice plantation on James Island. I remember Marjorie being a quiet girl. An accomplished pianist and a graceful dancer. Pretty, with soft brown eyes and red hair.

Red hair.

The first victim—Sally—was a redhead as well. I pull on one of the reddish curls adorning my own head. Denise George was also a redhead. Is there some correlation? A niggle of unease runs through me. All three of them. Redheads. And Denise and Marjorie knew one another, at least tangentially.

Miss Mabel brings me a fresh cup of tea. "Varina's nearly finished with her final reading. She'll perform soon." She glances around the room, which has grown quieter since our arrival. Only a few tables remain occupied. "These murders are taking a toll on my evening business," she says. "Ladies are too frightened to be out after dark."

"It's terrible. I heard two of them remarking about it, just now."

"Yes," Mabel says, shaking her head. "I suppose I'll need to begin closing earlier."

"I'm so sorry."

"Well, I want my patrons to feel safe. Perhaps I'll have Varina for matinee performances instead." She looks over my shoulder and waves. "Ah! Here she comes now. Have you ever heard Varina sing?"

"No, I haven't."

"Well, you're in for a treat. She deserves a bigger stage than mine, but I'm glad to have her all the same."

I turn in my chair and watch as Kate sweeps through the room. She ascends to the small, raised dais, gathers her skirts, and sits at the parlor piano, greeting her meager audience with a smile. Her eyes flit to me, then quickly away. She begins playing the opening lines of a song, one filled with poignant longing. And then she opens her berry-stained mouth, and sings.

Sebben, crudele, mi fai languir, sempre fedele ti voglio amar . . .

The hair rises along my arms at the rich, sensuous sound of her voice. All my thoughts of murders, grief, and fear fall away. There is only Kate, lit by a single limelight, luminous as the sun, her voice falling over me like starshine. She begins another verse, and her eyes lock with mine as she sings. My belly swoops and I slowly begin to understand that my infatuation with the person in front of me has nothing at all to do with her outward presentation to the world, and everything to do with her essence. Her energy. Her light. I've never longed for someone more. It's as shocking to me as it is delightful.

But when the song changes, her eyes drift to another in the crowd, a pretty dark-haired woman dressed in yellow. As Kate sings directly to her, I see the woman's shoulders droop, see the color rise on her face. My jealousy flares. I will Kate's eyes back to mine, but they never return.

After two more Italian arias, she finishes her performance and descends the stage, pausing to greet the woman in yellow with a kiss to each cheek. They share a few words, and then Kate comes my way. When she brushes past me, her hand grazes mine. My stomach tumbles at her touch. "Meet me outside," she whispers. "I'll collect my pay, then we'll go."

Flummoxed and agitated by my tumultuous feelings, I rise, smoothing out my skirts. I glare at the woman in yellow, who is completely oblivious to my presence. She leans her head on the shoulder of the well-dressed man sitting next to her, who seems unaware that "Varina" just seduced his beloved right under his nose.

I go outside and wait beneath the café's striped awning, my foot tapping on the pavers with impatience. The chill in the evening air cools my blazing cheeks, but does nothing to soothe my jealousy. But I must master my emotions if I'm to remain with Kate. My situation is precarious, and now that she knows who I really am, I don't want to make her doubt my gratitude or give her any reason to turn me out. Angel's Rest now feels like my home, and I long to stay.

Kate emerges from the alley a few moments later, her gown falling off one shoulder, exposing the faint freckles there. She winks at me. "Well, what did you think?"

"You were spectacular," I say, meaning it. "Your audience loves you."

"Well, it pleases me to entertain. I was born for it."

"Who was the woman in the yellow dress?" I ask the question lightly, with a smile to disguise my jealousy.

"Barbara Kincaid. One of my patronesses. She and her husband have me for parties sometimes. She's hired me for next Friday evening, matter of fact."

"I see. To sing?"

"Yes." Kate gives me a puzzled look. "To sing." She pulls me by the hand into the adjoining alley, out of sight of the street. "I can tell you're wondering about Varina. About what I do. And I don't want you getting the wrong idea. I know what people say about actresses. Singers. That we're loose. Easy. That we sell ourselves. And some do fall into prostitution. But I am not one of them."

Her eyes are limpid, blown-out pools, but there's a sharpness there all the same. "I flirt, Lillian. I perform. I give them what they want to see, because that's how I survive. But I have never, ever been forced to sell my body. That alone is mine to give." She tilts her head down, her breath smelling sweetly of raspberries and mint. "Do you understand me, darling?"

I'm too breathless to answer, but manage to nod. She's so close to me that if I tilted my chin up, her lips would be against mine. I've only ever been kissed once, by William, on the evening of our betrothal. He was poor at it, his tongue slipping into my mouth and startling me with its intrusion. I didn't enjoy the sensation. I wonder how different it would be, to kiss a woman. *This* woman. The nearness of her body is a firebrand. I long to feel her pressing against me, like she did this morning, when I knew her only as Alex. But as reckless bravery takes hold of me and I tilt my chin up to seek her lips, she pulls away.

"Let's go home. You're tired, and your leg must be in an awful state by now," she says.

She's not wrong. My leg is throbbing by the time we reach the wharves where we moored our shallow skiff. We row across the Cooper in silence under the full moon, then up the snaking, narrow tributaries to Angel's Rest. On the front piazza, a small stringer of drum lies next to the door. Kate picks up the fish and leaves a handful of coins in their place for Ruby and Noah. "I'll fry these for us tomorrow," she says.

I follow her up the path to the kitchen house. She places the fish in the sink, then lights an oil lamp, the flame illuminating her face with glancing light. She places it on the kitchen table, then stokes the embers in the cookstove. "I'll draw you a bath. I'll just need to change clothes and fetch water from the well," she says.

"You don't have to do that. The bath."

"Nonsense. It's no trouble. The warm water will ease your pain. Now sit and rest your leg. There are some things we need to discuss when I get back." Before I can protest further, she leaves. I settle into one of the hooped-back chairs to wait, wondering what she wants to discuss. A few minutes later, I see her through the window, lantern bobbing in the underbrush. When she returns, carrying two buckets of water, she's dressed in men's clothing—trousers with suspenders and a billowing white shirt. The blond wig is gone. Her dark hair hangs in unkempt waves above her shoulders. After her performance as Varina, the change in her appearance is jarring, but I have a feeling this is Kate at her most honest—somewhere between Alexander Mayhew and Varina.

She sets to work, placing a large stockpot on the stove and pouring the water into it. She fills the teakettle, then sets it next to the pot to warm. "Would you like some tea? Chamomile, to help you sleep? I drink it myself, every night before bed."

"Only if you'll read my leaves after I'm finished," I say, trying to lighten the tension between us.

"You know that's just a parlor trick. A game. But all right."

Once the kettle has boiled, she places a cup in front of me with crushed, earthy-smelling flowers and leaves covering the bottom. This is the other component to her distinctive scent, then. Camphor, menthol, and chamomile. She joins me at the table, crossing her arms over her chest as she studies me in her calculating way. "If I'm to help you, and if you're going to be staying here, under my roof, I must know everything about you, Lillian. And I do mean everything. About your past. Your family. I read the article in the paper this morning. It mentioned that you poisoned your sister. That you were due to be hanged for her murder. I remember hearing about all of that now. Did you kill her?"

"No," I say. "I promise you. I did not."

Kate studies my face and then smiles "Well. Then that would be the *first* honest thing you've told me."

"I don't know who killed Rebecca. Not really. I have my ideas. But they're . . . risky."

"In what way?"

"If I told you, it would imperil someone I love a great deal."

"Who?"

"I can't tell you that, either." I blow across the surface of the tea and take a tentative sip. It's light and warm, like sunshine on green grass.

She sighs, running her hands through her hair. "All right. How on earth did you survive being buried alive?"

I've asked myself the same question so many times. "I'm not certain. But once, when I was younger, I had an odd sort of spell."

"A spell?" Kate leans forward in her seat, elbows on the table. "Like a fit of some sort?"

"Yes. I was playing in our garden when a strange sensation came over me. All my joints seemed to freeze in place, and I fell. My father happened to be there. He saw it happen. I was unconscious for two days. Our doctor had never seen anything like it before. I had the same sensation when I was on my way to the gallows. I think it must have happened again. Only it lasted much longer this time. When I woke, I was in a coffin in our family mausoleum. I was able to break free, pick the lock, and escape."

"That must have been horrific." Kate steeples her fingers, studying me with her fathomless eyes. "I've heard of this phenomenon. What you've described. I used to read my father's medical journals. There's something called catalepsy, in which the subject becomes paralyzed and senseless. The heartbeat becomes so faint and shallow it can't be heard or the pulse felt. Breathing so faint it can hardly be detected. The person could easily be mistaken for dead. It's said that Saint Teresa of Ávila suffered from this condition when she experienced her ecstasies."

"And you think this might be what I have? This catalepsy?"

"I'm not certain. But it's a possibility."

I ponder her words. How strange to think that my body came so close to death that I resembled a corpse—that no attending doctor, nor the coroner, had detected the life still coursing through my veins. I think of my desperate prayers on the morning of my execution. Did God grant me a reprieve for a reason? Have I been called to a higher purpose, like Saint Teresa?

That last part seems preposterous. As good as I've always tried to be, I'm hardly a saint.

After I finish my tea, Kate takes my cup, turns it over on the saucer, then turns it right side up again. She studies the leaves clinging to the sides of the cup, a smile playing at the corners of her mouth. "There's a serpent in your cup."

"What does it mean?"

"Luck. Or a betrayal."

"That doesn't sound promising," I say.

"Could be that *you're* the betrayer." That same wicked smile again, sending a lash of longing through me. "There's also a coffin."

"No surprises there. My whole life it's been one coffin after another." I shudder. I don't like this game. "Is there anything hopeful at all?"

"A fox. Next to an angel. Which is a symbol for good news. And a new lover in the near future, as it's along the bottom of the cup." She smiles at me. "It's not a bad fortune, Lillian. Don't look so glum."

"I was hoping for better." A cramp runs through my calf muscle, making me wince.

"You're in pain, aren't you?" Kate puts my teacup down and scoots her chair closer to mine. "Here, give me your leg."

"What?"

She sighs. "I should rub it, before your bath. To loosen the muscles."

I raise my skirts above my knee and extend my leg, a frisson of unsettling excitement running through my belly as she takes my foot in her hand to unlace my boot. I've never felt these kinds of feelings. Not for anyone else. And I think somehow, Kate knows exactly what she's doing to me. When she reaches up my thigh and unties the garter holding my stocking in place, my heart gallops. Her hands are warm, but goose bumps rise all the same as she eases the fabric down my leg and off my foot. Though she massaged my injury with the camphor and menthol salve during my recovery, this feels different. Her eyes meet mine for a moment, a small smile playing at the corners of her mouth. She runs her open palms from my knee to my calf, and begins to rub, slowly and deeply. I can't help the sigh that escapes my lips. Can't help the want that throbs at my core.

"You have beautiful legs," Kate says, and I nearly come undone. "Firm, strong calves. Slender ankles."

"D-dancing," I stammer, utterly flummoxed by the way she's looking at me. Touching me. "I took dancing lessons, as a girl."

"Of course. As most gently bred girls do. How on earth were you getting by on your own?" Kate asks. "Surviving in the marsh?"

"I fished. Foraged."

"And before you came to the marsh?" That same calculating look. She bends my knee, her fingers working the arch of my foot now, her thumbs strong and sure.

"After I escaped the mausoleum, I went to my family's house. Took some food. Gathered some of my jewelry, too. I tried to pawn it, but the brokers thought it was stolen, or they only offered me pennies for its worth."

"I see."

"I learned to pick pockets, on the streets. I stole from the rich. On the Battery Promenade. And I'd wait outside the slave markets and steal from those awaiting the auctions. My father was an abolitionist. He hated those men. They hated him, just as much."

Another smile quirks at the corners of Kate's mouth. Her hands run back up my leg, kneading the puckered skin around the healed suture marks. "So, you're a thief."

"Yes, I suppose I am. But I'm no murderer, Kate, I promise you that."

Her hands go still, warm and soft on my skin. "How did it feel, when you stole from those rich men?"

I interrogate myself as she studies me. How *did* it feel? I remember the rush of excitement when I dipped my fingers into Patrick Calhoun's pocket and claimed his coins. I felt guilty at first, when I stole from the drunk man, but stealing from the rich was exhilarating. Perhaps a better person would feel ashamed. But these men sit in their great houses, unbothered by the fact that they made their riches by exploiting the enslaved, the fingerprints of their human chattel in every brick that built their lofty kingdoms. They shunned my family in society and wanted my father dead. No. I don't feel guilty. Or ashamed. I only feel justified.

I raise my eyes to Kate's. My heartbeat pounds in my ears. "It felt good. Really good."

She glides her hands up my leg, above the hem of my drawers, her fingers brushing the soft skin of my inner thigh, briefly, before returning to my calf. My belly tightens, wondering if she'll dare to touch me in a more intimate way. Hoping. But she doesn't. She lowers my foot onto the floor.

"And my massage? How did *that* feel?"

"Even better," I say, bashful.

"Good." She smiles, slowly. "I was hoping you'd say that."

THIRTEEN

After readying my bath, Kate leads me to the main house, to a wing of Angel's Rest where I've not yet been. Portraits line the walls of the long hallway, papered in flocked velvet. These somber-faced strangers stare at me as we pass, the flickering light from Kate's candelabra glancing off their varnished images. I follow her to a set of open double doors. Inside, a fire crackles in a marble hearth. The copper bathtub she hauled up to my room last week stands there, steaming. Above the mantel, a large portrait of a beautiful woman holds court, her dark eyes boring into mine.

"I haven't the strength to carry you up the stairs tonight," Kate says. "You can sleep here instead." She gestures to the imposing bed, topped by a pleated canopy and draped on all sides with bronze velvet curtains.

"Is this your room, then?" I ask, my eyes flicking up to the raven-haired woman in the portrait. I'm certain she's Lucrezia.

"Yes. It is."

"I don't want to take your bed."

"Nonsense. It's no imposition. I'll take a room on the second floor. Good night, Lillian."

She turns to go, shutting the doors behind her, and I disrobe, removing the green silk gown and placing it over a chair to prevent it from wrinkling. Lucrezia watches from above as I sink down into the bath, steaming water lapping over my bare skin. I close my eyes, wetting the scrap of woolen cloth Kate left on the side of the tub and sweeping it between my breasts and over my throat. I think of everything Kate and I discussed tonight. I think of her hands on my flesh, the sure way she soothed my pain with her ministrations.

Though we share little in common, I can't deny the attraction between us. I've *tried* to deny it. Tried to excuse the warmth radiating through my belly when her eyes linger on mine, the memory of how she looked at me when she sang, as if the lyrics of her song were meant for me. How my skin blazed when she touched me tonight and how badly I wanted her to test my boundaries and touch me in ways I could only imagine. I glance up at Lucrezia and imagine the sorts of things she and Kate might have done.

I know very little about sexual congress, but I saw two women together at the jail once, during my kitchen duties. I was emptying the slop bucket when I heard a low moan coming from the yard. I turned the corner and saw a young woman, her face pressed against the wall, her back arched, eyes closed, lips parted. As I watched, hidden behind the shrubbery, a whimper escaped the young woman's lips, her face reddening as she trembled. I almost went to her, thinking she was having some sort of seizure, given her obvious state of distress, but another woman emerged from beneath her skirts, wiping her mouth. She seized the young woman by the hair, pushed her down on her knees, then lifted her skirts and covered them both. Realization broke over me, and I fled, frightened and embarrassed.

Yet I was excited by what I'd witnessed, much to my chagrin. When William had kissed me, I'd felt nothing but mild disgust. Although I was fond of him, the thought of what might happen in our marriage bed only filled me with dread. Mother had always been circumspect about such matters, and the women in her circle never spoke of their marital intimacies in polite company.

But that day, behind the jail, I discovered something about myself. Something I'm not entirely comfortable with but that fascinates me all the same. Women are beautiful, after all. Infinitely more appealing to me than men. Their lines, their supple curves, the softness of their skin, and the easy pleasure of their company. I've heard stories and rumors of spinsters living together as married couples—so-called romantic friendships—and of nuns who chose their vocation because of their aversion to men and marriage, more than a desire to serve God. Might I be the same?

I've never had a large coterie of friends, like Rebecca did, but the closest thing I've ever felt to true love was with Eleanor, who died of measles in the winter of 1846. We sent one another valentines and fond letters (even though the Meades lived only three streets away), and spent every spare moment we could find together. Her death left me unmoored. I remember what I heard Arabella say at Miss Mabel's. *I'll never forgive her for leading my sister astray.*

What did she mean by that? Did my and Eleanor's girlish affection for one another draw suspicion? Looking back now, I'm quite sure my bond with her exceeded friendship, though neither one of us had the words or the courage to ever speak such things aloud. Such love was forbidden. Yet, all the same, Arabella may have known Eleanor better than I. Perhaps Eleanor confessed her feelings for me to her younger sister, and Arabella resented me for it. I never understood why Arabella hated me so, when I was always kind to her . . .

I ponder all these thoughts as I step out of the bath and dry myself, then don the clean cambric gown Kate set out for me. I nestle beneath the covers of the massive bed and close the drapes around me, hiding myself from Lucrezia's intense gaze. I can smell the scent of Kate's hair pomade on the pillows. As the tea takes hold, sending me adrift into sleep, I imagine her next to me, her lips seeking mine in the dark, her mouth hungry and eager.

My sleep is anything but restful. Rebecca accosts me in my dreams, chasing after me, her mouth wide, her teeth sharp like an animal's. Her beauty has become terrible in death, her eyes vacant black pools. I run from her, inside some endless, looping maze without corners.

But no matter how fast I run, her anger falls around me like sharpened swords, her howls and screeches inhuman. She's like something out of a myth, a nameless horror bent on vengeance. The worst of it is, even in the midst of this surreal, unnatural dream, I know too well the source of her anger and why it's justified. I didn't kill her, but she's pitted her wrath against me all the same. There's no lie in my plea of innocence. But there are so many ways I failed her daily. So many ways I might have saved her if I'd only been brave enough to speak my mind. All the doctors Mother hired over the years stream through my memories. Most of them quacks and charlatans, offering their tinctures and tonics. Yet still, Rebecca's illness remained uncured. And then there's the matter of what I witnessed, just days before she died. A truth I can hardly bear to confront, even after all this time.

The next morning, I wake to find Kate staring at me. I startle, sitting up, the covers falling around me. It's barely dawn, with only a faint pink glow filtering through the oaks outside the window.

"You sleep like the dead," she says, arching her brow. "No wonder they buried you alive."

"That's not a very nice thing to say," I retort. "And I slept horribly."

"There'll be time for a nap after breakfast. You can help me with the morning chores." She pats the bedcovers. "Get up. You need to build your strength."

I groan, swinging my legs over the side of the bed.

She smiles. "You've had plenty of cosseting, Miss Carmichael. I mean for you to stay. I *want* you to stay. But a house this size needs attention and you have able hands. Lying abed won't help you heal."

I turn my head so she can't see my smile. She wants me to stay. I stretch, sighing at the pull in my muscles.

"I washed your trousers and brought them for you to wear while we work," Kate says, handing me the folded breeches. "You should look through Lucrezia's things later. She wasn't as shapely as you, nor as small, but we can alter any of them you like. Take up the hems." She lights an oil lamp, then pours a ewer of warm water into the basin on the dressing table. "I haven't known what to do with her things . . . since she passed." A flicker of sadness crosses Kate's features in the mirror.

"That's her, isn't it?" I gesture to the painting over the mantel.

"Yes. Her husband commissioned that portrait when they were newly wed."

"She was beautiful."

"She was." Kate sighs, folds and unfolds the scrap of washcloth next to the basin. "But she was so much more than her beauty."

I have the urge to go to Kate, to lay my hand on her shoulder to offer comfort, but I don't. Instead, I stand there awkwardly in my nightgown, watching her. I can't stop watching her. She's absolutely magnetic, every emotion amplified by the contours of her face, by her expressive eyes.

"I'll leave you to get dressed," she says. "After breakfast, and after Ruby's lessons, we'll practice your act. If you're going to live here with me, your transformation as Mary Jones must be convincing. You must become her anytime we encounter someone else."

A shiver of delight runs through me. *If you're going to live here with me.* There can be no doubt now that living here is what I want. To remain at Angel's Rest, and see where things might lead. Even though I know very little about Kate's past, I've grown to trust her. "I'll do my best," I say. "And I want to work. To help. I don't want to be a burden to you."

Kate stills. She fixes me with an icy stare. "Don't you ever say that again."

"What?"

She doesn't answer me, but stalks off, closing the door with a sharp snap. I stare at the closed door for an inordinately long time, willing her to return. When she doesn't, I wash up and dress hurriedly in the chilly bedchamber, frustration and hurt cycling through me. I care too much about what she thinks of me. But this has always been my problem—caring too much for what other people think. It's a condition that's plagued me throughout my life. Even prison didn't absolve me of my inclination to diminish myself to make others more comfortable.

I find Kate on the side porch, overlooking a small patch of lawn, where a gaggle of hens peck at the ground. She turns to me, her expression inscrutable. She doesn't seem angry, merely indifferent, as she hands me a hooped basket. "Have you ever gathered eggs before?"

"No. Our maid always did that."

"Of course." Kate rolls her eyes. "It's not difficult." She motions at the rickety chicken coop, with its sloping roof. Two rows of holes line the top and bottom. "Just reach in the hole and pull them out. There's usually one or two eggs in each cubby."

I go to the coop and reach through the first hole. I'm rewarded by a smooth, brown egg, speckled with ruddy freckles. I carefully place it in the basket and continue on until I have six more. I squat and reach through the first hole on the bottom row, feeling around. My fingers brush against something smooth, cool, and dry. It moves under my hand. I shriek and pull back. A rat snake streams out, and races like a whip to the blackberry thicket bordering the yard.

Kate cackles. I turn around and glare at her. "That wasn't funny."

"Oh yes it was!" She smirks. "Your eyes were big as teacups. Gather the rest, then we'll clean the coop."

But there's no "we" to it. Kate takes the basket of eggs, then brings me a barrow of fresh straw. She supervises me from the porch as I open the hatch and remove the old nests from the other side of the coop, where I can clearly see whether there are more snakes in hiding. She stands against the porch post, one long leg insouciantly cocked, her arms crossed over her chest. "You're doing such a good job, Lillian," she calls teasingly. "So thorough."

I mutter a curse beneath my breath, but her teasing praise lights a glow in me all the same. I want to please her. To prove myself worthy of staying here. The chickens watch me with their beady, gimlet eyes, clucking as I work. I never had to lift a finger as a girl, but as a ward of the jail, I was forced to labor until my knees gave out. This isn't so bad by comparison. Not with the calls of birdsong overhead and the scent of spring in the loamy air. I find a rhythm—scrape out the old nest with the heel of my hand, then replace it with fresh hay—and before I know it, I'm finished. I wipe my hands on my trousers and join Kate on the porch.

She gives me a sly smile. "How are you feeling?"

"Hungry," I say.

"Come in and wash up. I'll make you breakfast. You've earned it."

FOURTEEN

Later that day, after Ruby comes for her reading lesson and I've had a dreamless nap, Kate and I return to the room full of costumes. I'm wearing the auburn wig again but otherwise dressed in only my petticoats, shift, and corset, for which Kate gave me another busk—scolding me for my slumping posture. Afternoon light slants through the windows, warming my skin as she slowly walks around me, inspecting me.

"Who *is* Mary Jones?" she asks, stopping to fix me with her calculating look.

"A woman."

"Yes. But what kind of woman? A servant, a well-to-do lady? You must know these things about her."

"A well-to-do lady. A young widow." Like Marjorie Blanchard. I shudder, remembering Alice's words. *I heard that when they found her, her throat was torn to shreds, as if some wild beast had gotten to her.*

"Good," Kate says. "Is she Welsh? Jones is usually a Welsh name."

"I'm not sure I can do a Welsh accent."

"Can you do any kind of accent?" Kate asks, lifting her brow. "It isn't vital, but it could help with disguising your voice."

"My father was Scottish. He was born in Lanarkshire. My sister and I used to imitate his speech."

"Was." "Used to." So much of my life now exists in the past tense. I swallow hard and look away.

"Your eyes are shining, Lillian. You look like you're about to cry. What's wrong?"

"It's nothing." I blink rapidly, avoiding her gaze. "I'm fine."

"But you aren't. Every emotion you're feeling dances across your face. Your eyes are beautiful. But they're your biggest tell. You must learn to master yourself." Her fingers grip my jaw, turning my head. "Look at me. Watch me. Very closely."

I meet her gaze, my breath hitching at the sudden coldness in her eyes. In an instant, all her sly wit, her warmth, everything that makes her Kate vanishes. "What do you think I'm thinking about?" she asks, her voice as frigid as her looks. Low and menacing, and distinctly male.

"I . . . I don't know."

She traces one fingertip down my throat and rests it in the hollow between my clavicles. I shiver at her touch, desire and unease tangling together in a confusing knot. "I'm thinking . . . how much I'd like to ravish you."

Even though Kate ravishing me was all I could think about last night, a visceral fear crawls over my skin, because this person standing in front of me right now is decidedly not Kate. Nor Varina. Or even Alex. I think she's acting. Merely trying to prove her point—to demonstrate her talent for becoming someone else in an instant. Still, I take two steps back. She smiles at me, but with no kindness. "You're all alone with me, Mary Jones. My helpless plaything to toy with, for as long as I like."

She stalks toward me, each footstep a staccato beat, her lovely features wolfish and sardonic, as if some dark spirit has overtaken her body.

"No one knows you're here," she says, backing me against the wall. "You can scream all you like, but no one will hear you. And once I'm finished with you . . ."

"Stop," I say, panting. "Please. You're frightening me."

In an instant, Kate returns, shedding the wicked persona like a coat falling to the floor. She steps back and I release my breath. "I'm sorry. I thought you'd know it was just an act."

"I . . . I did," I stammer. "It's just that you were so convincing."

She smiles sheepishly. "I know. I'm good, aren't I?"

I laugh, nervously, my face aflame. "Very."

"You must know I would never hurt you." She reaches for my hand, and I pull away.

"I certainly hope not."

"I won't let Winthrop inhabit me again in your presence," she says. "He'll be relegated to the stage, where he belongs, tying helpless maidens to railroad tracks."

"Inhabit." The word sends a chill through me. Though her promise is meant to comfort, the tenuous trust between us has narrowed. She's frightened me. Badly. I hardly know anything about her. I've been too afraid of seeming rude by asking her too many questions, but even though I owe her a debt of gratitude for saving my life, and for her hospitality, if I'm to stay here, I need to know more about her. "Where did you learn to do that?" I ask, sheepish. "Become someone else?"

"I've been practicing for most of my life, Lillian."

"Even before you met Lucrezia, then?"

Kate's head tilts. She regards me calmly, but there's a wariness behind her eyes. "Yes. Lucrezia helped me hone my talents. But they've always been there. I grew up in poverty. I spent my earliest years in a workhouse, with my mother. My imagination saved me back then, I think. Pretending to be someone else was a fun game, but it also got me out of a few scrapes."

That explains why she scoffed when I told her our maid used to gather our eggs. She's had a difficult life compared to mine, at least in her younger years. My sympathy rises, imagining Kate as a child in some dingy, lightless workhouse.

"Has anyone ever figured out that you aren't who you claim to be? Do Ruby and Noah know you aren't really Alexander Mayhew?"

"No. You are the only one I've ever revealed my true self to, Lillian, apart from Lucrezia."

I find it astounding, her ability to shift personas so completely and convincingly. And I'm surprised that she trusts me enough to disclose her biggest secret. Even though she is in the position of power here, it's still risky.

Kate clears her throat. "Now, Mary. Tell me about *your* past."

"My real one? I already have. Most of it, anyway."

"No, the fictional one. It needs to feel just as true as the other."

My breathing returns to normal, and I close my eyes, letting a story unspool behind them. "I'm Mary Jones. Aged four and twenty," I say, broadening my vowels, "from Wishew, Lanarkshire. I was married, but my husband died, three years past."

"Good. Very good." Kate laughs. "Almost Glaswegian. I could barely understand you."

"My mother used to say that very thing to Papa. She was ever telling him to slow down when he spoke to her."

"All right then. Jones is your married name, but your maiden name is Wallace. Can't get much more Scottish than that." Kate grows serious. "Is any of your story true, Lillian? Did you have a husband?"

"No. But I was betrothed for a short time. A very short time." I look down. "To a naval lieutenant."

"Was he killed?"

"No." A whisper of sound comes from behind me. My skin prickles. I turn away from Kate and see Rebecca's ghost standing in the open doorway. She glares at me accusingly. The memory of last night's horrid dream accosts me. How dare she intrude on me here, in these waking hours, in this new life I'm making? Rage simmers beneath my skin. "My sister . . . he fell in love with my sister instead."

"The one you're accused of killing."

"Yes. He took the ring from my finger and gave it to her. Said she needed him more than I did. That she was softer, more suited to his temperament." I bark a bitter laugh. "How ridiculous. He's a soldier. He needed a stalwart, practical wife, who would be able to endure his long absences during times of war. But Rebecca fawned over him. He didn't see the value in my strength of character."

"So. You were jealous of her. I'm not surprised."

I stiffen, whirling to face Kate. She gasps.

"What?" I ask.

"You looked like someone else, entirely, just then."

"I did?"

"Yes. Whatever you were just feeling, Lil, nurture it. That woman . . . is formidable. That woman is someone no one will cross. She's your Mary Jones."

While her praise invigorates me, Kate is wrong. I don't feel jealous of Rebecca anymore. I'm angry. An emotion I've never been allowed to feel. Anger that my entire life revolved around Rebecca and her needs. That I was ignored, rejected, and finally made the scapegoat for her death.

Anger, then.

Anger is my key to becoming someone else.

A VAMPIRE'S DIARY

Arabella

I've devised a solution to my conundrum. It's brilliant, really. What happened with Marjorie will never happen again, and my progress will march on, unimpeded. Especially now, thanks to Miss Carmichael's misfortune. I chuckle every time I read the newspaper. It's laughable that anyone could believe her responsible for my *work. Still, the attention is on her. The limelight. Which affords me the luxury of time, and opportunity. I will relish it for as long as I can. Let them have their silly superstitions. Their idle gossip and imagination are potent tools for my gain.*

For tonight, I will have the lovely Arabella. I try out her name on my tongue, my voice stroking over each syllable. While I'm disappointed that I won't enjoy the pleasures I've enjoyed with my other conquests, discretion has become necessary. It will be easy to isolate Arabella. She knows me well. She trusts me. Has trusted me for many, many years. I look forward to claiming the spoils of victory, while remaining safely in the shadows.

FIFTEEN

On Friday evening, Kate readies herself to go to the Kincaids' party. This will be the first time I've ever been left alone at Angel's Rest—something that makes me nervous but also demonstrates Kate's growing trust. My strength has returned to a point that I can manage the stairs without assistance, thanks to my new chore routine.

I'm playing the piano in the parlor when Kate descends, dressed in a subdued shade of rose pink. The blond wig cascades over her bare shoulders in long, freshly ironed ringlets. Her cheeks are flushed with rouge, eyes belladonna bright. Her transformation as Varina is stunning. She goes from rangy, loose-limbed Kate, with all her rakish charm, to a vision of such loveliness she makes me swoon at the sight of her. I lift my hands from the keyboard and rise to greet her.

"You play beautifully, Lillian," she says. "You needn't have stopped."

"Not nearly as well as you. And I can't sing to save my life."

"Well, it's lucky for you that I can. Barbara pays me handsomely to do so. Her patronage is enough to keep both of us in satin and pearls. Hopefully, after tonight, I'll earn more commissions from some of her friends as well."

"Are there still parties, then? Even with the murders? Miss Mabel said she'd been losing business."

"There have been fewer, for certain." She brushes her hair back to tighten the screw on her earring, showing the delicate, fey curve of her ear. "I used to have private performances on the books every week. Events have diminished, which is why I'm grateful for Barbara."

The flare of jealousy rises again, remembering how enraptured Barbara was by Kate's performance at Miss Mabel's. The way they embraced. Barbara was bewitching. Far more attractive than I. Still, I compose my features and smile. "Mrs. Kincaid seems very fond of you."

"We're old friends. We met through Lucrezia. Barbara is from an old Huguenot family—they've been here for over a century. And Mr. Kincaid is very influential. Their house is next to the Gibbes mansion."

I've never heard of the Kincaids, so he can't be *that* influential, despite his prestigious address. Mother practically kept diaries about the comings and goings of the planter aristocracy. The Kincaids are new money, most likely. And as a French Catholic, Mother and Huguenot Barbara wouldn't have frequented the same circles.

Kate takes a silk cape from the hat tree and fastens it around her shoulders. "I'll return by morning, Lil. Keep a lantern lit in the parlor. Don't answer the door for anyone."

"I won't."

I watch her leave through the windows, the moonlight falling over her like poured milk. Though I recognize her need to work and earn a living, I don't want her to go. Apart from my jealousy over Barbara, I worry about her safety. There have been three murders to date—enough to recognize a disturbing pattern. All three women were redheads. Is it a mere coincidence, or a purposeful choice on the part of the killer?

Sally. Denise. Marjorie.

Who will be next?

It's harrowing to assume there will be more murders, but until the culprit is captured, it's as likely a scenario as not. I return to the piano to distract myself and peck out a Bach Invention I memorized in my youth, finding solace in its steady, mathematical precision. But the music does little to lift my worries.

I keep imagining Kate in some silk-shrouded boudoir with Barbara Kincaid, kissing her, caressing her, loosening the pins from Barbara's black hair. Despite Kate's assurances, I wonder whether she might have a price. And even if she doesn't sell her body, perhaps she shares herself with Barbara all the same. There's still so much I don't know about Kate. She's been circumspect. Secretive.

As the night wears on, my curiosity gets the best of me. I go to Kate's room. I slept here only one night, after our outing to Miss Mabel's, but the room welcomes me with a low, crackling fire. The bed is turned down, as if in invitation. I cross to Kate's bureau and slide open the top drawer. It's filled with underthings—chemises, corsets, and men's and women's garments alike. The next drawer contains her shirts, the earthy, sweet scent of lavender and chamomile wafting up from the folded cambric.

The rest of the drawers contain only clothing, until I get to the bottom. I find letters nestled there, tied with a faded ribbon. I lift them out. They're addressed to Kate, from someone whose name I don't recognize—a Dr. Horatio Sutherland. Was he her father? She mentioned he was a doctor. I skim through the letters. There's nothing of interest, only a fatherly concern over Kate's health and well-being, until I get to the final letter, dated March 7, 1841. The doctor's penmanship is markedly different in this letter—an untidy, barely legible scrawl compared to the neat hand in the others.

> *Dearest Katherine,*
>
> *I have suffered an apoplectic fit, which has left me greatly impaired. Given my age, there will surely be more to follow. This may be the last time I am able to write to you. Please take this humble offering as an apology for all the misfortune you have endured on my account. It comforts my heart to know you've found happiness, but once I am gone, he will try to find you, Kate. I know it. He is a man obsessed. Driven by some inner demon. I can no longer control him or make him see reason. You are safest to remain as you are now, and where you are. Do*

not attempt to come to me. I have burned all your letters, though it pained me to do so. Let this be our farewell. Be wary. Be vigilant.

Your loving father,
H. Sutherland

I refold the letter and place it at the bottom of the stack, where I found it, retying the ribbon.

You are safest to remain as you are now.

Did Dr. Sutherland know Kate's secret? That she was living as a man, with Lucrezia? The letter certainly hints at it. And who was he frightened of, on her behalf?

He is a man obsessed. Driven by some inner demon. I can no longer control him or make him see reason.

A chill shivers through me. Someone from Kate's past wished her harm. An old beau? An old enemy?

I replace the letters in the drawer and slide my hand deeper, toward the back. I gasp as something sharp pierces my finger. I withdraw my hand and suck on the bead of blood forming on my fingertip, then slide the drawer open more fully so I can see what's cut me. It's a picture frame, its edges sharply figured with brass scrollwork. I draw it out to study the daguerreotype within. I recognize Kate immediately, dressed in a frock coat and breeches, though she's much younger in the photograph. Her dark hair is hidden beneath a powdered wig, but that same sly smile slants across her lips as she leans over a woman reclining on a couch. It's Barbara Kincaid, her full lips open in a seductive pout, her hand wound around Kate's neck as if pulling her in for a kiss.

The caption below the daguerreotype reads: Barbara Ardouin as Countess Almaviva with Katherine O'Malley as Cherubino. *The Marriage of Figaro*, Dock Street Theatre, 1845.

I want to dash the framed photograph against the wall. Or burn it. Instead, I sit on the edge of the bed to study it. So, Kate lied to me. Her history with Barbara is much more complex than she let on.

Lucrezia must have been introduced to Barbara through the theater, not through the planter aristocracy. She and Lucrezia both married above their station, that much is apparent. And between them, there was a connecting thread. Kate. I consider the photograph again. Yes, Countess Almaviva and Cherubino were not-so-secret lovers in Mozart's opera, and the photograph was obviously a staged promotional image for the theater, but the attraction between them is palpable. I witnessed their affection for one another firsthand, at Miss Mabel's. Did Barbara and Kate begin an affair after Lucrezia's passing? Are they carrying on still, beneath her husband's nose? Or perhaps the three of them are embroiled in an open affair. Though scandalous, such things happen.

It's enough to set my jealousy, and my curiosity, aflame. I place the photograph back inside the bureau drawer, wiping my hands on my skirt, and make a decision. It may prove to be foolhardy, but all the same, by the time the clock chimes ten, I'm dressed in the periwinkle gown I wore to my library dinner with Kate, my hair covered by the auburn wig. Barbara Kincaid is about to host an uninvited guest.

The house is garishly lit and filled with people from my former life, just as I worried it would be. Hidden behind the spiky leaves of a dwarf palmetto, I can hear scraps of their conversation drifting down from the upper piazza. The clink of glassware. A woman's high, distinctive laughter rings out over the gardens. Georgina McClintock, prima donna of the chivalry. I quell my nervousness and wait in the shadows for the right opportunity to make my entrance. Finally, a maid exits the side door, leaving it open behind her. I wait until she makes her way to the kitchen house, then rush across the lawn, face concealed by my cloak. Once inside, it's easy enough to pretend I belong here. I stash my cloak in a corner of the hall, then follow the sound of laughter and music up the servant stairs until I reach the third floor, where the ballroom awaits.

The Kincaid mansion drips with newfound wealth. Fine damask covers the furniture—likely from China—and with the array of other items from the Orient, I wonder whether Mr. Kincaid is an import merchant like Papa. Gorgeous, nearly translucent porcelain decorates the sideboards, and beneath my feet, Turkish rugs soften my step as I approach the ballroom. I pause before entering and glance at my reflection in a nearby mirror. My color is high, and I've gone through quite an adventure to get here. Though my leg protested, I walked to Mount Pleasant, in my gown, then took the steam ferry across the river. At this time of night, I was one of few passengers, but my apprehension only grew as the steamer churned the Cooper, carrying me back to the city that wants me dead.

Now, outside this ballroom, where I will undoubtedly encounter familiar faces, I feel foolish. Reckless. I've never been the impulsive sort. I've always been cautious and followed the rules. But seeing that photograph—Barbara's swooning desire, Kate's lecherous grin—stirred such anger and jealousy in me.

And then I hear her. Kate. Her voice soars over the din of conversation inside the ballroom. A few measures later, another voice joins hers. A woman's voice. I have no doubt who it belongs to. My heart pounds as I push past a couple standing in the doorway and make my way into the crowded room. The cloying scent of perfume mixes with the heady fragrance of gardenias. And at the end of the ballroom, on a raised dais, I see her—Kate, resplendent, beautiful, seated at a piano. Barbara stands near her, dressed in yellow once more, their voices twining together. A string quartet accompanies them as they sing, their voices rising in soul-piercing harmony. My fists clench at my sides. Kate is unabashedly flirting with Barbara as they sing, sending coy glances up at her through her lashes. Mr. Kincaid looks on, beaming. He's either oblivious to what's going on, or he's encouraging it. No longer able to stomach the seduction happening onstage, I turn my attention to the crowd.

Next to the stage, I glimpse Arabella Meade holding court, surrounded by men and women alike, her fan languidly sweeping the air. Her beauty is incandescent under candlelight. Now that Rebecca is gone, Arabella has no rival. With her looks and her father's standing as a wealthy shipowner, I'm shocked she hasn't yet married. Perhaps the rumors are true—that the Meades have lost their fortune, that they're hiding behind a mountain of debt. I can think of no other reason for Arabella's lack of suitors. With Papa gone, Captain Meade lost one of his chief merchants and silk-buying customers, which would surely take a toll as well. Perhaps Captain Meade and Mr. Kincaid have formed a new alliance, which would help to explain Arabella's presence here. I'll have to do my best to avoid her, as she's the most likely to recognize me. Other familiar faces drift past me as I hover along the outside edges of the room, trying not to draw too much attention. I exchange bland pleasantries with the guests, remembering my Scots burr. I am no longer Lillian Carmichael. I'm Mary Jones tonight, and for every night outside the walls of Angel's Rest.

Though I hide my disdain behind a gracious smile, the simmer of cold anger that Kate witnessed in me is easy to nurse here. I hate so many people in this room. Leroy Burrows, haughty and overdressed, took great pleasure in denouncing my father to the papers. Georgina McClintock resembles a cream puff in her toffee-colored gown, white hair bundled at her nape in a knot of complex braids an enslaved maid likely spent hours accomplishing. As the chivalry's chief matchmaker, she helped arrange my and William's betrothal and was once my mother's closest friend. Once.

Part of me worries that Mother will be here. But even in the unlikely event she was invited to this party, she'd still be in full mourning for Papa. Besides, our family name fell off the society invitation lists long before tonight.

A footman passes by, carrying a tray with drinks. I accept his offer of champagne to calm my nerves and find a seat near the back of the room. The irritating duet ends, finally, thankfully, and Barbara descends the stage, her cheeks flushed. She goes to her husband, who kisses her temple. She's a talented singer, I'll give her that. Begrudgingly. I'm sure she and Kate owned the stage together in their heyday.

"Varina" resumes playing, and the chatter in the room fades to a hush as she lifts her voice to sing. Distracted as I am by her performance, and my still-boiling jealousy, I hardly notice that someone has taken the chair next to mine. It's his *smell* that finds me first. Fresh limes and tobacco smoke. I turn my head slowly and see his long, elegant fingers clutching his silver-topped walking stick. *Remember, you're Mary Jones.* I repeat the phrase over and over in my head as Dr. Broadbent, my former physician, angles toward me. "She's a bit tawdry, isn't she?" he whispers, gesturing to Varina.

"Yes," I concur, remembering that Mary Jones is a wealthy widow and would, in fact, look down her nose at performers like Varina. "That dress is ill-fitting. Cheap." Though my jealousy adds a bitter drop of poison to my words, it's no lie. As the daughter of a silk merchant, I know good fabric when I see it. Most of Kate's costumes are made of poor-quality satin—meant for the stage, not a fine ballroom.

Dr. Broadbent assesses me coolly, his refined, aquiline features unchanged since the last time I saw him, in the courtroom where he provided the damning testimony for my conviction. "I'm so sorry, have we been introduced?" he asks. "I didn't see you at the reception."

"No, sir. I'm afraid I was late." I demur even though I've known this man since childhood. He nursed me through countless illnesses, only to betray me in my hour of greatest need. "Mrs. Mary Jones."

"You're Scottish." He smiles. "How charming. Lionel Broadbent, physician."

"Pleased to make your acquaintance, Dr. Broadbent," I say. My pulse hammers beneath my skin. A few moments pass. I glance at him as he watches Varina. If he recognizes me, he's doing a tremendous job of concealing it. He doesn't, I determine.

"Is your husband with you tonight, Mrs. Jones?" he asks abruptly, still watching Varina.

"No, sir. He's been gone three years now. The war." I'm grateful that the periwinkle gown is somber enough in color to count as half mourning but curse myself for not studying Great Britain's recent wars more deliberately. William always kept me well schooled in such matters—one thing I enjoyed about our courtship. Our shared love of history.

"In Africa, I assume?"

"Yes," I say, my mouth dry.

His gray eyes rake over me. "You're quite young for a widow. Are you here visiting family?"

My scalp prickles beneath the heavy wig. A bead of perspiration runs down my temple as I nod. "My cousin. She was supposed to come tonight. She fell ill."

"How unfortunate." He clears his throat. "How much longer will you stay?"

"At the party?"

"No, ma'am. In the States."

"I'm not . . . certain. I haven't yet booked passage home."

His eyes scrape over me again, and quite suddenly, I realize why he's asking me these questions. He's *interested* in me. Perhaps romantically. I'm not surprised. The doctor is a confirmed bachelor and a rumored playboy, handsome, with a reserved charisma. I remember that many of the young women in my cohort secretly admired him, though their standing in society would never have allowed betrothal to a doctor. But that never kept him from his dalliances. From the way he's looking at me, it appears nothing has changed.

"If you'd be inclined, Mrs. Jones, I'd very much like to call on you while you're here," he says, giving credence to my suspicions.

Disgust roils through me, but I master it before it alters my expression. Still, I'm pleased my disguise seems to be effective. He doesn't recognize me. Perhaps my acting is better than Kate thinks. "I'm afraid my elderly cousin doesn't have the patience for entertaining gentleman callers, sir. She's quite infirm."

He hums thoughtfully and withdraws a small metal case from beneath the lapel of his jacket. He takes out a crisp calling card and offers it to me. "I see. Should you—or your cousin, for that matter—ever find yourself in need of a doctor during your stay, I do call on my patients at home. Or if you happen to be near Savage Street during your visit, you might stop in. I keep office hours between one o'clock and three. You may bring your cousin, if you'd prefer to have a chaperone."

I take his card gingerly. "I'll keep that in mind, sir."

"As a matter of fact, I'm quite surprised your cousin allowed you to come out alone tonight. Surely she told you."

"Told me?"

"About our murders. There's a curfew. Women are no longer allowed to be out past eight o'clock without an escort."

I take out my handkerchief and dab the bit of lace-trimmed fabric along my temple. The air is much too close. My confidence fades. While I appear to have fooled him, I don't even know Mary's full story yet, and my ruse is full of holes. The longer I engage in conversation with him, the more likely he will see through my unpracticed veneer. I shouldn't be here. I shouldn't have come.

Varina ends her song, and the room explodes in applause. In the brief pause before the next song, Dr. Broadbent leans close and whispers, "I can see by your expression that I've frightened you. But we *do* have a persistent murderess, Mrs. Jones. A she-devil who hungers for the blood of young women."

"How terrible." I nearly slip out of my Scots accent but catch myself just in time to roll my *r*'s.

"Yes. As a physician, it's harrowing but fascinating. I've been practicing medicine for over twenty years, and I've never seen anything like it. Bodies completely drained of blood."

"And it's a woman? This murderer?"

"Yes. Lillian Carmichael. She's been seen about town since her apparent death. She collapsed on the morning of her execution, on the way to the gallows. She murdered her own sister. Poisoned her."

At this, I flinch.

"Miss Carmichael was a former patient of mine. I examined her corpse myself. Her body, though absent of heartbeat, pulse, and breath, was remarkably preserved. I've never seen the like."

"How uncanny," I say. Although I manage to keep my voice steady, inside, I'm tied in knots. With his cool manner and probing questions, I have the feeling Dr. Broadbent is toying with me. That he senses my dissembling. I must find a way to extricate myself from this party, undetected, before my lies get the better of me.

I try to control my emotions, as Kate admonished, focusing on the glittering tableau of wealth surrounding me—the plasterwork ceiling with its swirling clouds, the whale oil chandeliers, the fashionable taffeta-clad ladies with their ruffles and lace. Vanities I once believed important.

"I've read a story written by a fellow physician, Dr. Polidori," Broadbent continues, losing no interest in the topic at hand, "though as a lady, you're unlikely to have read it yourself. I'm convinced Miss Carmichael must be akin to the creature Polidori describes in his novella. A vampire. I'm curious whether he ever encountered such a creature himself. I'd give anything to study one. To capture Miss Carmichael and investigate her physiology. The science that might come about . . . it would be truly uncharted territory."

I could almost laugh if I weren't disgusted. But even though the killer isn't me, what if he's right? What if there *is* some beastly creature walking the streets of Charleston, draining women of their blood? Whether it's a human or monster, I'd be in just as much danger as any other lady here. So would Kate. Suddenly, everything feels like a waking nightmare. I recall my terrible dream of Rebecca. Her sharp teeth and wild, rage-filled eyes. Surely . . . no. The thought is abominable. My sister has been dead for nearly three years. It couldn't be her.

"I *really* should escort you home," Broadbent says, turning the subject effortlessly. "Should we become separated, come find me before you leave. I'll safely see you returned to your cousin." His persistence is jarring. His interest unsettling. The urge to flee screams through me. All my petty jealousy over Kate and Barbara, my foolish curiosity—none of it was worth the risk of this encounter. Suddenly, the neckline of my dress feels much too snug. The air too thin to breathe.

As soon as Varina begins the next song, I excuse myself with a smile and slip down the hall and up a set of stairs. I hide behind a hutch, clawing open the neck of my bodice as I try to catch my breath. I bite my lip until I taste blood. A Negro maid comes out of one of the rooms, her eyes widening. "Ma'am, you're bleeding. Are you all right?"

"Is there a room where I can hide, until the party is over? Please. I beg of you."

"Certainly." A moment of immediate understanding passes between us. "Come with me."

She ushers me down the hall and unlocks a door, motioning me inside. "This room belongs to the mistress's daughter. She's with her grandmother tonight, across town. No one will find you here."

"Thank you," I say, sobbing, barely comprehending the fact that Barbara is a mother.

The maid gives me a shy smile, presses a clean handkerchief into my hand, then leaves me. I collapse onto the thick Aubusson carpet and try to push aside my memories, but they come anyway. They have nothing to do with blood-drinking monsters, but they're nearly as vile. My mother, swooning with pleasure in Dr. Broadbent's arms, while on the other side of the house, Rebecca lay dying, with Papa in prayer at her bedside.

SIXTEEN

I stay in the room until I can no longer bear it. I need fresh air. Though all my fears have coalesced—Dr. Broadbent's questions, along with the very real possibility of encountering the murderer, alone and defenseless on the streets—I need to get out of this house. The sound of Kate's singing filters up to me as I sneak into the hall and slink down the servant stairs, gather my cloak, and slip out of doors, undetected. I hurry to White Point Gardens, where I'll hide and watch for Kate. She'll have to pass by the gardens on her way to the wharves, where our rowboat is surely moored. Though I shudder to think of her anger when she discovers I've followed her, I don't feel safe walking to the wharves alone, where it's unlikely I'll find a boatman willing to ferry me over the Cooper at this time of night.

I nestle against the trunk of one of the sheltering oaks near the entry gate, hidden in the shadows beneath its low branches. I pray Kate's performance ends soon. I long to be back at Angel's Rest, where the fear overtaking the city can't reach us.

I'm there for only a few minutes before I hear a soft whimpering from somewhere deeper in the park. It sounds like a hurt animal. My ears perk up. The sound grows louder, more desperate, until it becomes a high-pitched mewling like a kitten or a rabbit in pain. I can't bear it. I've always had a soft spot for animals. We rescued our wolfhound, Walter, from drowning as a puppy—someone had tied him into a bag and tossed it into the Ashley River.

The mewling rises in intensity, then diminishes again. To my shock, I make out a word: *"Please."* It's not an animal. It's a woman. All my instincts tell me she's in danger. My conscience spurs me to action. I rush from my hiding place and up the path. What I see next makes my blood turn to ice. A man—for it is a man, there's no denying it—crouches over a woman lying on the ground, her legs akimbo. A person happening upon them might think they were mid-tryst, but her cries are of pain. Not pleasure. Everything in me screams to run. To turn away. But I can't.

"Stop!" I screech. "Get away from her!"

The man stills. Lifts himself from between the woman's legs and, without looking at me, lopes into the low-hanging oaks. I catch a glimpse of a pale face. Dark, feral eyes.

I rush to the woman and kneel at her side. Shock and disbelief wash over me. It's Arabella Meade, her prim curls unbound, skirts rucked above her waist, her drawers ripped. The ground beneath her is soaked with blood. A wound on her inner thigh pulses. I pull her skirts down and try to use the fabric to stanch the flow, but it does little good. The silk taffeta soaks through in seconds. She lifts her head weakly, her eyes wide and frightened. She attempts to speak and cannot.

Time slows. If I don't get help, and soon, she'll die. Dr. Broadbent. I pray he's still at the party. "I'm going to get help, Bella," I say, using the diminutive Rebecca had used. They were always Bella and Becca. "I'll be right back. I promise."

Arabella's eyes plead with me. *Don't leave me.*

But I must. I fly through the park, back to the Kincaid mansion. I push through the double doors and up the stairs, into the ballroom. Most of the guests have left, but Dr. Broadbent is there, conversing with Georgina McClintock. "Help!" I scream. "It's Miss Meade!"

Dr. Broadbent turns, surprise and confusion knitting his features . . . Kate ceases playing the piano, her voice falling away as her head swivels toward me, eyes wide.

"Arabella. She's . . . it's the killer. In the park. Come quickly!"

Realization dawns over Dr. Broadbent's face. "My god," he says, setting aside his drink. "Send a footman for a carriage, Mrs. McClintock. Hurry."

As Dr. Broadbent rushes from the house and the remaining guests stream out onto the promenade, Kate appears at my side. Her fingers grip my arm like a vise. "What in heaven's name are you doing here? We have to leave, Lil. Now."

"But Arabella . . ."

"You little fool! They think it's you, remember? The killer. You broke character. I don't know whether anyone noticed but me, but you were decidedly *not* Mary Jones from Lanarkshire when you burst in here."

I should worry. I should be afraid. But as Kate steers me out of the drawing room, hastily thanking Barbara Kincaid as we leave, all I can think about is poor, frightened Arabella, dying alone in the dark.

Confirmation of Arabella's death comes to us two days later. The headlines blaze with gruesome proclamations. I can't bring myself to read the details. I'll never excise Arabella's pleading look from my memory. Her fear. The horrific sight of that monster crouching over her. Though Kate is still angry at me for following her to the Kincaids' party, she does her best to comfort me, but guilt chases me all the same. I should have tried harder to save Arabella. And why was she in the gardens alone without an escort? Who was that man . . . or was he a man at all?

Later that afternoon, Ruby arrives, though I hardly have the wherewithal to teach her. I haven't slept more than an hour since the Kincaid party, the shock of witnessing Arabella's murder still fresh in my mind. Kate, dressed in her typical trousers, ushers Ruby into the parlor, falling seamlessly into her Alexander Mayhew persona. It still astounds me, how easily she does it. She accepts the brace of shining drum Ruby offers and bids her to sit. "I'm afraid Miss Mary is indisposed today, Ruby. Perhaps after a few days, your lessons might resume."

"I'm sorry to hear that." Ruby perches on the edge of a damask-covered chair, shyly folding her hands in her lap. I pour her tea, my hands shaking with tiredness, and she accepts it with a smile. "But I can't keep up my lessons anyway. I came to tell you all it might be a while before I see you again," she says. "The whole city's in an uproar, and it's spreading here. There are search parties out, looking for that killer, so Daddy says we'll need to lay low, until this is over. The Gullah warned us to move deeper into the swamp with the other maroons. Look out for ourselves."

"That's certainly understandable," I say.

"Daddy has a friend in town, a free man, who brings us provisions sometimes. He says he's never seen anything like it. People hiding in their big houses, businesses closing early. We're afraid, too. Not so much of the killer, but of what it'll mean for us colored folk."

With the murderer still on the loose and Arabella's death, paranoia and suspicion have surely risen to a fervor. No one took much notice of Sally's murder. But now that the killer is targeting wealthy, white debutantes, panic is spreading. Charleston's elite care only when something affects their own.

"What have you heard, Ruby? About the killer?" Kate asks, leaning forward in her chair.

"Well, Daddy's friend said they *were* saying it was a colored man. But they always blame our kind first. Now they're saying it's a woman, that she's some kind of . . . creature." Ruby's eyes flash to mine. "I don't know much more than that, or what to believe."

Out here in the marshes, Ruby must not have seen the papers. Must not have seen my image, plastered on wanted notices throughout town. And though her reading skills are improving with my tutelage, she wouldn't have been able to read a full newspaper article even if she encountered one. "None of that is true," I say, bristling. "It was a man. A white man. I saw him attacking Arabella."

Ruby's eyes widen.

"I couldn't identify him—it was much too dark—but I'd swear it on my life."

Kate clears her throat. "I'll go across the river tonight. See what I can find out."

"I'll come with you," I say.

"No, Mary," Kate says, her voice firm. "I'll go alone. It's too dangerous for a woman to be out after dark." I rankle at this, but do my best not to let it show. I dislike how patriarchal Kate becomes as Alex. "I've a friend with connections to the City Guard. I'll find out what he has to say."

Ruby looks from me to Kate. "I'd better go. Daddy's waiting for me outside. We'll bring you more fish later this week, though, before we leave."

"Understood," Kate says. "If there's anything we can do to help, Ruby . . ."

Ruby nods and rises, smoothing her calico skirts. "Thank you, Mr. Mayhew. Miss Mary."

I walk her to the door, and before she goes, I press her hand in mine. "Thank *you* for everything you've done for me, Ruby. You saved my life, you know. Make sure you practice what I taught you. Someday soon, I hope we'll read more of *Sleepy Hollow*."

"I'd sure like that." She smiles and ducks her head, squeezes my hand, and then she's gone, disappearing into the marsh's wild, unkept beauty.

That night, Kate leaves me alone again at Angel's Rest. She's dressed as Alex this time, handsome in a cutaway coat and high-waisted breeches, a crimson silk cravat knotted at her neck. As she prepares to leave, my anxieties gather. I'm frightened to be left alone, but I'm also worried about what might happen to Kate, in the city with a murderer still at large. I think of that horrid figure, bending over Arabella. Her helpless cries.

And there's still a part of me, a shameful part, that wonders whether she's going to meet Barbara for some clandestine tryst. When Kate confronted me about why I followed her to the Kincaid party, I was too ashamed to admit my jealousy. I didn't confess to finding the photograph or the letters from her father. Instead, I apologized profusely and weathered Kate's scolding with contrition.

Now, as if sensing my worries, Kate brushes the back of her hand against my cheek. "Please don't do anything foolish tonight, darling. Don't follow me again. If anything were to happen to you . . . well, I can't think like that, can I?" She trails her hand down my neck, sending a tremor of longing through me. "I trust you, Lillian. Don't do anything to make me regret that trust." She gives me a rakish smile. "Now, be a good girl and stay put. I've stoked the fire in my room. It's going to be a chilly night. I'd better find you in my bed when I return."

I nearly swoon at the innuendo in her tone. A flush crawls up my neck, setting my ears afire. When she looks at me the way she's looking at me now, my mind goes soft as pluff mud.

"Please be careful," I say. Because, despite her appearance, her swagger, her confident air as Alexander Mayhew, I know she's still a woman beneath her clothes. And women are in danger in this city.

She dons a tall satin hat and winks at me. "Always."

Though a wintry chill is on the air, I follow her onto the piazza and watch as she strides down the tabby path, to where our rowboat is moored in the marsh grass. I stay and listen until I hear the steady sweep of her oars, then go inside to try to distract myself with a book, to no avail. I wander about downstairs, dusting and straightening picture frames and trinkets, then go to Kate's room. A low fire crackles in the hearth. My eyes go to the bottom drawer of her bureau, where the loathsome picture and letters are hidden. I'm tempted to take the picture out again, but it will only inflame my insecurities and betray Kate's trust.

Kate *did* tell me to look through Lucrezia's things—to choose anything I liked from her wardrobe. Apart from the periwinkle gown I wore the night of Barbara's party, which is ruined, stained with Arabella's blood, I haven't tried on anything else. The thought of wearing Lucrezia's clothes disturbs me. Not because she's dead. But because of everything she and Kate shared together. Of the memories and love they made in this room. My envy is undeniable. I glance up at Lucrezia's portrait, at her imperious, regal gaze. How could I ever hope to compete with this formidable woman? I'm nothing at all like her. I open the high Chippendale wardrobe and look through the gowns and petticoats. Most of them are in the mode of the last decade—with puffed sleeves in the slope-shouldered silhouette favored then. I take out one brilliant-blue dress, its bodice trimmed with delicate, beaded lace. I cross to the dressing table and hold it against myself, studying my image in the mirror. While my cropped hair does little to flatter my features, my cheeks are rounding out again, and the contours of my body have softened, thanks to Kate's cooking. The blue gown brings out the violet color of my eyes. I take off the calico day dress I've favored since my arrival and slip the gown over my undergarments. The hem, on the shorter side given the era of its making, grazes the floor. With my petite frame, and a stiff, corded petticoat, it will be the perfect length for walking. The dress fits as if it were made for me, scooping low over the plump line of my bust and hugging my corseted waist.

I open the drawers in the dressing table and find paste jewels, gloves, and a pot of rouge. I take up the boar bristle brush on the dressing table and coax my hair to wave around my face and chin as becomingly as possible, then adorn myself with a chevron-accented necklace. I sweep through the room, twirling and dancing. I feel beautiful for the first time in years.

And then guilt strikes me. Here I am, dancing, playing at being a grand lady in a dead woman's dress, while Arabella Meade lies in a morgue, her body cold. I left her alone, to die on that path. Did she expire before Dr. Broadbent arrived, or later? Yes, she betrayed me—lied to the court and told the judge that I was jealous of Rebecca, that Rebecca was frightened of me, and that she'd heard me threaten her. Arabella's testimony destroyed my innocence. But she was so young then, like my sister—only eighteen.

And she and her family had remained loyal to us. Even when others turned Mother away from their doors when we went for Sunday calling, Mrs. Meade welcomed us into their home. Unlike us, they had Negro servants, but they were free men and women. The Meades paid them well and treated them with dignity. Captain Meade had traveled the world and witnessed the differences between cultures. He and Papa spent many an evening discussing the South's future, and while Captain Meade wasn't publicly an abolitionist, he contributed money to the cause.

All the same, I can think of no specific reason why the murderer targeted Arabella. She was well liked by all. And Denise George, the other murdered debutante, came from a respected family. So did Marjorie. The only other thing the three women had in common was their youth and their red hair. The first victim, Sally, was a redhead as well. It's the only tie that binds all four of them together.

I pace through the rooms, going over the scene I witnessed in the park. That man. The way he'd moved was strange. He scurried away, like a startled animal. His eyes were so dark they didn't appear to have pupils. What if . . . what if he wasn't a man, but a monster in the guise of one, an undead creature, as the papers claimed about me?

A chill walks between my shoulder blades, despite the warmth of the fire. All of a sudden the house is too quiet, the rooms too large, the space between each of my breaths loaded with fear. Kate is out there. And I'm here, alone. Defenseless. What if?

I jump as a shrill scream comes through the cracked window. It's only a fox in heat—I've heard the sound before—yet I rush to the window all the same, peering out into the darkness. There's no moon tonight. The sky is an unfathomable scrim of black, pocked with stars.

In the shadows, I imagine all sorts of creatures. I slam the window shut and draw the curtains, my heart pattering.

I didn't tell them. I didn't tell them and look what happened. You *should have told them, Lillian.*

I whirl at the ghostly sound of Rebecca's voice. I'm certain I heard her, but I do not see her. There's no one there. My head spins, and I press the backs of my hands to my eyes. My mind is playing tricks on me. My anxieties, and my lack of sleep, have eroded my senses. "Please stop. Please leave me be."

I crawl into Kate's bed, not bothering to undress, but I don't sleep. I can't. All I can think of is Kate, wandering the streets alone. Vulnerable. And if I sleep, dreams will come. Dreams of Rebecca. Her haunted eyes. Her anger. My guilt.

When dawn breaks, I'm still awake. I lift my head from the pillow. In the distance, I hear the telltale swish of oars. I rush to the upper piazza, relief flooding through me as I see Kate's tall form striding between the oaks, her hat in her hands. I fly down the stairs to meet her, flinging open the front door.

Red-gold light breaks over her, gilding her hair. "My god, Lil. Look at you," she says. Her eyes rake over me, taking in the blue ball gown, the jewels. "Have you been up all night?"

"Yes," I say, breathless. "I couldn't sleep. I was too worried about you."

She climbs the steps. Stands over me. "Well. Here I am. Unscathed."

"Don't ever leave me alone again," I say. "Please."

"Are you all right? Did something happen while I was gone?" She places her hat on the porch railing, and grasps my arms, her forehead wrinkling with concern.

"No. But I imagined all sorts of things happening. To *you*. Terrible things."

She smiles. "I'm quite fine, I assure you. I can take care of myself."

"I . . . I know. It's just . . ." A tear snakes down my face, and I swipe it away angrily.

"Lillian. Are you sure you're well?"

"No. Not really. But I'm better now. Now that you're home."

Kate stills, her eyes holding mine. She smiles slowly. Catlike. "You've fallen in love with me. Haven't you?"

I peer up at her shyly, taken aback by her boldness, but no longer willing to lie. "Is it that obvious?"

"Yes," she says, laughing. She tips my chin up. "You look stunning, by the way."

"I found this," I say, anxiously grasping the blue dress's skirts. "You told me to . . ."

"I did." She bites her lip, her eyes drifting down to my high, hoisted bust. "It fits you perfectly. As I knew it would."

My heart beats furiously as she winds her fingers through the hair at the nape of my neck, as she presses herself against me. "Oh, Lil. You're shaking," she murmurs. Then she lowers her head and kisses me. At the feel of her lips against mine, all my senses ignite, my body thrumming with desire. I sigh, winding my arms around her neck as she explores my mouth with her tongue, as her hands rove over my body. How right this feels. How natural.

"This dress," she says, kissing my neck, "is beautiful on you. But I'm far more interested in what's beneath it. When I told you I wanted you in my bed, I meant it."

SEVENTEEN

I have no idea what time it is. I wake alone, the sheets tangled around me, the sun blazing through the windows. I sit up, dizzy with hunger. I haven't had anything to eat. After Kate swept me off to bed this morning, I didn't care about anything but the feel of her body against mine, her hands, her mouth . . .

My god, the things she did to me.

I stand on wobbly legs and reach for my chemise, discarded on the floor along with the rest of my undergarments, although Kate had the foresight to fold the blue dress and place it back in the armoire. I find her in the kitchen house, standing at the stove, her shirt unbuttoned, suspenders draped around her hips, trousers slung low. Her hair riots in dark curls around her shoulders. She's never looked more enticing.

"There you are," she says. "Hungry?"

"Yes. Very," I say, sinking into a chair.

"I gathered the eggs since you were sleeping."

She presents me with coffee, two sunny eggs, and toast. I can barely meet her eyes, remembering the feverish way we came together. "Ruby was right," she says, turning back to the stove. "I hardly saw another soul about town last night. Miss Mabel's is closed. Indefinitely. Apparently, the ladies are too frightened to go out, even during the day."

"Goodness."

"Without her, I'm not sure what I'll do for work. I have a private party on Saturday, in Mount Pleasant, but I may be forced to go back to mashing if there are no more commissions."

"Mashing?" I ask.

"Doing breeches roles at the theater. Dock Street is still running shows, at least. But private parties are where I make the best money. And those mostly came about because of Mabel. And Barbara."

I think of the photograph of Kate and Barbara again. Cherubino was a breeches role. I push aside my thoughts of Barbara. My jealousy. No matter what their past together entailed, Kate wants *me* now. She showed me that this morning, in every way possible.

She sits next to me with a sigh, and tucks into her food, stabbing at her eggs with her fork. She seems agitated. Irritable.

I place a hand on her forearm. "Surely all of this will be over soon," I say. "The police will find the real killer."

"That's just the thing." Kate gives me a tight smile. "They're still convinced it's you. As I feared, you were recognized at the Kincaids' party. That doctor—Broadbent—reported that he spoke to you at length. That you were in disguise, but he knew who you were. I also talked to my friend at the City Guard. You were seen fleeing the park. They've increased the bounty on your head. It doesn't look good, Lil."

Dr. Broadbent. He saw through my guise. Of course he did. Fear trundles through me, anew. If they capture me, I'll be put to death. Possibly on sight, knowing the City Guard and their penchant to shoot before asking questions. And what if Kate now sees me as more of a liability, too? I think of her passionate nature, of how she's opened my eyes to a new way of being. I'm loath to let my freedom—and this new life with her—go.

"What are we to do?" I ask.

"You'll have to hide away here. No more coming to town. Ever. If all my work dries up, I won't be going to town anymore, either. I'll have to rely on my apothecary skills to sustain us." She finishes her breakfast and paces the room, running her hands through her hair. Although I have nothing to do with these murders, I feel guilty all the same. I've complicated her life. Made things more difficult. She's been nothing but kind to me, with her hospitality, her care, and now, her love. She has no reason to do these things—to take in a fugitive like me—and I don't want to be a burden. I want to contribute, to be her partner in all ways. To prove myself worthy of her. There's also the matter of learning more about the killer and the rumors about me. There's no better place to overhear gossip than a ballroom.

Though Angel's Rest is now my home, the thought of never leaving here again makes me feel unsettled. Beautiful as my surroundings are, being locked away like a princess in a tower is merely another form of prison, even with the pleasures Kate affords me.

Suddenly, it dawns on me. A way I might help and slake my boredom and curiosity at the same time.

"I can help you, Kate, just as much as you're helping me. I want to."

She lifts her brow. "How?"

"I can pick locks. If you have the guest list for the party in Mount Pleasant, I can go to the guests' houses. Break in and steal while they're away."

"And who do you think would get the blame for that, Lillian? Most of these people are slave owners."

I wilt. She's right. If precious jewels and money went missing from a wealthy home, the enslaved would be the first suspected. And punished. Sometimes with their lives.

"One last party, then," I say, lifting my eyes. "I'm quick with my hands. When I stole to survive on the streets, I was never caught. I'll dress like a boy again. The only person who ever recognized me besides Dr. Broadbent was Arabella, and well, she certainly won't be there. People are so enraptured when you perform, they'll be completely distracted."

"No, Lil. It's too dangerous." Kate leans against the kitchen sink, crossing her arms. Her eyes harden. "This isn't a game."

I clench my hands in my lap. "I cannot just sit idle in this house, feeling useless. I need a purpose, Kate. I want to help."

"You're not useless, sweetling. Besides, I have money in reserve. Lucrezia's jewelry and antiques."

I also have money, and the jewelry I took from home, still hidden at my campsite. I need to go back for it, at some point. But the cautious side of me believes I should keep it a secret, just in case things between Kate and me ever sour. I pray that they won't. But I've learned not to trust anyone completely.

"We'll get by," Kate says comfortingly. "You needn't worry."

"Yes, but you said yourself that work is drying up. We can't depend on more parties. I'll cut my hair shorter. Like a boy's. Tailor one of your suits to my size. I'm afraid of being caught, too. But I won't be a b—" I cut myself off, remembering Kate's reaction the last time I said the word "burden" aloud. "I promise to be careful."

She sighs, rolling her head back on her shoulders. "Your obstinance is maddening. I'll need convincing. Can you really pick pockets that well?"

Her doubt rankles me. But it also challenges me. "Lay a trap for me. Put coins in your pockets. Wear jewelry, just like the ladies at your parties. I'll prove my skills to you within a day."

"Oh, you will?" The corner of her mouth quirks up. "I'm not sure I believe you."

"We'll see, won't we?" I say haughtily.

That night, after supper, I lay three coins and a pocket watch out on the dining room table. Kate fishes in her pockets, patting her breeches. Then she smiles at me, slowly. "I'll be damned," she says. "How?"

I sit up a little taller, lifting my chin. "I took one coin while you were hanging laundry to dry. I took the pocket watch when you kissed me in the hall. The other two coins, I pilfered when we passed one another, tidying the house."

"I didn't feel a thing."

"And neither will they."

"You've convinced me, you little minx." Kate sits back in her chair, a wolfish gleam in her eyes. "Come here."

I cross to her. She pulls me onto her lap, one hand knotting in my hair. My breath catches in my throat. "You deserve a reward, my sweetling. My clever, quick girl." She traces her tongue along my neck as she positions me squarely against her, one arm latched around my waist while her other hand rucks up my skirts and finds the opening in my drawers. I twist as her fingers explore my bared flesh.

"Please," I whimper.

"Please, what?" she says, her hand tightening in my hair again. "Tell me what you want, Lillian."

"You," I say.

She chuckles, opening my legs with her knees, locking me in place. Right where she wants me. Her dominance over me is intoxicating. Heady. With practiced ease, she strokes the knot of throbbing want between my legs. In a matter of moments, she brings me to the edge of oblivion, and then ceases her ministrations, even as I writhe and beg for more. She lands a stinging slap on my thigh. I gasp in surprise. The sensation makes my skin tingle, sends molten heat catapulting to my core.

"Not until I'm ready, sweetling," she scolds. "And I do mean to take my time."

Kissing me deeply, she unbuttons my bodice, shoves her hand down my corset, and brings my left breast out. "Perfect, so round and fitting for my hands," she says, pinching my nipple. I whimper as her other hand travels back to my nether regions, as she dips one long finger inside me, plumbing my depths. "You're soaking wet." She brings her finger to my lips, teasing them open. "Taste how honey sweet you are, my pet."

I take her finger into my mouth, suckling it. She groans. "I need to see you. All of you. Take off your clothes. Then climb onto that table and offer yourself to me." She pushes me off her lap and watches with heavy-lidded eyes as I shed my clothing, until I'm naked and trembling before her. Her eyes blaze with desire as they travel over me. Being on such flagrant display feels salacious. Wicked. But if our sort of love damns me to hell, I'll burn willingly.

"On the table," she says. "I won't tell you again."

I hoist myself up onto the table, the cool marble top kissing the backs of my thighs. My heart races as Kate stalks toward me, her eyes hungry. I reach for her, but she grasps my wrists, pushing me onto my back. She takes one of my nipples in her mouth, tugging at my sensitive flesh with her teeth. The candles in the center of the table flicker with our movements, casting leaping shadows onto her face. Once she's had her fill of my breasts, once she has me panting and begging, she pulls her chair closer and sits between my open legs. I lift my hips, aching to feel her touch, needing her as much as I need my next breath.

"Look at you," she says, tracing the line of my sex with the tip of her finger. "Such a delicious feast. So ready and eager for my mouth."

She scoops her hands beneath my hips and pulls me to her roughly, hooking my legs over her shoulders as she nuzzles between my thighs, nipping and licking. I nearly levitate off the table, gripping the edge with my fingertips as she buries her face in my wetness, as she lavishes me with her tongue, from bottom to top, like I'm the most delectable dish she's ever tasted.

Her hands grip my buttocks, holding me captive to her mouth, my cries echoing from the high ceiling as I beg for the release she so cruelly withholds. She brings me to the precipice, again and again, circling the source of my pleasure with the tip of her tongue, then diving back into my depths to drink from me, until finally, she shows mercy and, with a relentless, steady rhythm, drives me past the point of no return. My crisis breaks over me, and I clench and cry out, pleasure blooming within me like a hidden rose.

Once my trembling ceases, she lowers me gently back onto the table and returns to my mouth, kissing me long on the lips. I grasp at the waist of her trousers, longing to taste her, to give her the same satisfaction she's just given me. She pulls away, shoving my hands aside. "No, Lil." Her face is hard. "Don't ever touch me there. Not ever. Do you understand?"

I sit up, confusion looping through me. The first time we were intimate, I excused her reticence as a reaction to my inexperience. She initiated me into the ways of pleasure, but when I reached for her to do the same, she gently pushed me away, then gathered me in her arms and held me, distracting me with loving words and caresses.

"But what about you?" I ask. "Don't you want . . ."

"No. I don't. My satisfaction comes from being the one in control."

"Oh." I try to hide my disappointment. My wounded feelings. I don't understand.

"Please don't be hurt. It's not about you, sweetling," she says, softening. "I just . . . I prefer it this way. Can you accept that?"

"I suppose so. But it seems selfish on my part. To only receive pleasure. And never give it."

Kate's wolfish look returns. "Oh, but you do give me pleasure, Lil. Seeing you come apart is an ecstasy. The sounds you make. The way you move. To know that I have that kind of power over you . . . it's hypnotic." She cups my jaw with her hand. Her thumb brushes my lower lip. "You are so beautiful. Your body. Those eyes. Your spirit. The way you taste. You just might be my undoing, you know."

She bends to kiss me, and before I know it, I'm consumed by her desire again. And this time, I succumb completely.

A VAMPIRE'S DIARY

I am restless. My work is suffering. Arabella afforded me nothing. Her essence, her precious vitality was wasted, spilled on the ground.

That foolish, stupid girl. Lillian. Her interruption cost me dearly. I take comfort in only the fact that the finger of blame is now firmly planted upon her head. No one suspects me. I'm as invisible as I ever was. As I always have been. I walk among them, dance among them, and serve them, yet they ignore me. They think themselves above me and always have. Well. Someday, everyone *will know my name.*

The prostitute I took home after my failed conquest of Arabella did little to slake my urges. I considered killing her and using her blood, but her red hair was only a ruse. A wig. The thatch of hair between her thighs was dark as pitch. After she left, I felt nothing. Only emptiness. It's in these moments that I miss Rebecca the most. Warm, willing Rebecca. How I mourn her.

I must extend my hunting ground. I need more blood. I will go utterly mad if my work bears no fruit. It must.

EIGHTEEN

Kate slides the cut-throat razor through my damp hair, neatening the layers and shingling the nape. When she's finished, she smooths my waves with a bit of whale oil pomade, combs everything into place, then plants a kiss on my forehead. "There, sweetling. Have a look."

I eye my reflection in the mirror and decide there isn't much my lover can't do. I no longer look like a ragamuffin, but a polished young gentleman. Though the cut is fetching, emphasizing my high cheekbones and pointed chin, I miss having long hair. As a girl, it was one of my few vanities and, along with my eyes, the only mark of beauty I inherited from my mother. The day I arrived at City Jail, a guard pushed me into a chair, gathered my thick chestnut locks in his hands, and sawed through them as if he were threshing hay. I was "deloused" with harsh, lye soap that made my sensitive skin burn, then given a scratchy gray woolen gown. My bombazine mourning dress, which I'd worn only three times, was taken out to the prison yard, added to a heap of clothing, and burned. There was no room for vanity at City Jail.

I shove aside my bleak memories, lower the mirror, and smile at Kate. "It looks wonderful."

"Well. You resemble a boy, as much as you can." She takes my chin in her hand, turning my head from side to side as she studies her work.

Later that evening, Kate dresses as Varina and then helps me bind my breasts with lengths of muslin. I don one of her Alexander Mayhew suits that we've altered to fit my petite frame, and she drips belladonna into my eyes to disguise their color. We decide that if anyone asks who I am, she'll tell them I'm her nephew, visiting from the countryside. As the sun sets, we row downriver to Mount Pleasant in silence, passing the stand of trees where I once made camp. I think once more of the pouch of jewelry and coin I buried beneath the roots of the sycamore tree but say nothing of it to Kate. I'm anxious about tonight. Afraid. But I'm excited to prove myself to her and use my skills again, all the same. Mount Pleasant, removed as it is from the panic in Charleston, could be our salvation. The wealthiest members of Charleston society live in the city proper, but there's money to be had in Mount Pleasant, too.

The party is at a raised Palladian home nearly the size of the Gibbes mansion. I recognize a few faces, but not nearly as many people as at the Kincaid party—something that helps me relax into my role a bit more. As I prowl through the reception hall, looking for easy marks while Kate sings, I tune my ears to the gossip around me. I learn Arabella's funeral is to be held on Monday in a small, intimate ceremony at Saint Mary's. There will be no wake. The Meades have drawn the curtains and are refusing callers.

As I eavesdrop, I pilfer a diamond bracelet, three liberty heads, and two silver dollars within the first hour. By the end of the night, my pockets are obscenely heavy with jewels and coin, and I've learned that while there have been no more murders since Arabella, the killer is still on the loose, the Calhouns have canceled their spring ball, and some of the most illustrious among the chivalry are planning to summer in Mount Pleasant, where it's safe.

Back at Angel's Rest, I empty my pockets. Twenty dollars in coins and a ransom's worth of jewelry. I smile at Kate, biting my lip. "I told you I was good," I say proudly.

"You are. And so am I. I received another commission—a party next week near Fort Moultrie. Say you'll come with me?"

"I wouldn't dream of missing it," I say. "From what I heard tonight, Mount Pleasant will be quite the social hive come summer."

"Yes. There's a rumor the 'vampire' can't cross water." Kate laughs. "Whether that's true or not, I'm anticipating many more opportunities for commissions."

I clutch a handful of jewelry. "And many more opportunities to steal. Perhaps we can use some of this to help Ruby and Noah. Or others like them. Help them buy passage north. Have you heard of the Underground Railroad?"

"No, I haven't."

"My father . . . he told me about it. It's a network of safe houses, mostly owned by free Negroes, but some are white abolitionists. They call themselves agents. They help enslaved people escape to the North, on hidden trails, river crossings, and such. It's very secretive, but Papa told me the Gullah Geechee know about it and they're a part of it."

"I can pawn some of this," Kate says, sorting through our quarry. "Take the money to the Gullah elders, to distribute how they see fit. And we'll save the rest." A gleam shines in Kate's eyes. "I have big dreams for the future. For our future."

"You do?" I say, with a teasing smile.

"Indeed, my delectable little crumpet."

I tilt my chin up, and she kisses me ravenously, then takes me to bed, where she makes love to me the whole night through. We're now partners in every sense of the word. Bound by our secrets. Bound by our contempt for the chivalry. Bound by our forbidden love.

But as I drift off to sleep, satiated and heavy-limbed in Kate's arms, I can't help but think about the bloodthirsty killer still prowling the streets of Charleston—a killer everyone now believes to be me—and that our bliss is on borrowed time.

As we prepare for the next party, Kate's mood is somber. "There will be officers from Moultrie at the party tonight," she says. "Do your best to fade into the shadows, Lil. Don't take any foolish chances."

Officers. I immediately think of William, and a pit of dread lodges in my belly. Last I knew, he was garrisoned at Sumter, not Moultrie, but the two forts are close enough together that anything is possible. What would I do if I saw him? Hide my identity, like I hid from Dr. Broadbent at Barbara Kincaid's party? Little good that did me. Broadbent saw right through my disguise. If I encounter William, surely he will, too.

But all the same, the thrill of stealing—the rush it gives me—is too undeniable to avoid. I have very little agency in my new life, and taking this risk is worth it, to prove that my life still has purpose and meaning. Not only do I feel the need to earn my keep, but the thought that we could use some of the chivalry's stolen wealth to help those in need—people like Ruby and Noah—feels a lot like justice, underscored with spite. The planter aristocracy turned their backs on us. Ruined my family financially. Only the Quakers, a smattering of Jewish merchants' wives, and a handful of sympathetic friends would trade with my father after his secret identity as L. M. Pilco was revealed, thanks to that scoundrel Leroy Burrows and his lurid journalism.

That evening, we row out again at sunset. Spring has come in full bloom to the marshes. Loons cry from the spartina, which ripples like an undulating, green ocean as our skiff parts the waters. The air is fresh with tender promise. We haven't seen Ruby or her father for more than a week. As I scan the horizon from the bow, I wonder where they've gone. Wherever they are, I pray they're safe.

The steam ferry from the city is making port at Haddrell's Point when we arrive. Well-dressed ladies and several men in uniform disembark on the quay. I instinctively duck my head as we pass the dock site.

"Some of our guests tonight, I'd imagine," Kate says. "This is a big party, Lil. A proper ball. There'll be an orchestra coming later. We'll stay until the reception is over, and then we'll head home. I don't want to linger."

The mansion is large and imposing, its entry gate guarded by two grand palmettos, the gardens beyond lit with oil lamps. I follow Kate inside, where the butler takes her card, then ushers us into a receiving room. I hang back as she greets the lady of the house—a tall woman with a regal bearing, who looks vaguely familiar. Kate introduces me as her cousin from Greensboro, and the lady—Mrs. Henrietta Cole—gives me a tight, dismissive smile. It's not until Kate begins performing in the front hall that I recall why our hostess is familiar to me. She's William's maternal aunt and the widow of the naval captain who recruited William into the Citadel. He'll be here tonight. I'm certain of it. A social event of this magnitude would demand his attendance.

My skin prickles with anticipatory dread as I move among the guests. The belladonna in my eyes makes them sensitive to the blaze of lights inside the mansion. The wall sconces bloom like overblown roses. As a result, I blink constantly, my eyes watering. Still, I manage to steal a pocket watch within my first half hour . . . and an emerald bracelet off one unsuspecting lady's wrist. Though I'm tempted by the glittering necklines all around me, I check my ambition. All will be for nothing if I'm caught.

Kate's performance is magnetic, her voice soaring to the high ceiling. She looks beautiful in her green taffeta gown, its bodice dipping low, showcasing the graceful line of her shoulders and her long neck. I watch the men watching her and can imagine their thoughts. As Varina, she's the very picture of femininity. But I prefer her as she is at home, when we're alone at Angel's Rest—just Kate, with her trousers slung low over her hips, her shirt unbuttoned above her small breasts, the earthy smell of her sweat after our chores. I'm more in love than I ever thought I could be. While these rich men stare at her, lusting after her uncommon beauty, I have the smug satisfaction of knowing she belongs to me.

I weave through a cohort of naval officers, dipping my hand into one distracted man's pocket. I'm rewarded with a silver dollar and a small, ivory-handled knife, its blade folded. I hide it in my trousers pocket and disappear into a feather-adorned coterie of ladies. I'm crossing to the other side of the room when I finally see William. He's leaning against the wall, handsome in his formal uniform as he converses with a plump young woman in pink shot silk, her head adorned with a halo of curly blond hair. She laughs at what he says, fanning herself. I watch them from behind a potted palm as he leans forward to kiss her neck, just below her ear. They must be betrothed for him to make such a display of affection at a public assembly. Sure enough, when she lifts her left hand, I see a slender gold band around her finger. Not betrothed, then. Married. She's his wife.

A flare of jealousy runs through me. No doubt she's enjoying all the privileges of being Mrs. William Cameron. The fine house on the Battery, the carriage with its team of four, all the pretty gowns and jewels his riches will allow. The children he'll surely put in her belly, if he hasn't already. An ache of loss runs through me. The thought of our marriage bed filled me with dread, but I wanted to be a mother. Badly.

It would have never been me, though, at his side. It would have been Rebecca. His young wife resembles my sister, in some ways. Her rosy cheeks, her laughing eyes. I wait until William departs, until his wife is engaged in conversation with a trio of ladies, before I make my move. I approach from behind and, in one deft motion, unhook the glittering diamond fob dangling from her fan. I pocket it swiftly and turn around. My eyes lock with William's. He saw what I did.

"You, boy!" He pushes through the crowd, his face a thundercloud.

Panic crests over me, flooding my limbs as I turn to flee, knocking over an enamel vase, sending it crashing to the floor.

"Thief!" William cries.

I rush from the reception hall to a small parlor, looking for a place to hide. I try the door on the opposing side of the room, but find it locked. William enters the parlor, a sneer lashed on his face. "There you are. I saw what you did. Give it to me, you little thief." He closes the distance between us, his eyes filled with fire. I freeze, like a rabbit stared down by a wolf. He shoves me, sending me toppling to the carpet. My head collides with the floor, sparking a shower of stars behind my eyes. He crouches over me, his hands everywhere, searching. He draws the pocket watch from my jacket, and then the diamond fan fob. As I try to wriggle away, he strikes my face with his open hand. I gasp. And then he looks at me. Really looks at me, his green eyes widening.

"My god. It's you."

I say nothing, stilling beneath him.

He smiles, slowly, menacingly. "Well, Lillian. You've certainly changed."

I feel the weight of the stolen knife inside my trouser pocket—a place he hasn't yet searched. I dare not. I don't think I can hurt him. But then he withdraws a whistle from his waistcoat and puts it to his lips, sounding a shrill alarm. "She's here! Miss Carmichael!"

He's calling his fellow soldiers, like dogs. I hear a rush of footsteps from the other room, ladies' panicked voices rising in alarm. Have I really become so notorious?

As the phalanx of uniformed men rushes in, instinct takes over. Survival takes over. I shove my knee into William's groin, as hard as I can, and then swiftly bring the stolen knife out, opening it with one hand and stabbing him in the upper arm. He yelps and rolls onto his side. I leap to my feet, though my head protests with a wave of dizziness, and seize a horse-faced bust of Andrew Jackson from a side table. I pitch it at one of thc high, arched windows. The glass shatters. As the uniformed men surround me, I dive through the broken window, ignoring the pain of glass slicing into my hands. I land in a hedge of bougainvillea and roll onto the grass. The men peer down at me, shouting. I growl at them like a tiger, showing all my teeth. One of them draws his gun and shoots. A bullet goes whistling past my head. I duck and run through the gardens as more shots ring out.

I have no idea where I'm going. Whether Kate will be able to find me. Whether she's in peril, too. People saw us arrive together. But I can't help her right now. I can't do anything if I'm dead.

I run until I reach Shem Creek, until there's no breath left in my lungs, till my knees give out, and the distant sounds of the men fade. My old injury from the boar trap cramps painfully, reminding me that

I still haven't completely healed. I crumple into the bracken, my hands a bloodied mess, Kate's beautiful, tailored suit ruined. After a while, my racing heart slows, my breathing calms. I lie there, listening to the sounds of the marsh. I pick shards of glass from my palms, undo my cravat, rip it in half, and use it to bandage my hands. And then I start walking, slowly, to favor my injured leg, which is still throbbing. I find a skiff tied to a tree alongside the creek and climb inside. Though my hands ache in protest, I row, slowly and deliberately, up the creek to Hog Island.

After a brief nap in the hull of the skiff, moored in the spartina, I find my way back to my old campsite at dawn. The shoddily built hermitage has fallen down, and the spring growth has consumed the clearing, but I won't go back to Angel's Rest. To Kate. I can't. I'm only a liability to her. I briefly consider taking my own life—for what choices do I have now? They'll find me eventually, and I'll die anyway, either at the end of the noose or from a bullet. I palm the knife, opening and closing it several times before putting it away. I think of my mother. Of Papa. I bed down in the ferns and cry myself to sleep, my heart sick with longing for a time when life was easy. When I was just plain, quiet Lillian Carmichael, and not the monster they've made me.

NINETEEN

Memories of Rebecca in the days before her death haunt my sleep. Our mother's vigil by her bedside. Dr. Broadbent's frequent visits. Papa's prayers. The bottle of syrup on the table by Rebecca's bed, thick and unctuous, flavored with lavender and honey—and laced with the arsenic Mother had been dosing her with for years, in ever-increasing amounts, to calm her persistent coughing. The arsenic that no one knew about but me. The selfsame arsenic that was my undoing. I tasted the syrup once, out of curiosity. It was pleasingly sweet, the tasteless poison hidden without a trace of bitterness to serve as a warning.

There were other things that no one knew about. No one but me and Rebecca. And it's those things that haunt me the most.

During the days before Rebecca's death, I spent hours in the chair next to her bed, reading to her. *The Bride of Lammermoor* was her favorite. We'd seen Donizetti's opera at its American premiere in New Orleans, then again in Charleston, that summer. The soprano in the role of Lucia resembled my sister, with her red-gold hair and haunting blue eyes.

Now, in my dream, I am once more in my chair by the foot of her bed, but instead of reading, I'm working on a hoop of embroidery. My stitches are haphazard and crazed—I can make no sense of what the work is meant to be. Rebecca reclines against the pillows, watching me, her face pale, dark circles etched beneath her eyes. A bowl of blood sits next to the bed, from her latest bloodletting. A futile attempt to save her life, despite Dr. Broadbent's insistence otherwise.

"Do you remember . . ." she croaks. "Do you remember when Mother took us to the opera. In New Orleans?"

"Yes," I say. I stab the needle through the stretched muslin, once, twice. An angry circle of red blooms on the fabric. I've hurt myself. Yet I feel no pain.

"There was a man there. At the opera. Do you remember?"

I pause, resting the embroidery hoop on my lap. Blood trickles from my finger. Drips onto my skirts. I do nothing, inexplicably, to stanch the flow.

"No, I don't remember."

"I do," she says tiredly. "He brought Mother champagne. Gave us sweets and joined us in our booth."

I vaguely remember a young man—handsome, blond, broad-shouldered—who sat next to Mother for part of the opera. "I recall that he was there for a time. Then left rather quickly."

"Yes. But *she* left, too, right in the middle of the mad scene." Rebecca smiles tightly. "No one leaves during the mad scene."

I know what Rebecca is getting at—one of the secrets we share. Our mother dallies and toys with men. Flirts. Craves their eyes upon her. The blood courses faster from my finger now, pouring out in a steady stream. I nonchalantly watch it plop, plop onto the floor, where it creeps toward the edge of the rug. "What are you trying to say, Becca?"

"Mother. She's always been vain, hasn't she? She craves attention. When I'm sick, she gets it."

My defensiveness rises. My blood pulses. "No more than you. You enjoy the attention, too. She dotes on you because of it. Everyone does."

"You're wrong. I hate it." Rebecca sighs, her eyes finding the corner of the room. "You don't know how lucky you are. You think beauty is a blessing. But beauty is a curse."

"So says the beauty." I stab with the needle. But I'm no longer sewing through the muslin. I'm piercing my skin. I force the needle through my forearm, drawing the thread along with it. I do it again, then once more, stitching a tidy *x* on my flesh. Blood beads around my work.

"You can't understand, Lil. You don't see what's happening to me. What she's *allowing*. No one sees it. And I dare not speak of it."

"I don't know what you're talking about. You're not making any sense." I sew another *x* close to the first.

"There are bad kinds of attention, you know," she says, and coughs. "Something broke in her, after Ruth and Emma died. She keeps me sick, because it gets her what she wants. Water, please. I'm so thirsty."

I bring the glass to her lips. Blood drips from my wrist onto her coverlet. She ignores it and drinks the water, then collapses onto the pillow. I return to the chair, take up my needle, and add another stitch to my skin. I now have a neat row of cross-stitches. It's the best work I've ever done. I raise my arm, admiring the evenness of my stitches, and vow to always practice my embroidery in this way.

Rebecca begins to cry, faint tears tracing down her face. "I'm so sorry, Lil. I just want it to be over. All these years . . . you've wanted what you *thought* I had. But you'll never know what it's been like."

"Hush now, you're only making things worse." Another stitch.

"Do you know? I think I would have been happier if I'd been a thing made of porcelain instead of flesh and bone." She whimpers, then goes silent. I raise my head. She's gone, her coverlet pulled taut, like she was never even there at all. Her doll, with its flurry of red ringlets and softly parted lips, lies upon her pillow instead, its glass eyes void of life.

I wake in a panic, inspecting my arms in the pale shaft of moonlight passing through the trees. There are no stitches. Only Kate's ruined cravat, wrapped around my hands. I sit up, remembering where I am, and what happened. William. The party. The soldiers. Kate. I'd abandoned her.

As dawn lightens the sky, I begin rebuilding my hermitage, slowly and deliberately. Rain comes, soaking my clothing and destroying my progress. I huddle in the underbrush, crying with frustration. Everything seems futile. My continued existence a mockery. Once the rains abate, I resume building my shelter. I have the walls completed by early afternoon. After I'm finished, I search the underbrush and find my pouch of money and jewelry, my kitchen knife, and the two remaining fishing hooks and twine Ruby gave me. I dig up some earthworms, then trudge to the creek to fish. I shed my jacket and roll up the trousers, letting my feet dangle in the current to soothe their soreness. Though I miss Kate fiercely, I've missed this, too. The solitude. The sense of self-reliance I cultivated in the wild.

I catch two redfish, then head back to my campsite. When I arrive, I find a box of matches lying on the sycamore stump. I smile. "Thank you, Ruby."

I sense her nearby, and sure enough, with a quiet rustle, she emerges from the shadows, dressed in dark muslin, her hair covered by a green kerchief. "Why are you back out here?" she asks.

"This is the only place that's safe."

"Does Mr. Mayhew know you're here?"

"No," I say. "And I don't want him to."

"Why? What's happened?"

I set about gathering twigs for a fire, not knowing how to answer this question. Kate and I are good together. I love her. But in this world, in these circumstances, what could ever come of our partnership? I'm a convicted murderer on the run. She had a steady, predictable life before I came along. "It's for the best that I left, Ruby. That's all. Mr. Mayhew helped me, and I'll always be grateful to him, and to you, but I must exist henceforth in solitude."

Ruby sucks her teeth, making a sound of displeasure. She sweeps her skirts to the side and sits on the tree stump where we leave our offerings. "Daddy and I will be leaving soon," she says. "For good this time. The other maroons told us a ship comes through every spring, on its way to Canada. *The Cassidy.* They take freedom seekers back with them."

For a moment, I wonder if such ships take other kinds of fugitives north as well. It would be tempting to escape to Canada and disappear. But then I think about my mother. The thought of abandoning her still unsettles me. "I have something for you." I pull the ivory-handled knife and the emerald bracelet I stole last night from my trouser pocket. I hand both to Ruby. "You may need the knife, for protection on the ship. You can pawn the jewelry once you go north."

"Well, it's not a sure thing. Our going."

"Still . . . it's a hopeful thing."

She nods, tucking the knife and bracelet into her bodice. "It is. And risky. But Daddy's tired of hiding. He wants to make an honest living on a real fishing boat. He can do that, up north. And he wants me to marry well. I think about that a lot. Having a husband. A family of my own."

"You will, Ruby. You're a bright, lovely young woman. Any man would be so lucky."

"Don't *you* want to get married?"

I shake my head. "I was betrothed once. Things didn't work out."

She hums. "Mr. Mayhew is sweet on you."

I say nothing, only concentrate on building my fire.

"He must get mighty lonely, all by himself in that big house. He needs a helpmate. A wife."

I strike a match and set it to the dry kindling. A thread of smoke curls up, and then a small flame begins to flicker. Building a fire is risky, but during the daytime, with the overcast sky, the smoke will be less noticeable. And as well fed as Kate kept me, my belly protests its emptiness. "Thank you for the matches, Ruby. Would you like some fish?"

"If you have enough."

"I do."

After the fire burns down to a soft glow, I set the fish atop the embers, and crouch on my heels, watching them cook. The smell is delectable, and the taste is even better. Ruby and I enjoy the warm meal, using the tree stump as a makeshift table. We pick every bit of the tender, white flesh from the bones, not wanting to waste a morsel. After we eat, she helps me cut spartina for the roof of my shelter, and together, we finish the hermitage before the sun sets.

She leaves me at nightfall, turning to wave at me once through the trees. I know this is the last time I'll see her. My friend. My saving grace. I think of her future life, safe and free in the North, and pray that she gets everything she wants and deserves.

As for me? The marsh will have to be enough. But the perpetual emptiness of my future conjures dread. Alone out here, my dreams and memories have full rein—a chorus of regrets eager to chase away any peace I might hope for in solitude. It's all coming back to me now. What I witnessed. What I denied. What I refused to speak aloud, for speaking it aloud would have made it all true. And finally, it occurs to me. I allowed myself to take the blame for Rebecca's death because, on some level, I *was* guilty and felt like I deserved my punishment. If I'd spoken up, if I'd said something sooner, she might still be here.

I lie back, trying to harness my emotions as night descends. I listen to the soft, resonant call of a great-horned owl. The distant splash of a dolphin plying the riverine landscape. The sawing of cicadas. But even surrounded by these comforting, familiar sounds, the marsh, once my haven, offers me no respite from my tortured thoughts.

My solitude doesn't last long. I wake to the sound of dogs baying in the distance. I scurry out of the hermitage, jump to my feet, and tamp out the remains of the fire, throwing dirt over the embers. The dogs are getting closer. And beneath their baying, I hear the voices of men. A search party. My heart gallops as I gather my most precious possessions—the kitchen knife, my jewelry pouch, the matches, and the fishing hook and twine, which I hastily cut from the limb I've tied them to. I scoop handfuls of pluff mud, covering my skin and clothing with it to mask my scent before crossing the shallow creek to hide in the underbrush. The men's voices grow louder, the glancing light from their torches and lanterns flickering through the trees. I slow my breathing, every muscle in my body quivering as I will myself to remain still.

"Here! Over here!" The crunch of boots carries from my clearing. The hounds' baying becomes a cacophony. "She's been here. There's a fire. I knew I saw smoke earlier."

The men talk among themselves excitedly. I catch snatches of their conversation. Enough to know they mean to lynch me if they find me. I heard the same threats made against my father, many times. And lynching has been the fate of many an escaped slave. This is sport for men like these—hunting human beings. The reward on my head will likely be the same, whether I'm dead or alive. Anger wells up in me, hot and fierce. I hate these men. What they stand for.

My muscles tense as the men spread out, parting the underbrush with the butts of their rifles, their dogs at their heels. It's only a matter of time before they find me. I pray, silently, against all hope.

A ragged snuffling meets my ears. Through the fresh, green undergrowth, I see a bluetick hound on the other side of the creek, her nose to the ground as she prowls nearby. She lifts her head and bays. I flatten out, slowly, soundlessly, until my belly presses into the cool mud. I'd rather risk sinking in the sulfurous quagmire than what they have planned for me.

The men gather at the edge of the creek, peering across. There are fewer than I thought—only three. "She must be on the other side of the creek," one of them says.

"She won't get far."

They splash into the creek, their hounds at their heels.

This is it. It's over.

Suddenly, a gunshot cracks overhead. Then another, from somewhere behind me. I tuck my head under my arms as I hear a bullet whiz past and hit the water. "Off my land!"

The men still, talking among themselves, confused.

"You cross that creek, you're dead men," the booming voice says, menacing, angry, and distinctly British.

It's Kate. She's come looking for me. Longing and relief and love flood through me, along with the fear that she might die here, with me. These men are hardly the sort to respect her warning.

"We're searching for that escaped convict. The murderer," the tallest man says, eyes scanning the spartina. It occurs to me they can't see her.

"I don't give a damn. You're on private property. *Mayhew* property." Kate's voice seems to come from everywhere all at once, as if amplified. She fires another shot. One of the men yelps.

"Goddammit. Show yourself!" the tallest man screeches.

"The next time I shoot, I won't miss. Now leave, gentlemen, and don't come around here again."

The men confer with one another, strangely subdued, all their earlier bravado gone. Kate has exposed them for the cowards they are. Men who hunt the desperate and hopeless. I watch as they splash back through the creek, and trudge up the bank, then disappear into the trees, their hounds padding dutifully by their side. I remain on my belly in the marsh grass, trembling.

"You can come out, Lil. They're gone." Kate's voice is stern, but tender.

I push up onto my hands and knees, my joints aching. I see her then, silhouetted against the twilight sky, tall and imposing, like a warrior queen of old. "Come on," she says. "Let's go home."

A VAMPIRE'S DIARY

Tomasina

Mount Pleasant is ripe with possibility. The chivalry have ferreted many of their daughters away here, while others have abandoned the city altogether, fleeing to their plantations, despite the dangers summer will bring. Yellow fever. Cholera and dysentery. All less of a risk than I, apparently.

From my boardinghouse quarters, which I reserved under the name Eugene Crabtree, I have an unimpeded view of the young women as they parade together in the evening. That's where I glimpsed sweet Tomasina, her parasol tilted on her shoulder, the bright flame of her hair gathered atop her head.

After a few days of observing her habits—always the evening constitutional, at six, escorted by her middle-aged companion—I approached her. While her dour-faced companion was less than gracious, Tomasina smiled at me, offered her hand, pleased to make my reacquaintance. She said she remembered my visits to her with fondness and thought of me often. She was now married, with a husband away. A railroad man—an investor. Her loneliness was manifest, the hunger in her smile unmistakable. Before we parted, I whispered an invitation to dine with me the following evening at the boardinghouse. Alone.

She came to me, dutiful, lonesome creature, and met my ardor with fervor, falling apart in my arms. After we spent ourselves in passion, I plied her with wine and drew her a bath. While she was thus distracted, I invited the monster in. It was over with quickly, cleanly, and silently. In the hours before dawn, I carried her body to the marshland ringing the edges of town and left her there, then returned to the boardinghouse and enjoyed the most refreshing sleep I've experienced in months. Tomasina's contributions have allayed my despair over Arabella. My work can continue unimpeded here in the hinterlands, especially given the news Tomasina shared with me before she met her fate. In a fortnight, there will be a ball upriver, at a plantation on Daniel Island—one with invitations to debutantes and fine matrons from far and wide. My anticipation is boundless.

TWENTY

"Don't ever do that again," Kate says. "You little fool." We're in the bath together, Kate behind me as I recline against her, nestled between her legs. She wrings out a washcloth and strokes it over my breasts, along my arms. "I thought you were dead."

"I'm sorry. I didn't know what to do. They were chasing me. I was worried . . . I thought you'd be . . ."

"Better off without you?" She laughs softly. "Ruby told me. She came straight here after leaving you. Oh, sweetling." She dips the washcloth in the water, wrings it out over my belly. "How could you think that?"

"I've only brought you trouble."

"Maybe." She chuckles. "But my life was rather boring before you turned up."

"What happened at the party, after I ran?"

"They sent a search party after you—most of the soldiers there. And your William detained me. Gods, Lil, he was the one you were betrothed to? You should have set your sights higher."

"Hush. I was young. And his family is very rich."

"Well, all the same. He looks like a ferret. But even with his prodding, I never broke character. He asked me question after question—had I known you were Lillian Carmichael all along? Had I been aiding and abetting you?" She sighs. "So, I lied. Unlike you, I'm good at it. I told them I thought you were my cousin, who I'd only met once when we were children. I played the victim. Pretended you tricked and stole from me, too."

"And he believed you?"

"Yes. I cry rather prettily, you know."

I laugh, imagining her act. "So, what do we do now?"

"We'll come up with another plan. But you must stay here, from now on, and let me provide for us. You've run through all your disguises, my dear. It's no longer safe for you to accompany me." She strokes the washcloth over my skin, softly, tenderly. "And there's been another murder. A young woman in Mount Pleasant. Now that you've been spotted there, the killer has mysteriously widened his margins. I find that interesting."

"How so?"

"I've performed many plays. Operas. There's often double-crossing in those stories. Vendettas. And I think the killer is using you. As cover. So that he can continue his rampage, unchecked. Who better to blame things on than a convicted killer who rose from the dead? A vampire." She clucks her tongue. "Do you know anything at all about vampires?"

"No, not especially." I know they consume blood, that they supposedly walk about only at night. That they are exceedingly difficult to kill. I think of that dark figure, crouched over poor Arabella in the gardens. How he moved so quickly, so inhumanly. "Might there be a real vampire? The man I saw . . . Arabella's killer. He was unusual looking."

Kate hums beneath her breath. "A real vampire . . . that's far-fetched. There's something distinctly human about this murderer. Conniving. My father had a book in his library. I read it as a girl. It had a story in it, about a vampire lord. He moved among the upper classes, undetected. He seduced and targeted young women of means, just like this creature. It's possible the killer modeled himself after Lord Ruthven—the vampire in the story. And made you the foil."

"So, you think he might be part of the chivalry?"

"Perhaps. Or someone who secretly hates them. By pinning the murders on you, he won't be subject to scrutiny. Do you have any enemies, my dear?"

"Not any one person in particular I can think of." Plenty of people wished to see my family fall into ruin because of Papa's cause. The chivalry bore ill will toward us, but I can think of no one who would specifically target me, apart from Arabella, and now she's dead.

"There's something else I've noticed," I say. "The women he's killed—they've all been redheads."

"The young woman in Mount Pleasant—Tomasina Graham—was as well."

"My sister was a redhead. It could be another way for him to tie the murders to me."

"Possibly," Kate says, thoughtfully. "But why redheads? And is he killing for sport? Or another reason . . . I can't be sure."

"Nor I." Even though I'm relieved to be removed from Charleston society and all its vanities, the thought of staying hidden away while a murderer—human or otherwise—prowls the city, unchecked, pricks at my conscience. My compassion for the murdered women stirs my guilt. Their lives mattered.

"What's the matter, sweetling?" Kate asks.

"What can we do, to make it stop? It seems as if we're the only ones who have the slightest inkling of what's really going on."

"I've been thinking about that. I've an idea. My grandest one yet. But for now . . . there are other matters that need tending to. I've missed you. Desperately."

One of her hands disappears beneath the water, as the other cups my breast. I sigh and lean my head back, welcoming her hungry kiss and how it soothes my worries. Before long, she has me whimpering and pleading, just as she likes me. I twist and arch against her, water splashing over the side of the tub as she wrings pleasure from my body.

"There. Isn't that better?" she says, her tongue flicking against my cheek. "You sound so lovely when you fall apart."

I sigh, my heartbeat slowing back to its normal cadence. "I'm lost for you," I whisper.

"I know, sweetling," she says. "I know."

Life resumes as normal at Angel's Rest. I gather the eggs; Kate cooks our breakfast. We do our chores, make love, and then nap for most of the afternoon. After supper, she goes out as Varina. Alone. I worry myself sick, often pacing the floors until she returns. She brings home news—there have been no new murders since Tomasina, and the society matrons have begun to entertain the thought of resuming their summer balls in the countryside. Their daughters need husbands, after all, and life must carry on. While this is good for Kate—she receives three more commissions for private parties—I can't help but worry that the killer is merely lying in wait. Biding his time.

Unfortunately, my prediction comes true. During the grandest ball of the season, held at a plantation on Daniel Island, another debutante disappears. Her bloodless body is found in the Wando a few days later by a dockworker. Sophie Butler, a young woman from Florida, visiting her aunt. Also a redhead. My name is once more splashed across the pages of the paper, along with a reward for $1,000 for anyone who kills me or informs the authorities of my whereabouts. A crude, overtly sexual cartoon accompanies the article, penned by that loathsome Leroy Burrows. The cartoon pictures me feasting between a swooning woman's legs. I laugh at the sensationalism.

Kate looks up at me. She's expertly peeling an apple, the red skin dangling from her hands in a perfect spiral. "What's so funny?"

"That ridiculous cartoon," I say.

"I saw it. If only they knew it's *me* with the insatiable appetite for the tender flesh of maidens," she says with a wry grin. "Though not in the way they think."

"Stop," I say, blushing. "You're terrible."

"Yes. But you love me." She cuts a slice from the apple and feeds it to me. I bite the tip of her finger as she pulls away. "Naughty thing."

I sit back in the chair, the tart sweetness of the apple making my mouth water. I study my lover in the sunlight filtering through the dining room window. Her crisp jawline, that precious divot beneath her plump lower lip. My good humor fades. "I don't think you should go out anymore, Kate. Cancel your performances. Please. I'm sick with worry anytime you leave."

"How are we to make money, sweetling? Varina isn't the killer's type. Too blond. Too tall."

"How can we know he won't divert from his habits?"

"We can't," she says. She puts the apple and knife down on the table. "But I've been thinking. The only thing that may stop these murders is if the real killer is exposed. If we prove it's not you."

"How can we do that? I can't very well show up at the City Guardhouse and say I didn't do it. Besides, they'd still hang me for my sister's death, even if I could prove myself innocent of these vampire murders."

Kate studies me. "Perhaps . . . perhaps we should give them what they want."

"What do you mean?"

"You'll become the very thing they believe you to be."

It sounds ridiculous at first. Kate's idea. She spends the rest of the morning explaining it to me. How we'll rehearse. Costume ourselves. The ruse will begin with a letter to the papers announcing the arrival of the renowned Dr. Ezra Winthrop, scientist and vampire expert.

"It will be perfect, Lil. You saw for yourself how intimidating Winthrop is. He'll be convincing, don't you think?"

A shiver runs through me, remembering the coldness in Kate's eyes when she transformed into Winthrop the first time we rehearsed together. How badly she frightened me. "Yes, very."

She paces through the costume room, pulling out dresses and examining them. "You, on the other hand, are far less convincing. Remember how I told you that your anger is your best tool?"

I sit back on the chaise and sigh. Sometimes, when Kate is in a mood like this, all creative passion and frenetic energy, she exhausts me. "Yes."

"You must tap into it. Our audience won't want to see a meek, submissive vampire. They'll want to see a fight." She snarls, showing all her teeth. Tosses her headful of dark curls. "Gnash your teeth. Growl. You must leave every trace of modesty behind and become their monster of myth."

"All of this is well and good. But say we're successful. Say the real killer comes to this spectacle and realizes his game has run its course. Even if the audience is convinced the vampire is vanquished and their daughters are safe once more, what about the authorities? How are you going to remove my body, without suspicion? And what do *we* do after? Just come back here, to Angel's Rest, and hide away forever? I'll have *died* twice at that point. I can hardly resurrect again."

"You underestimate my persuasive abilities *and* the level of corruption in the city," Kate says. "I have it on good authority that the coroner is debt-ridden. He's old. Disinterested. He'll be easy to pay off."

"I'm not so sure about that. He certainly seemed interested in what happened to poor Sally. And having a real live vampire to study? If I were a doctor, I'd be fascinated."

"Trust me, Lil. Nothing talks louder than money."

"Just how much are you thinking?"

"Including the jewelry and money you stole from the party, we have well over five thousand dollars, by my estimate."

I turn away, considering. I intended at least some of the stolen money to go toward helping fugitive slaves. Not to line the pockets of an already corrupt coroner. "I thought . . . I thought we were going to give that money to the maroons to aid in their escape. Or for them to buy their freedom."

"Well, we won't give all of it to the coroner. But . . ." Kate bounces on her heels. "Don't you think it's worth it? You deserve freedom, too, sweetling. To have the sun on your face again, without fear." She comes to my side, takes my hands in hers. "Have you ever been to England?"

"No. I have not."

"Nor have I." She laughs. "My mother despised the English. But for an actress . . ." Kate sighs wistfully. "There's no better place. I could make it big in London, Lil. I know I could, with my talents. We have more than enough money to get by until I find my feet, even with paying off the authorities. We could leave here by autumn. In another country, you'd be truly free."

I consider her words. How wonderful they sound on the surface. But just like everyone else in my life before me, she's *telling* me what we'll do. Not asking me. Just like Mother. All my life, I've been soft, compliant. Uncomplaining. In the hopes that my mother's love was as unconditional as my own, I stood by and allowed her to slowly kill my sister, too, didn't I? Her motives might have been loving, initially, but her obsession over Rebecca's health drove her to do the unthinkable. And I did nothing to stop it. My sins were those of omission, but all the same, I lacked the fortitude to stand up for myself or Rebecca . . . I never once stopped to consider the consequences of my inaction. I could punish myself for my mistakes forever, or I could change, and take agency over my own life.

I pull my hands from Kate's. "I hear it gets dreadfully cold in England. I'm not sure."

Her face falls for a moment, then brightens again. "You'll come around, darling. Just think about it. I certainly won't go without you." She pulls me close and kisses me, biting my lower lip. "If we rot and grow old here, with golden dreams unmet, then at least we'll rot in bliss together, won't we?"

She draws me down onto the chaise, and while I revel in her kisses and caresses as I always do, I consider the fact that I'm almost as much of a prisoner here as I was at City Jail. Even though Kate's heart makes for the loveliest prison I've ever inhabited—and one I'm not entirely sure I want to be free of, it's a prison all the same.

TWENTY-ONE

In the days that follow, Kate works me to exhaustion with rehearsals. She chooses a scarlet gown for me out of Lucrezia's wardrobe and alters it with a clever pocket above my left breast, where we'll hide a sheep's bladder filled with blood on the night of our performance. An actor's trick, she says, to make my "murder" look more convincing. She also carves two sharp teeth out of the ivory handle of a serving spoon and attaches them to my own with gum arabic. The false teeth are uncomfortable but effective. Their sharp points are menacing. Wickedly realistic.

I've grown more comfortable with my vampire persona. When we rehearse, I growl and slink and roll my eyes. But I never become quite comfortable with Ezra Winthrop, my would-be slayer. It's uncanny, how much Kate transforms within his role. Everything, from the way she walks to the contemptuous sneer she takes on as Winthrop, fills me with dread . . . and an undeniable frisson of sensual attraction. Winthrop is dangerous, cunning, and coolly intelligent—like a snake coiled to strike. But there's an appeal to his salaciousness all the same. One that sends my heart tripping over itself when I feel his arms go around me, his breath on my neck.

Kate has made me fall in love with every one of her characters. Even this one. They're all a part of who she is. Her darkness and her light.

We rehearse my death scene again, though the afternoon heat in our rehearsal room has grown feverish. Winthrop stalks toward me, a sharp oakwood stake in one hand, a mallet in the other. I crouch and growl, like a cornered wildcat, rolling my eyes dramatically. Winthrop tackles me, dragging me to the center of the room, his arm hooked around my neck. I struggle in his arms, but he holds me fast. My heartbeat races. "Fight all you like, little one," he sneers. "Your fate is sealed."

He wrestles me to the ground and crouches over me, the stake held high. He plunges it downward, and I instinctively flinch. Even though we've rehearsed this scene countless times, my trust is still tenuous. The stake is real—twelve inches of solid wood Kate has honed to a point sharp enough to kill. But our props, our costumes, this final act, must be thoroughly convincing.

Winthrop hovers the stake a hairbreadth from my bosom, then brings the mallet down. This too requires trust. Because the stake must be driven with enough force to penetrate my clothing, then pierce the sheep's bladder, without piercing *me* in the process.

I cry out, thrash in place for a moment, and then still.

With a shout of triumph, Winthrop stands over me, then nudges me with his foot, rolling me over to face the audience. It's imperative that I stare blankly ahead, without blinking, during this part, so that the onlookers will believe I'm truly dead. Winthrop then bends, lifts my "lifeless" body, and carries me to the chaise, which will be a wagon at the real event. The whole thing would be humorous if not for the gravitas and grim sense of purpose Kate brings to her role.

"Excellent." The fearsome Winthrop departs, and my Kate returns. She brings me to my feet, kisses me, and spins me around. "You were spectacular. That moan of despair as I hammered the stake home! Absolutely perfect, my darling girl."

"It wasn't too much?" I ask, glowing in the light of Kate's praise.

"Heavens no. After those lurid comics, the more moaning the better."

"Oh, stop. Did you send the letter to the papers announcing Winthrop's arrival?"

"Yesterday."

I sink onto the chaise, my good humor fading. Everything is suddenly all too real. "Kate, what if we do this, and he still doesn't stop? What if this murderer is more animal than human? Our performance won't matter then, will it?"

"Think, sweetling. All of the victims have been young white women. Most of them, apart from the first, wealthy. An animal predator wouldn't discriminate. No. This monster is fully human. I'd be willing to bet my life on it."

"Please don't tempt fate," I say, looking up at her. "*He's* going to know it's all an act. Don't you worry that he might seek revenge? *I* worry, Kate. I'm no vampire, and much as you relish playing him, you're no Winthrop. We're both just women, like all the other victims. What if he comes after us next?"

"He won't." She kneels at my feet, taking my hands and bringing them to her lips. "If it makes you feel better, I won't go out again as Varina until we've forced this killer to cease his rampage. And we will, mark my words. It's almost over."

"Do you really think so?"

"Yes, sweetling. And then we'll be on our way to England, where I'll take the Strand by storm. Now, let's go over things again. More thrashing and moaning this time. They'll want to see a fight."

I groan. "You exhaust me."

"You're getting good, Lil. We don't want to impede your progress, do we? I'll reward you later." She pulls me to my feet, binds my wrists behind my back (loosely, as part of the excitement for the audience is me breaking free from my bonds), and tugs me back to the center of the room, where we run through the scene. Again. And again. Until my body aches, sweat pools beneath my breasts, and hunger claws my belly.

That night, after Kate treats me to a hearty supper, I sleep heavily, and dream once more of my sister.

She's older in my dream, inexplicably—closer to our mother's age, her copper curls streaked with gray. She hums to herself as she dresses her dolls, lining them up on her bed. There are four altogether. One of them is the faceless doll from my previous dream, two smaller dolls for the twins, and Rebecca's doll, with its coiled ringlets. "Don't they all look pretty, all lined up in a row?" Rebecca croons.

"Why can't you rest, Rebecca?"

She sighs, turning to face me. It's disconcerting, seeing her older, knowing that she'll never be this age in real life. "Because I worry about you."

"Worry?"

"Do you trust her?"

"Who?"

She only smiles wistfully.

"Who, Rebecca?"

"You know who I'm talking about." That same wistful smile. "Love has made you a fool, sister." She strokes the faceless doll's brown hair. "Open your eyes."

I startle awake, my heart pounding. I catch my breath, staring up at the canopy. Kate sleeps next to me, breathing steadily. My vision adjusts to the dim light filtering through the curtains, as I study my lover in her sleep. She is beautiful, yes. It's undeniable, with her long, dark lashes at rest on her cheeks, her full lips slightly parted. She could be male, or female, or a sexless archangel in repose. How quickly she's become my world. How gamely I've offered myself to her.

Do you trust her?

Do I? Because of course Rebecca was talking about Kate. Who else would it be?

I think of her passionate dominance over my body, her coy, flirtatious machinations. Kate would never hurt me. Or anyone else. Would she?

I sit up, suddenly in need of fresh air. Everything feels too close. Though it's only late springtime, the humidity is already suffocating.

But when I swing my legs over the side, Kate stirs. "Where do you think you're going?" She grasps my waist from behind, pulling me to her. Her hands wander over my body, squeezing, groping. Desire blooms low in my belly, as it always does at Kate's touch. "God, you're so soft. So warm."

She burrows her face against the nape of my neck, and I go limp and weak as she lifts my nightgown and works her way down the length of my body, trailing kisses along my bare spine. She hoists me up onto my knees and, with a low groan, sets to her hungry work, sending all my thoughts of leaving our bed into flight. In moments, she has me shaking, then suddenly ceases her ministrations, tumbling me onto my back. She straddles me, looking down at me with a wicked grin. I arch my hips upward, eager for more. "I would have you, sweetling," she says. "Completely." She takes one of my nipples in her mouth, still encased in the thin cambric gown, and pulls with her teeth. I whimper as pain and pleasure knot together in a tangle.

"Please," I say, gasping. The ache between my legs is a torrent of want. I reach down, touch myself.

"No, I don't think so." She tugs my gown over my head, and twists it around my arms, binding me. "I'm going to give you what you want. But you must be a good girl and wait." She leaves my side, opens a drawer in her bureau. I hear rustling, the sound of something being buckled, though the shadows hide her actions. "I have a surprise for you, my pet. Something I had made, just for you." Her voice has shifted, grown darker. More masculine. I tense, my nerves quaking. She's transforming. Changing.

Kate turns back to me. My eyes widen. Through the dim, I see a thick phallus between her legs, harnessed at her waist, its length curved slightly upward. She strokes it, as if the device is part of her body, her eyes locking with mine. She's become Winthrop. Completely.

Fear and desire and fear and desire wrestle with one another. I cannot find words. I pull at my bonds, testing them. They hold fast.

"Look at you," Winthrop growls. "How you tremble for me. How your body beckons."

And god help me, he's right. I *want* him. Just as much as I wanted Kate only moments ago. I'm unsure of what it will feel like to be claimed by him, to surrender completely to a man, and that alone is as tantalizing as it is frightening—the good kind of fear, like jumping into a cold spring on a summer day. There might be rocks beneath the surface, unseen, but all the same, you jump, the exhilaration of having survived the fall the reward.

Winthrop runs his palms over my breasts, and my body responds . . . eager for his touch. He lowers his face to kiss, suckle, and tug at my skin with his teeth. I arch upward as his fingers find my sex, as he teases me open and strokes me. "Are you afraid, sweet Lillian? Do you want me to stop?" he asks, biting the tender flesh of my belly.

"No," I say, sighing. And I mean it, because in this moment, I've never felt more alive. "Please."

"Good," he murmurs. "Do you want me here, inside you?" he asks. His fingers move deeper. Testing me. Readying me.

"Yes," I say, though a quiver of fear runs through me, remembering the girth of the phallus. Its length. Can my body withstand it?

I groan as his fingers retreat, leaving me empty, longing, aching to be filled once more.

"I'm going to take you now, my darling," he says, settling over me. "You're more than ready."

My heartbeat ratchets higher as I feel the phallus prodding against my nether lips. Suddenly, its flared head slides into me in one deft, smooth motion. I gasp at the momentary pain of my claiming.

"There now," Winthrop says, chuckling low. "You fit me so well. My tight little sheath. My sweet, wet cunny."

He begins to slide in and out of me, in a slow, steady rhythm, rocking me out of pain into pleasure as I wrap my legs around him, eagerly meeting his thrusts. He whispers filthy, decadent things in my ear as he brings me nearer and nearer to the edge, as his pumping increases in urgency, shaking the bed. My nightgown untwists, freeing my hands from their bondage. I tangle them in his hair instead, rising up to kiss him.

As our lips meet, he scoops me up onto his lap, still inside me, and drives into me with a pistonlike fervor as I grip his shoulders and cry out, my crisis breaking over me. To my surprise, his breath quickens in concert with my own, and with a loud groan, he grasps my waist and buries himself to the hilt inside me. I smile, knowing what that deep groan means, and trace my tongue along my lover's throat, tasting the salty sweetness of sweat. Knowing my love, my darling, has reached the same heights as I have is the greatest pleasure of all.

Winthrop departs, and my Kate returns. She lays me down and holds me as I recover, gently kneading my belly as the waves of pleasure subside. "Did you like that?" she asks.

"Yes. It was thrilling, and a little terrifying, all at once. Did you? Like it?"

"Oh, yes. Couldn't you tell? I'm eager to do it again." She chuckles, propping herself up with her elbow and looking down at me. She's satisfied with her artful mastery of my body, as she should be. She traces lazy circles over my bare skin with her fingertips. If I were a cat, I'd be purring. "Winthrop has utterly ruined you, though, I'm afraid."

A pleasant soreness between my legs lingers, as a reminder of what just happened. "Being ruined isn't so bad. I liked your surprise."

"Came all the way from France," Kate says. "And worth every pretty penny I spent. I knew you secretly wanted Winthrop to ravish you. I could see it in your eyes when we were acting. And then there's Alex. I'd imagine he's a more tender lover, but no less enthusiastic. Perhaps he'll visit you next. Or sweet Varina. Who knows what new delights we might conjure?"

"How could I resist such a delightful selection of lovers? But you're my favorite, Kate. Never forget that."

"My god, Lillian." She strokes my face, her eyes soft. "We're perfect together, aren't we? How lucky am I, to have something so beautiful."

No one has ever called me beautiful. No one before Kate. I've never been wanted like this. Desired. I kiss her again, then lie back on the pillow with a contented sigh. My disturbing dream of Rebecca—and her warnings—fades from memory as the soft morning light caresses Kate's long limbs. She wraps herself around me. "Don't you dare leave me, Lil," I hear her whisper as I drift back to sleep. "Never again."

A VAMPIRE'S DIARY

Sophie

My hubris has once again gotten the best of me. I was too bold. Too careless. Always before, I've pursued those who trusted me. Who knew me, if only in passing. But Sophie and I shared only a single dance before I asked her to stroll with me in the gardens.

When I gave the signal for my man to attack, I wasn't as cautious as I should have been. A servant witnessed the scene and alerted his mistress. The commotion that ensued forced me to flee before I could be assured of Sophie's demise. I do not think she survived her wounding, but I cannot be certain. I am gripped with anxiety. If she was still able to speak after the attack, to describe the course of events, my name will undoubtedly be mentioned. There were too many people at the ball who saw me. Who know who I am. Lillian cannot be my scapegoat this time.

Lillian must die. And I must leave this city to begin anew, somewhere else.

TWENTY-TWO

Two days later, a new headline splashes across the front page of *The Charleston Daily Courier*: VAMPIRE SLAYER PROMISES TO VANQUISH CHARLESTON'S BLOODTHIRSTY KILLER

Kate reads the article aloud with bravado, pacing through the parlor. "Famed vampire scholar Dr. Ezra Winthrop, lately from Massachusetts, will arrive in our fair city on the morrow. He will commence his search for the dreaded vampire immediately. Dr. Winthrop will host a presentation this Sunday, on the Battery, near the corner of Water Street, at seven in the evening, to address community concerns."

"A presentation?" I cock my head, quizzically.

"Yes. I must prepare the way, sweetling. Give them a taste of what's to come." She grins. "It will drum up enthusiasm for our performance. We want a robust crowd. One the real killer won't be able to resist."

"Do you really think he'll expose himself so readily?"

"No. I don't. I think he'll come to watch, blend in with the crowd, as he's done for months. Then I believe he'll go away once he no longer has a scapegoat in you."

I think of the six murdered women. Their families. Will their deaths merely be forgotten? "But where's the justice in that, Kate? He should be made to pay some sort of price. What if he just leaves, and goes somewhere else to do the same thing?"

Kate's shoulders sink. "We can't worry about that, Lil. Ending the murders here and now, that's our imperative. And securing your freedom. *Your* safety."

"It just seems sort of . . . selfish."

She ceases her restless pacing and sits next to me on the divan. "What are our choices? Capturing him ourselves? Do you think they'll grant you clemency for your sister's murder, and laud you as some kind of hero? Do you think they'll believe a word you say, even if we discover who's behind all of this? The killer must be someone important. Someone influential, with money, to be able to infiltrate the upper echelons of the chivalry and gain access to these women. This is a man who knows how to cover his tracks and hide. It's not worth the risk." She cups my jaw, resting her forehead against mine. "I'll go to town. Build excitement. In a few days, I'll send notice of your capture to the paper, and we'll perform our grand finale. And then, to London."

But as I watch Kate dress in her smartest suit that night and transform into Ezra Winthrop, I become more and more anxious. I think of all the ways our ruse might go wrong. Yes, she looks completely different as Winthrop, with his lean, rangy swagger. There's no chance anyone will mistake her for Varina. And no one in the city—or here in the marshes, for that matter—likely knows her real name: Katherine O'Malley. But what if someone follows her? What if a nosy guardsman or detective pries into Winthrop's background, studies his lofty credentials a little too closely?

After she kisses me goodbye, in character as Winthrop, I admonish her to be careful. She gives me a cocky smile. "When I return, I want you ready for me," she says. "Do you understand?"

"Yes," I say. "Just please . . ."

"I have a gun, Lil, remember?" she says, breaking character for a moment. "A Deringer. It's how I scared off those men who were hunting you, in the marsh. And I've a knife in my trousers." Her face shifts, transforms back to Winthrop's calculating, cold gaze. "Don't doubt for an instant that I'll use them if necessary. Now. Be good while I'm gone." I watch her go, my apprehension keen. Everything depends on how convincing she is. Everything depends on her. And that's what frightens me.

I'm not suited to being a kept woman. Of that, I am certain. During the long hours Kate is gone, I go to the library and straighten the shelves, missing Ruby and our lessons together terribly. Since my return from the marsh, a restive dissatisfaction has settled deep in my bones. I'm grateful to be back at Angel's Rest, certainly. And I *do* love Kate—of that, there can be no doubt. But I've survived near-death time upon time. There has to be a reason—some higher calling or purpose I'm meant to fulfill besides being her companion and lover. But until I'm free and able to explore and interrogate that purpose more fully, I'm stuck. It's not a feeling I relish.

But this is the sort of life I'm used to. Placating. Pleasing. Unlike my mother, whose anger would rise if I ever challenged her authority, Kate uses other means. Coercion. Pleasure. Charm. So I moan for her. I sigh, I lay myself out for her, like an offering on an altar. And yes, being desired is powerful—something my mother and Rebecca both knew and used to their advantage. But desire is also a trap.

Still, when Kate returns, hours later, I am in her bed, just as she requested, my skin perfumed with rosewater. She wakes me with a stinging slap to my bare rump, then has her way with me as Winthrop, until my knees give out and I collapse onto the mattress, trembling and exhausted. But *she* isn't tired. Not in the least. She washes up, dons her nightgown, and then with much excitement, tells me about the presentation. "You should have seen it, Lil. There were droves of people! Droves. From every walk. I swear, when I demonstrated how I would slay you, a woman swooned. If it weren't for her husband, she would have fallen to the ground. I had them in the palm of my hand!" She laughs, her enthusiasm infectious. "They believe it, all of it."

I pull my shift on over my sex-flushed skin, resting my chin on my knees. "I've no doubt, my love." Though I smile and give her the praise she craves, envy runs through me at her freedom. That others got to bask in her performance, her presence, while I worried and fretted here alone.

"Were the authorities there?"

"Yes. Guardsmen and detectives. Even a doctor, who they've got studying the case. He's a bit of a skeptic, that one, but all the same, I convinced him. They all asked about my education, my background. I told them everything I've rehearsed, and they were duly impressed."

"Yes, of course," I say, rolling my eyes playfully.

"And the coroner was there, too. He thanked me profusely for coming. I was able to pull him aside and persuade him to allow me to retain your body, for my studies, with the promise I'd share my findings with him. I oiled the wheels a bit, and he was amenable."

"And you're certain they believed you?"

"There's no doubt. They even offered to take me out for a pint after my presentation, but I refused. Winthrop must keep his head clear, you know." Kate tugs the hem of my shift. "And after his triumphant performance, he was very eager to return to you. It wasn't all a lie. I *do* plan to study your body for the rest of my life, though my findings won't ever leave our boudoir."

"You're shameless," I say, pulling my hem free from her grasping fingers. "I'm glad it went well."

"It's going to be spectacular," Kate says. "We'll rehearse as many times as we can, in preparation. I'll visit the butcher for some pig's blood and a sheep's bladder tomorrow, so we might have a full-dress rehearsal. And then"—she snaps her fingers—"three nights from now, I'll vanquish Charleston's dreaded vampire forever."

I scowl. "You do realize you're talking about *me.*"

"Oh, yes, my darling girl," she says, slipping easily into Winthrop's baritone as she pins me to the mattress, holding me by the wrists. "You'll be utterly conquered. Ravaged to oblivion."

"I think you enjoy being Winthrop a little *too* much," I say, wriggling free. "I'm tired, Kate. Let's go to sleep."

She groans. "Fine. There's always tomorrow."

I blow out the candles next to our bed and lie back. Kate curls around me, warm and smelling faintly of sweat. Spring's pleasing mildness has fled, and the air now carries the sultry feel of summer. For the first time this season, we don't draw the bed curtains. Lucrezia's portrait gazes down at me, tangled with Kate in the bed they surely must have shared. I wonder what she would think of me. If she would be jealous or give us her blessing.

"If it bothers you, we can take it down," Kate murmurs, as if reading my mind. She weaves her fingers through mine.

"Would it be asking too much to do so? I always feel as if she's judging me. That she would be upset at my being in her bed, with you."

"She wouldn't be. She would understand. She was softer than she looks. We were only lovers briefly, for a very short time in the physical sense of the word. Lucrezia was much too frail for the sorts of things you and I do. She was nothing like you. She was stoic. Almost holy, like a Madonna of old. I worshipped her. But you . . ." Kate chuckles. "You bring out something primal in me, Lil. Something possessive."

"I've noticed," I say, smiling in the darkness. "I'm a little jealous that you don't find *me* worthy of worship, though."

"But that's where you're wrong. I covet you. I crave you. Completely." I turn to her. To my surprise, I see tears gleaming in her eyes. She traces my cheek with her thumb. "Please say you'll go to London with me. Build a new life. Marry me—become Mrs. Mayhew. Or Winthrop. I care not which gentleman you prefer. Just be my wife, my world. I cannot bear the thought of ever being parted from you. You are my Portia, my Eurydice. I'd go to the depths of hell for you."

Suddenly, it occurs to me that Kate might need me more than I need her. There's a vulnerability in her voice, a tender, childlike pleading that disarms me completely. I think of the little girl she once was, singing and acting to escape the grim circumstances of her life.

Something breaks in me then, and the last of my reservations fall to the floor, like ill-fitting clothes. My lip trembles, my throat clenching around my words. I hesitate for only a moment. "Yes. I'll go to London with you."

She laughs. "Oh, Lil. You'll never regret it. I'll make you so happy, I promise."

⁂

"You're not present. You need to concentrate, Lillian. Get up," Kate says sternly as she stands over me, hands on her hips.

"I'm tired. Can't we take a break?"

"I'll let you have a break after we run through it with the sheep's bladder. You'll need a bath after that, anyway."

I drag myself up from the floor. Is this truly an actor's life? Repetitive rehearsals, exhaustion, the endless quest for perfection? I can't say I see the appeal, frankly. Thunder rumbles outside, as rain sheets the roof and lightning flickers through the windows. Our first summer storm.

I face Kate, scowling. "Once more. Only. I'm on my courses, Kate. I'm not well."

It isn't a lie. My menses came on this morning in a maelstrom of cramping pain.

"There are no excuses in acting, my love. I once played Rosalind with a shaking fever. It was my best performance yet. This is your *only* role. Your life—our future—depends upon you mastering it. Summon the strength." She's so smug that I want to scream.

"Turn around," she orders. I sigh and do as she commands, wincing as she pulls my arms behind my back and roughly binds my wrists. She produces the swollen sheep's bladder, and stuffs it in the pocket above my left breast. It smells foul. The coppery scent of the blood inside makes me gag.

She falls right into Winthrop's chilling cadence, jerking me forward so hard that I almost stumble. We go through the preliminaries—the struggling, the wrestling—and I hold nothing back as I growl and hiss. I'm angry with her, and I let it show. When she finally pins me to the floorboards, I stare at her defiantly, baring my teeth. Winthrop's cool gaze appraises me in return. He raises the stake. "Foul creature. I take great pleasure in sending you to the depths of hell."

This time, when he brings the mallet down, I feel the stake pierce my bodice, then tear through the sheep's bladder. The sharp tip grazes the flesh of my bosom. I yelp at the pinch of pain, and then, remembering that this is my final act, and that I'm sick to death of rehearsals, I roar and writhe, just as a massive clap of thunder shakes the house.

Winthrop pushes me onto my side. Dark blood streams from my bodice, onto the floor, soaking my rehearsal dress. It's cold. Sticky. "Stay still," he hisses. "Don't you dare blink."

Once we finish, Kate heats water for a bath and strips the dress from me to wash later. I glimpse myself in the looking glass. The pig's blood streaks my body, drying and flaking. There's a small wound on my breast, where the stake scratched me.

"Come bathe, Lil," Kate says. "I'll wash your hair."

I let her help me into the steaming tub. The storm still rages outside, rain lashing the darkened windows. I sink in, up to my chin. Kate brushes my hair back from my forehead and cups water in her hands, letting it stream over my scalp. I've let it grow since she cut it, and it now brushes my jaw in soft, becoming waves.

"I'm sorry I was harsh earlier," she says, working soap into my hair. "I do realize this isn't who you are, or what you want to do. The things I aspire to aren't your passions. One more night. And then all of this will be over. We leave for London next week. I booked our passage on a steamer when I went to town today."

I sit up, water splashing over the sides of the tub. "A week? I thought you said we would leave in autumn."

"It will be a safer passage in summer. We don't want to wait. The storms come late in the season. Besides, I'll want to try for a few roles when we arrive, to see us through our first winter."

Anger claws through me. I bite my lip against the harsh words that want to tumble free. She wasted no time, nor did she consult me. "Couldn't you have spoken with me first? I thought . . . I thought we'd have more time."

"You're angry with me."

"I am, Kate!"

She sighs. "What do we have to gain by waiting? There's nothing left for us here, sweetling. Only the risk of discovery. Even this house has become a prison."

I laugh. "You know nothing of prison."

"I know more than you think. And I'm only trying to give you a life again, Lillian. To give *us* a life. Together. There's nothing more for us here. You know this."

She's right that there isn't anything left for me to cling to here. If we don't leave, I'll never be free. But then I think about my mother, alone in our house on Tradd Street, with so many words left unsaid between us. I don't know what I want. What sort of closure, or absolution, could be gained at this point. Mother thinks me dead—or worse. It would frighten her if I turned up at her door. But still . . . the thought of being an ocean away from the only family I have left in the world is suddenly too much.

Tears bristle in my eyes. I wipe at them angrily. "I can't expect you to understand, Kate. You've always lived the way you wanted to. Done what you wanted to. But I haven't. I *haven't.* I've only ever done what others wanted of me."

She kneels next to the bath. "Oh, sweetling. But can't you see? This is *how* you discover who you are. What you want! If you'd like to become a governess once we're in London, you can. You can't do that here, it would be impossible. There, you can begin again. Afresh. With no taint of crime or sin to prohibit you. In a place where no one knows you. *That's* freedom. The best kind." She picks up my limp hand, kisses it. "And you're wrong about me. I haven't told you everything about my life. I ran away from something once, too, you know."

She moves to the head of the bath and eases my shoulders back, then massages my scalp with her fingers. The scent of the verbena soap is soothing, her touch tender. "I wasn't born here. I came from North Carolina. My mother was an indentured servant from Ireland. Her master impregnated her at thirteen. When his wife discovered Mama was with child, she tossed her out."

"Oh, Kate. I'm so sorry. I knew about the workhouse. That your mother was Irish, but not the rest."

"You couldn't have known. I don't like to talk about it. My mother endured too much in her short life. It was a blessing when she died. A mercy." Kate pulls in a shaky breath. "She birthed me in the workhouse and carried me on her back in a sling while she worked. As soon as I was old enough, I was put to work, too, sorting laundry. That's how we came to live with the man I called my father. Dr. Sutherland. He saw us in the workhouse when he made his rounds—saw my young mother's poor health and my angelic looks—and took pity on us. But we weren't the only foundlings under his care. There was a boy. Seven years older than me. Lionel. An orphan.

"We were raised as siblings. At first. But as I got older, Lionel's attention became amorous. Dr. Sutherland arranged our betrothal. I was fifteen when we married. Dr. Sutherland was an old man at that point. He knew that if I married Lionel, who was being primed to take over his practice, I'd have security and wouldn't be sent to a workhouse like my mother. No one ever asked me if it was what *I* wanted." She stills, her fingers dangling in the water at my sides. "Our marriage was horrid, as you might imagine. I ran away and came to Charleston. Found work as a scullery maid in a grand house. Then, once my education and talent for singing were discovered, I was elevated to companion for my elderly mistress. Mrs. Phillips. Her son owned Angel's Rest. That's how I met Lucrezia. After Mr. Phillips died, I came here, cared for Lucrezia, and in return, she taught me how to act. I became Alexander Mayhew. You know the rest."

I take Kate's hand, weaving her fingers through mine, my ill temper fading. "I'm sorry that happened. The marriage. Your having to run away."

"He beat me, you know. Lionel. Because I wouldn't submit. He wanted someone like Varina. Pretty, charming, an ornament in his home and on his arm. Someone willing to open her legs anytime he wished. But I always knew myself, Lil. Knew who I was. What I wanted."

She strokes the side of my neck, and I melt into her touch, nuzzling against her hand. I think of the letters in Kate's bureau. Her father obviously regretted arranging her marriage. The vengeful man he mentioned in his final letter must have been Lionel. It's what makes the most sense.

"I can't imagine what it must have been like for you," I say. "To be forced into that sort of marriage."

"And you'll never have to, thank heavens for that." She sighs, cupping my chin tenderly. "How fortunate we are to have found one another—that Noah and Ruby delivered you to me like some gift from the gods."

I tip my head back, and she kisses me. Later that night, after Kate drifts off to sleep, I consider everything she told me. Her lot in life brought her pain and misfortune. But it also made her resourceful. Ambitious. Perhaps too much so.

I still have my doubts that our ruse will work. That we'll succeed at our charade, force the killer to cease his rampage, and then escape blithely to England and live happily ever after. Life is hardly ever that easy. And our best-laid plans are often a trap we set for ourselves.

TWENTY-THREE

Our rented wagon rumbles over the cobblestones, jostling me roughly and making my teeth chatter as we roll toward our fated performance. We roll over a rut, and one of the sharpened ivory fangs cuts into my lip, but I can do nothing about the trickle of blood that runs down my chin. My hands are tied behind me, my feet bound beneath me. My belly lurches as we near White Point Gardens. Hundreds of people have gathered—a crowd so dense, their noise and excitement hum like a plague of locusts, even at a distance. Torches and lanterns glimmer in the darkness. There's even a band playing music. Vendors selling refreshments.

"Look at that, Lil," Kate says over her shoulder, slowing the horses. "Just look."

"I'm terrified," I whisper. I'm nearly in tears, my worries about all the ways in which this could go terribly wrong multiplying by the minute.

"Good. I want you terrified. Terrified and angry. A trapped animal."

"This isn't one of your plays, Kate! Those people want to see me dead."

But Kate is gone. As we approach the path leading into the park, Winthrop's stiff, formal coldness steals her bravado. The shift in her demeanor sends a quiver of unease down my spine.

When we enter the park, the crowd roars. Something sails toward me, and lands next to me in the wagon bed. It's a rotten apple, crawling with maggots. I gag as more rotting fruit, offal, and spoiled oysters bombard me, stinking and foul. I can do nothing to shield myself from the volley. I'm bound and helpless.

Suddenly, a rock bounces into the wagon bed. Then another, this one glancing off my shoulder painfully. I duck, cowering against the side boards. If I was afraid before, I am utterly panicked now. Kate had better get things under control, and quickly, or they'll kill me long before Winthrop ever draws his stake. Still, I muster my courage, compose my fear into what they've come to see. What they want me to be. I growl, baring my teeth, my eyes wild as I whip my head from side to side, taking satisfaction in their wide eyes and fearful gasps.

Kate parks the wagon alongside the road, stands, and cracks the horse whip. The crowd stills. "Ladies and gentlemen. I have tracked, captured, and delivered your enemy. Just as I suspected, she was hiding in the marshes, lying in wait for her next opportunity to kill." Kate tosses a disdainful look at me. "And now, I will bring you justice. But I must insist on order at this execution. For your own safety, there must be no more heckling. No rioting. Am I understood?"

A murmur rumbles through the crowd of well-dressed animals. I see so many faces I recognize. Their expressions are a mixture of wonder, fear, and hatred. Georgina McClintock, dressed in a lavish gown, as if she's just come from a party. William and his wife, her pretty mouth set in a scowl. Patrick Calhoun, a young woman clutching his arm, her eyes brimming with tears. But there's no sympathy on her face. Only fright. Leroy Burrows is there, with his diary and pencil in hand, scrawling down all the details of my plight for the papers. Most disturbingly, children are everywhere, laughing and playing, and running about, as if this is a summer carnival.

And then my heart lurches. At first, I believe it to be a trick of the light. But it isn't.

My mother stands near the pathway cutting through the park, her face pale and drawn, dressed all in black. Her eyes meet mine, and

I nearly cry out with longing. Dr. Broadbent stands next to her, his mouth set in a frown.

Kate, now fully Winthrop, climbs down from the wagon, the whip still in hand, the stake and mallet lodged in the waistband of his trousers. He unlatches the wagon's rear boot, and stands there looking at me for a moment, calculating with his frigid eyes. With his free hand, he grasps the rope binding my feet and drags me toward him. I gasp as my head falls back and hits the baseboards of the wagon. A shower of sparks flickers over my vision.

He unties my feet and hauls me out roughly, holding me close, just as we rehearsed. If I were hoping for any warmth, any comfort, I'm sorely disappointed. Kate has so thoroughly become the scoundrel that no traces of tenderness remain. No love. Not even desire. Only the act.

"Move. Your. Feet," he commands.

The crowd, my mother's face, the torches all blur together in a swirl as he forces me forward, the onlookers parting for us. The clearing at the center of the park, shielded on both sides by an alley of live oaks, is to be my planned place of execution—mere feet from the place Arabella Meade died. The scent of jasmine mixes with the smoky tallow from the torches and the stinking sheep's bladder tucked into my bodice, sickeningly sweet with an earthy gaminess. Winthrop drags me forward, and the crowd gathers close, leering at me with curiosity. I do my part. I roll my eyes, sneer, wriggling in his arms. He grasps me by the hair, exposing my throat, and cracks the whip against the tabby path. I flinch, involuntarily. I can feel his heartbeat against my back. He's excited. He's enjoying this.

"A vampire—this undead creature—can be killed in one of two ways," he says, his voice commanding. "By fire, or by destroying the creature's heart. This evening, ladies and gentlemen, I'll slay this monster by the latter means." He drops the whip and produces the sharpened stake, brandishing it. "I promise you, after tonight, your daughters will no longer fear this monster's lurid hunger. They need no longer hide themselves away."

This is the challenge. The hidden message to the real killer. *You've been found out. If this continues, you'll no longer have a scapegoat.*

A scapegoat. Because that's all I've ever been. For Rebecca's murder. And now, for all the others after. I begin to shake. But this time, it's not out of fear. It's out of anger. Out of hatred for these well-bred men and women who would rather make me a monster than examine the rot corrupting their core. How they use the enslaved to prop up their vanity and build their kingdom, how they play at being royalty, when their souls are anything but noble. It is they who are the real vampires.

Suddenly, my long-hidden rage comes roaring out, fierce, hot, and hungry, like a wildfire burning unchecked. I thrash and howl, breaking free of my bonds. I lunge toward Patrick Calhoun, remembering the cruel way he spoke about my father. My sister. "Good god!" he swears. The young woman at his side swoons into the arms of the older gentleman next to her.

I laugh, wickedly, then turn and growl at Georgina McClintock. She places one gloved hand over her mouth, averting her gaze. None of them can bear to look me in the eye. As I scan their faces for any scrap of empathy, I come away lacking.

"Lillian!" My mother pushes through the crowd, her eyes brimming with tears, her heart-shaped face still lovely, despite all her years of grief. Dr. Broadbent reaches for her, restraining her, at the same time Winthrop tackles me, throwing me to the ground. She fights her way free and holds out her hand. I grasp it, desperately, her fingers gripping mine.

"Mama . . ." I say, reverting to my childhood name for her, hot tears falling from my eyes.

"Oh, Lil, my darling, my angel."

"I love you," I say. "I'm sorry. I wish. I wish . . ." The words come out as a garbled lisp, thanks to the ivory fangs, and my panic, but I fight for the right things to say to her all the same.

"Why, Lillian?" she asks. "What have you become?"

And then I realize. She *believes* it. She believes their lies. This ridiculous myth, that I'm a monster. An inhuman killer. The pain of it lances through me like a poisoned barb. But she convinced herself I killed Rebecca, too, didn't she? She believed her own lies, and mine. And I so willingly took the fall. Better I die than accuse the one I've always protected. The one who murdered her own daughter, slowly, year after year, until the poison finally overcame her.

Instead of saving my sister, instead of saving myself, I saved my mother.

And she *let* me.

"Mama, I didn't—"

"Enough!" Winthrop slaps a hand over my mouth, his knee in my back. "Shut up, Lil," he growls in my ear. "Shut up."

Dr. Broadbent pulls Mother away, though her heartrending wails hang in the air long after she disappears into the crowd. I'm thankful she won't witness what comes next. Winthrop flips me over, straddles my hips, pinning me to the ground. I strain and buck as he leans forward and grasps the stake. Its polished point gleams in the lantern light. I see a chilling hardness in his eyes as he regards me. The harsh torchlight etches the face I love—Kate's face—into that of a stranger. My heart gallops. This is it.

He lifts the stake and brings it down. The first, hard blow from his mallet sends it into the sheep's bladder. A fountain of cold, stinking blood gushes forth. The crowd gasps. I scream, and it's as if I'm watching the scene from above, as if my soul has separated from my body. The mallet comes down again, and I close my eyes. Pain cascades over me as I feel the sharp point pierce my flesh. He's gone too far. Too deep. Blood trickles down the collar of my dress, warm this time. *My* blood. My eyes snap open, shock cutting through the fog of my surreal, dreamlike state, followed by panic.

Winthrop smirks down at me, his eyes utterly devoid of feeling. Had he intended this all along? Had *Kate* intended this? *We must make it convincing, Lil. They have to believe it.*

Rebecca's words echo inside my head. *Do you trust her?*

My vision blackens around the edges, a high-pitched whine sharp in my ears. This time, when Winthrop rolls me over, I don't have to pretend. I don't have to act. I faint, dead away, the crowd, the lights, the screams of the onlookers fading as I plunge into oblivion.

A VAMPIRE'S DIARY

What a spectacle. A splendid farce! And those fools, those ignorant, superstitious simpletons, lapped it up like kittens with a saucer full of milk. The ruse has served its purpose and enabled my escape. The dreaded "vampire" has been vanquished, but my work will continue elsewhere. I've untilled pastures ahead of me. I'm so close. So very close now. Just a few more weeks, or months, until my labor is rewarded. Truly, I owe Lillian a debt of gratitude. The myth has died with her, along with any suspicion that might have been cast my way. Now, as I pack my trunks and prepare to take my wife and make a home elsewhere, I think only of the future, and the glory that awaits me.

TWENTY-FOUR

I wake in our bed, hours or days later—I've no recollection how much time has passed. A shaft of sunlight slices across my eyes. I blink, and then I see Kate, her form silhouetted against the window. "Ah, you're awake," she says.

Anger trammels through me. I sit up, ignoring the rush of dizziness. I brush the hair out of my eyes and look down at my chest, where she pierced me. A square of gauze, plastered in place, covers the top of my left breast, right below the neckline of my nightgown. "You hurt me," I say.

"I had to," she says, sitting on the edge of the mattress next to me. "You were breaking character, Lil. You nearly ruined our act."

"So you did it to punish me, then?" I spit, seething.

"No," she says steadily, as if speaking to a child. "To focus you. To bring you back into character."

"You could have killed me!"

She sighs, crosses her arms over her chest. "You forget that I know the human body. Intimately. You were in no mortal danger. I was well southwest of your heart. Your plump little breast might have a scar. That's all."

I want to slap her, hard, across the face. But I lack the courage to do so. Instead, I turn my head, unable to meet her steady gaze. Tears prick the corners of my eyes. How I hate her in this moment! Her smug look. Her condescension.

"You ought to be ashamed, Lil."

"Ashamed? Of what?"

"Of how you treat me. I've saved your life. Twice now." She looks up at the ceiling. "Or is it three times? Yes. Three. Counting the search party who wanted to lynch you."

"I trusted you! I trusted you not to hurt me."

She scoffs, shakes her head. "It's only a puncture wound. It will heal."

"It isn't just the wound. It's so much more than that." I push the covers back, scurrying out of bed.

Kate sighs. "I knew you would be upset. But you're acting like a spoiled child. I saved your life, Lillian! Saved countless others. There hasn't been another murder since our act. Not one."

I clench and unclench my fists, my nails biting into my palms. "How . . . how long have I been asleep?"

"Four days."

"It happened again, then. The catalepsy."

"Yes. And I've not left your side. I've dripped water into your mouth with a sponge. Washed you. Held a mirror to your face, to check your breathing." Hurt brims inside her eyes. "Come, let me make you something to eat. You have to be famished."

I scoff, turning my back on her, but she's right. Hunger gnaws at my stomach, just as it did when I woke in the crypt. She closes the distance between us and wraps me in her arms, resting her chin on my shoulder. I stiffen at her touch. "Please don't be cross. We're free now. Really and truly. Try to think of that."

"Don't you *ever* become Winthrop in my presence again," I say, whirling to face her. "Never. God help me, if you do, I'll leave you, Kate. I'll leave and I'll never come back."

"Do you know who Winthrop is, darling? Who I based him on?"

I bark a laugh. "The devil himself?"

"One would think. But I based him on Lionel."

"What?"

"I became *my* monster to exorcise him. Just as you had to become yours."

I still, horror and disgust running through me. I push away from her. "You . . . you bedded me as him. Twice. Can't you see how that sickens me now, Kate? Knowing what that means?"

"Yes, and I don't expect you to understand. But becoming Ezra Winthrop helped me vanquish Lionel. The memory of what he did to me. More than you could ever imagine. Becoming him gave me power when I felt powerless. Lionel inspired Winthrop. But I made him my own. He's *my* creation. Controlling him—even if it's only in my imagination—cages the lion."

"He beat you!"

She flinches. "Yes. He did. And far worse. That's the reason I can't bear submitting. To anyone."

The next question is sour, bitter as bile on my tongue, but I must ask it, all the same. "Were you . . . did you act like him? The things he did to you . . . did you do them with me?"

"No. And I never would. That was all me, sweetling. You were willing. You wanted it. What he did to you. My Winthrop, at least, is gentleman enough to require consent."

I let out my breath in a rush. Grateful, at least, that I didn't give myself over to something as evil as I feared.

"I promise you, Winthrop won't ever return. I understand why you're angry. I do. I've compromised your trust." Kate reaches for me. I pull away at first, then melt at the insistence of her arms. She enfolds me, swaying me from side to side. "Our performance was astounding," she says, kissing the nape of my neck. "They believed it as if it were gospel. Your catalepsy was the real miracle of it all. The coroner came forward, took your pulse, listened to your chest. Pronounced you dead. It was perfect. No one questioned it. You should have heard the cheering, Lillian. We brought the house down. Men came up to shake my hand and congratulate me. One girl wanted a lock of your hair, as a souvenir. I obliged her, of course." Kate grins. "I'm a hero, sweetling. It's really something."

A sickening tumble of horror runs through me. They cheered my death. Applauded my would-be executioner as a hero. Even though I know it was all an act, my feelings are hurt by Kate's glee.

"And what do we do now?" I ask, my mouth dry.

"After you're fully recovered, we'll pack our bags. We'll leave for London."

"And what happens when they discover you aren't who you said you were? You were supposed to report your findings to the coroner, remember?"

"By the time he realizes it was all a hoax, we'll be long gone, making our new life together." Kate nuzzles my shoulder. "I'm sorry I hurt you, Lil. Do you forgive me?"

"You frightened me. Terribly."

"Look at me." She turns me in her arms, fixing me with her eyes. "I'll never hurt you again. Ever. In any way." She shakes me gently. "Do you hear me? I *love* you. You're my wife. My North Star, my light."

"I . . . I love you, too," I say.

"All is forgiven then, eh?" She grins at me playfully, raising a brow.

Though I accept her apology and stifle my bitterness, my feelings are in tumult. We have breakfast together in our room, and then Kate goes out to do the chores, leaving me bundled beneath the covers. By evening, I have a fierce headache, and my mood has soured even more, though I do my best to hide it. After Kate falls asleep, I sneak out of bed, and go up to the library. Ruby's tablet is still there, with her name written across the slate in looping, even letters. She was so proud that day. She'd practiced writing her name, over and over. Tears spring to my eyes, unbidden. I miss her sweet smile. The way she bit her lip when forming her letters.

This can't be all there is for me—becoming Kate's doting wife. I reach up, feel the stubble at my temple, where she sheared off a lock of my hair to give to some pretty girl as a trophy. A souvenir. Kate didn't consider how that would make me feel. How my hair is one of my few vanities. She didn't care about anything other than their applause. Their praise.

We spend the following days preparing for our trip. We pack two trunks with Kate's favorite costumes, a few of Lucrezia's altered dresses for me, and enough cookery and utensils to set us up in a new home. We give the chickens to the Gullah Geechee elders and learn that Ruby and her father successfully stowed away on a ship bound for Canada. It's a relief to know they're safe.

The day before our departure, Kate goes to town for a few necessary supplies for our journey, and I wander the house, poking in all the rooms, taking stock of the memories we've made here. Finally, I make my way up to the widow's walk. Kate forbade me from going there, alone, due to the danger, but I want one last view of the marshes to capture in my memory forever—my place of salvation, where I discovered my first taste of freedom.

I climb the rickety stairs and emerge atop the roof as the sun sets. The view takes my breath away. The creeks and rivulets cut through the spartina, lit up like twisting roads made of molten gold. From here, I can see the hammock island where I built my hermitage, the lights of Mount Pleasant winking on in the dusk, and past that, the glittering sea beyond the harbor. I take a deep breath, leaning over the wrought iron balcony. It creaks under my weight and then gives way under my elbows, the iron rusted and weakened by the salt air. I step back as a section of it falls to the ground, far below. My heart gallops. If I'd leaned against it with my full weight, I'd have lost my balance and toppled over. Regretting my folly, I descend to the attic on shaky legs and stay there until I reclaim my senses.

Once night falls, I begin to worry. Kate told me her errand wouldn't take long—that she merely needed to go into Mount Pleasant to pawn some of the jewelry I'd stolen and shop for supplies. But as midnight passes, suspicion seeps along the edges of my mind. What if she's double-crossed me? Tricked me? What if she's already left for England, and never intended to take me with her at all?

When dawn breaks and she still hasn't returned, I hastily dress and hide my face with my cloak. She's taken our skiff, so I walk to the nearest wharf, hoping that one of the fishermen plying the morning waters will take me down to Mount Pleasant. It's risky. And with the rising temperatures, my cloak will draw attention. But I cannot sit idly at Angel's Rest, pacing the floors and worrying that Kate has betrayed me.

Luckily, an elderly Gullah fisherman rows by and offers to take me to town. I sit in the keel of his boat, my head lowered as he hums and checks his nets along the way. I give him a few coins from my pouch as payment, then make my way up the King's Highway into town. Though it's early, people are already out and about on their errands. I furtively scan the alleyways and shops, lingering in the shadows outside the pawnbroker's to see if I can get a glimpse of Kate, to no avail. Finally, exasperated, I steel my spine and go into the shops to ask if anyone has seen a man fitting her description. She went out as Alex—in full gentleman's dress, so as not to attract suspicion from the brokers.

But although I go from shop to shop, asking about my "husband," the shopkeepers only shake their heads. I'm becoming hot, and agitated, and my worry has grown teeth. I debate hiring a skiff to take me back up the Wando to Angel's Rest or boarding the ferry over to town proper. Finally, I decide on the latter. I won't go back home until I find her. As the steamer churns across the Cooper, I stand against the railing, my fear rising as we pass White Point—that place of my greatest fear and humiliation. I swore I'd never set foot on the Peninsula again after that night. Yet here I am, on a fool's errand for love.

Where is she? What has she done?

Do you trust her?

When the ferry makes port, I wait until all the other passengers have disembarked, then rush along the wharves, looking everywhere for her tall hat, her confident stride. Again, I search the pawnshops along the wharves, but she's not there and no one has seen her. I have no idea where else I should look. My mind spins out in a thousand scenarios. Perhaps she has another lover. Or she's gone to see Barbara, her paramour in yellow, one last time. Has Kate met her for a final farewell tryst? Eventually, the midday heat and my emotions get the best of me. I go inside Saint Michael's to rest and cool off, tucking myself into a box near the back. I need water. And food. I rushed out this morning without eating. All this seems foolish. Every bit of it. I resent Kate for her inconstant heart and broken promises.

The church bells chime two o'clock. I'm only a few blocks from our Tradd Street rowhouse, and my mother, who thinks me a monster. But she loves me still—I saw it that night, at White Point. Suddenly, such a longing overtakes me. Such an undeniable, powerful yearning to see her one last time, and to say all the things I need to say before we're parted forever.

I stand outside the ocher-painted door for a long time, thinking of the right words to say in greeting. A black crepe bunting adorns the lintel, and all the shutters are drawn. She's still in mourning, then. Surely for Papa. But perhaps for me, too.

I lift the brass knocker and tap three times.

At first, I hear nothing. And then, from inside, a rustle of stiff skirts. The sound of paws scratching the door and Walter's excited bark. The door opens, slowly. My mother stands there, blinking at me in confusion. "Yes? Is there something I might help you with?"

I lower my hood. She takes a step back, her hand flying up to cover her mouth and the whimper that follows. Walter dances at her side, hopping onto his hind legs and pawing at my skirts. Mother doesn't say a word, only snatches my wrist and pulls me inside. She shuts the door and bolts it behind me.

Then I'm smothered in waves of black bombazine as she embraces me, her thick rose attar perfume clouding my senses. Walter nudges my hand, and I bury my fingers in his rough fur. Tears spring to my eyes.

"Oh, Lil," Mother coos. "You're here. It's really you, isn't it? This isn't a dream?"

"Yes, Mama," I say, pulling back to look at her. I wipe my eyes and smile, showing my teeth. "And I'm no monster, I promise you. It was all a ruse. But you mustn't tell a soul. You mustn't tell anyone you saw me, or that I came here."

"Oh, Lil, I didn't dare hope." She squeezes my hand. "Yet here you are, as rosy-cheeked as I remember. You look well, daughter. Healthy. That color suits you," she says, motioning to the blue walking suit I wear. One of Lucrezia's, altered to fit me. Of course she would focus on my appearance, but I glow under the light of her approval all the same.

She leads me into the parlor, its velvet curtains drawn to block out the afternoon light. Walter trails us, his tail still wagging excitedly. "Come, sit. I'll lay out tea."

"Where's Siobhan?"

"Oh, she left me weeks ago. Her health. Rheumatism. I've been getting by on my own just fine, for now."

I look around the front parlor. The mirrors are draped in black crepe, the clock silent on the mantel, as is the custom for households in mourning. But a fine veneer of dust covers everything. There are cobwebs in the corners. The grate still holds ashes from the last fire. And on closer inspection, Mother herself is diminished; her acclaimed beauty, while still present, has faded. Her oily hair hangs in limp plaits from a pale center part. Only her eyes, the selfsame violet as my own, still shine, wet with grateful tears.

"Oh, Lil, my love. My darling girl," she croons, wringing her hands. "Tea. I'll fetch it. Would you like cake? I've made a sponge, just in case I had callers."

"I'm famished, Mama. I'd love cake."

I perch on the davenport, focusing my thoughts. There are so many things I want to talk about with her. This may well be the final time I see her in this life, and my heart is full of complicated feelings. There's Rebecca, of course, and Papa. I want to know the details of his death—I hope that he did not suffer.

When Mama brings the tea and pours it for me, my hand shakes as I lift the cup to my mouth. Her sponge cake is dry, and tasteless, but I eat it all the same. She sits across from me, in her favorite chair, and leans forward. Walter settles at my feet, nuzzling his head against my shins.

"Oh, Lil! I used to dream of this moment. Of being reunited with you on this side of heaven, by some miracle." She laughs, runs a hand over her oily hair. "I didn't believe him when he told me you were still alive. But he was right, wasn't he?"

I still, a shiver running through me. "Who told you I was alive?"

"Why, Dr. Broadbent. He examined you after Papa claimed your body at the jail. He's the one who insisted that we leave the lid to your casket unscrewed. He felt there was a chance, however slim, that you might have just had another one of your fits. He watched over your body, in the receiving tomb, for three nights before he agreed with Papa that it was all right to bury you." Mama sighs. "It was torture for me, Lillian. All of it. We didn't have a public funeral. There was a sensation about it all in the papers, so we did it quietly. Just me, Papa, and Father Flynn."

I sit back in my chair, flummoxed. Dr. Broadbent certainly knew I'd survived the grave, at least since Barbara Kincaid's party. He saw through my guise as Mary Jones on the same night Arabella died. But he substantiated the vampire claim as well. They quoted him in the papers—he told them my dress was covered in blood and that I was unnaturally pale when I came to fetch him from the party to see to Arabella.

"When did Dr. Broadbent tell you I was alive, Mama?"

"After Arabella died, darling. He saw you at a party. But Arabella told me she saw you, too. In town." Mama's eyebrows furrow. "Did you kill her, my dove? Or any of the others?"

"No, Mama. I did not. I've never been a killer." I grip the arms of the chair to keep my hands from shaking. "And quite frankly, it wounds me that you would even question it. We need . . . we need to talk about Rebecca."

"I can't talk about Rebecca," she says, her face crumpling. "I cannot."

"I didn't kill her, Mama." I say the words clearly, calmly. "I think we both know what happened. Who was responsible."

"Lillian, please . . ."

"I've forgiven you for it. For all of it. That's why I've come." I reach for her hand, but she pulls it away. "I know you had the best intentions. You changed, after the twins died. Their death wasn't your fault, Mama. Lots of people died. I almost died, too." My fingers find the smallpox scar on the back of my wrist, remembering how the fever raged through my body. Through our home. "You nursed us all, as best you could. I remember."

"It was horrid. I cursed myself for not having all of you inoculated. I should have. It saved my life." She sobs. "Do you know the guilt I felt, after losing my babies? So needless."

"Yes. And you didn't want to lose another child," I say gently. "You couldn't. So you believed every charlatan that came knocking at our door when it came to Rebecca. I remember, Mama. I remember when you started with the syrup. You thought you were doing the right thing. But it killed her. Slowly."

"How dare you," she says coldly, her tearful eyes narrowing into angry slits. "To come here, and imply . . ."

"It's not an implication. It's the truth. I watched you. I knew what you put in that syrup."

"It was helping her!"

My hands knot in my skirts. I bite my lip to quell the vicious words that long to jump free. "I know you believe that. I do."

"Of course I do. Because it's the truth."

"Then if it was so innocent, so well intentioned, why didn't you tell the judge? The jury?"

Her tear-reddened eyes skate from my own. "I . . . I was frightened, Lillian."

My anger crests, spilling over the edge of my fragile composure. "So was I!" I roar, standing. Walter runs from the room, his tail tucked between his legs. "Do you know what it was like? Prison? Papa's money, his bribes, saved me from the worst of it. But there were men there who wanted to rape me, Mother. Killers—real killers—who would have snapped my neck like a twig. I had to listen to the sounds of torture, day and night. Rats crawling over me while I slept. I suffered from dysentery and nearly died. There was no respite from the horrors. And yet I endured it all. And I would have, unto death. For your sake!"

"Stop!" she wails. She claws at her hair, one of her looped braids falling loose. "I didn't . . . it wasn't my fault. You can't understand what it was like for me."

As I watch my mother dissemble, the realization that I'm never going to receive her contrition, that she'll never admit her fault in Rebecca's death, washes over me. She isn't capable of seeing the world through my eyes. She isn't capable of loving anyone—not even her own children—more than she loves her feigned innocence.

I choke back a sob, steeling myself, regaining my self-possession. Kate has taught me well in that. "There was another killer," I say, calmly. "I saw him murder Arabella. I don't know who he is. His motives. I don't even know for certain whether he's fully human. But I did not kill those girls, Mother. Not a one of them." I look up at the ceiling, study the plasterwork for a moment before speaking. "I've come here to say goodbye. I only wanted you to know that at least one of your children survived."

"Goodbye? But where will you go?"

"To England. I'm betrothed. My husband-to-be is the man you saw that night, at the park. The one who pretended to slay me. It was merely a hoax, so that I could leave my old life behind, once and for all. We're leaving tomorrow. I'm not sure if I'll ever return to Charleston, so I wanted to see you one last time."

"But why? You could stay here, with me. You can hide in the attic when we have callers. So long as you never leave, no one will ever know."

Another prison. I sigh. Pinch my eyes shut and then open them. "No. You're not understanding, Mama. I'm getting married. I'm building a new life with my husband. A free one. I can't stay here. It's impossible, especially now."

"Who is he? This man you're running off with?" Her words are accusatory, judgmental. She's angry that I'm choosing someone else over her. And if she knew the full truth of my and Kate's relationship, I'd be dead to her, I'm sure.

"His name is Alexander Mayhew. He's a doctor."

"Oh." She studies the carpet, shamefaced. "A doctor. I suppose I must accept it, though it saddens me to think of you so far away. I do hope that you'll at least write."

"I will," I say, though I don't think I shall. I take a drink of my tea. It's already cold. "There's one more thing I need to ask you, before I go. It's about Papa."

"I already know what you're going to ask. It was his heart, Lil. It was sudden. He did not suffer. Dr. Broadbent assured me of that."

"Is he still . . . are you still seeing *him*? I've known for some time, so please don't lie to me about that."

"No. We haven't seen one another like that, for many months. He only escorted me to the gardens, to your . . ."

"My execution. What a circus."

"Your father and I loved one another. But it was never a grand passion, do you understand? I was so young when I married Richard. I knew little about the world."

"Did he know? About your affairs? Dr. Broadbent wasn't the only one. There were more men, Mama. Rebecca knew it, too."

She blanches at my forthrightness. So unusual for me.

"Yes. I believe he did know," she says.

So, she never told him. Only assumed he knew. Of course.

Her eyes skitter along the wall behind my head. "It shames me to speak of such things, Lillian. And the truth of the matter is Dr. Broadbent was a comfort to me after the twins died. And with Rebecca. I was hoping that after my mourning period for Richard reached a respectable end, we might marry. But it seems he's married someone else. I saw Georgina at the market, and she told me. I suppose I'll have to go live with Tillie now. I don't want to, but with you going away, I haven't many choices, have I?"

"I understand." Frankly, knowing that she'll have Aunt Tillie to take care of her in her dotage makes me feel less guilty about leaving her behind. We sit there in silence, letting time drip by, moment by moment. I study her, this woman who gave me life, and find that my feelings for her have grown numb. Indifferent. But there's still one more matter I must address.

"Mama, did Rebecca ever tell you anything . . . strange about Dr. Broadbent? I saw something. Just a few days before Becca died."

She puts her hand up. "Whatever it is, I don't want to hear it. It won't change anything."

"But I need to tell you. You need to know." I pull in a steady breath. "This is indelicate, but was Rebecca still a virgin when she died?"

"What?" Mama's face reddens. "Of course she was!"

"But I saw . . . I saw Dr. Broadbent. He was touching her. In a way that he shouldn't have been touching a maiden."

I squeeze my eyes shut against the memory of that day but force it to unspool all the same. I'd gone to the privy after keeping vigil at her bedside, then stopped in the kitchen for a glass of cold water, before going back upstairs. I'd paused outside our shared room, at the sound of Dr. Broadbent's voice.

Then I heard Rebecca whimper, as if in pain.

The door was cracked. In my dressing table mirror, I saw them. Rebecca, lying on her side, Dr. Broadbent behind her on the bed, her nightdress bunched above her waist, his arm latched around her neck. His other hand was a blur, it was moving so fast between her legs. Suddenly, Rebecca stiffened, her lips drawn tightly over her teeth. Dr. Broadbent bucked, the bedpost slamming into the wall as his face transformed into a paroxysm of apparent agony. And then Rebecca saw me standing in the doorway, her eyes widening. I stepped back from the door and fled, the water glass slipping from my hands and shattering on the floor.

Now Mother stares at me, incredulously. "Are you talking about the treatments? He was only trying to help Rebecca," she says, wadding her hands in her skirts. "He was convinced her asthma was brought about by hysteria. That when she was energized properly with manual stimulation, it would resolve. It did help her."

"What I saw, what I witnessed, was more than a treatment, Mama. He was violating her. Perhaps even raping her."

Mother's face blazes. "Nonsense. She never spoke of any such thing. I would have *known*. Whatever you think you saw, Lillian, it didn't happen."

"Yes, it happened. Mama, I saw it. I saw it and I should have said something. I should have told you. Papa. Dr. Broadbent must have known that I knew. I think that's why . . . that's why he lied, in court. I could have told the truth. I should have. But I was afraid you would be angry with me. That Rebecca would be ashamed."

My arms begin to tingle. The hair on the back of my neck rises. I lift my head. In the corner of the room, I see my sister's spirit. Her eyes are hollow, haunted, but there is love there all the same. And a sense of relief.

"I'm sorry," I whisper. "I'm so sorry."

Rebecca drifts toward Mother, rests her bruised hands on her shoulders. *She'll never understand, Lillian. She never will. But I forgive her. I forgive you. And* you *must forgive* me, *so I can go in peace. I only wanted it to end. I never meant for you, or anyone else, to suffer.* And then I know the truth. My sister wasn't murdered. On the morning that we found Rebecca dead, the bottle of syrup was almost empty. Everyone had overlooked the obvious. That she'd taken her own life.

Tears fall, dropping onto my skirt. I wipe them away with the edge of my sleeve. My guilt will always be with me. My grief. But I will no longer flinch from it. I'll embrace it. Learn to honor it, and my sister's memory, with the love and grace she deserved in life.

When I look up again, Rebecca is gone.

"You must understand, Lillian," Mother says, oblivious to Rebecca's visitation. "I was trying to be a good mother. To give Rebecca the best treatment I could. Lionel was convinced he'd found the cure for her affliction. And I believed him."

All the color drains from my face. I nearly drop my teacup. "Lionel?"

"Dr. Broadbent. Have you forgotten his Christian name?"

No. It's impossible. It can't be. The coincidence would be too great. Surely . . .

"How old is Dr. Broadbent, Mother?"

"Only a handful of years younger than I. Two and forty, I believe."

Kate is in her mid-thirties. The difference in their ages aligns with what she told me. "Where was he born?" I ask, my voice tight.

"In the Piedmont, dear. Near Greensboro. Why are you asking me these questions?"

The Piedmont. North Carolina hill country. The same place as Kate. A frigid wave of panic washes over me. I remember Barbara Kincaid's party. Dr. Broadbent's scathing assessment of Varina. How cheap and tawdry she looked.

I wasn't the only one he recognized.

I stand, trembling from head to toe. All this time I've been looking for the tiger, and he's been staring me right in the face. And now the tiger might have Kate.

"Goodness, Lillian. What's gotten into you?"

"I have to go, Mama. I'm so sorry. Give Aunt Tillie my love."

"Lil!"

I rush from the room, fear and dread tangling within me as I fly out the door, startling a trio of well-dressed ladies on an afternoon walk. I run past them, at full tilt toward Savage Street, and Dr. Broadbent's office, to confront whatever fate awaits me there.

TWENTY-FIVE

When I reach Broadbent's office, out of breath and boiling beneath my cloak, I throw it off in frustration and try the door. It's locked, the front windows dark. I bang on the door with my closed fist. Finally, a weary maid opens to me. "Yes, miss? Can I help you."

"I need to see Dr. Broadbent, please. It's an emergency."

With my reddened face and panicked breathlessness, it's hardly an act.

"I'm sorry, miss. He's out for the day. He won't be back until evening. He was sent to call on a patient in the marshes."

"The marshes?"

"Yes. He had a visitor this morning. A lady. They left together."

"Did you happen to catch her name. It's very important."

"No, miss. I didn't."

"What did she look like?"

"She was very pretty. Tall. With dark hair. I'm sorry I can't help you more. I must see to my work."

It could have been Kate. Or it might have been someone else. When she left Angel's Rest, she was dressed as Alex. I take some comfort in that knowledge. I sigh, my shoulders sagging. "Thank you. You've been very helpful."

"If you'll leave your card, miss, I'll tell him you called."

"That won't be necessary."

She nods and closes the door. I rush to Bay Street and hire a boat to take me back to the marshes, paying the oarsman handsomely for his efforts.

When I arrive at Angel's Rest, it's evening, and the house is lit up like Christmas, its windows blinking yellow through the oaks. Kate's home. Relief floods through me. I race up the path and onto the piazza, calling her name.

But when I fling open the door, she doesn't come to greet me. "Kate! I'm home!"

Nothing but silence. I walk into the parlor. A vase on the sideboard is tipped over, murky water spilled on the floor. I right it, and call for her again. I still, listening. Upstairs, I hear the floorboards creak. My skin prickles with wariness. Something isn't right.

"Kate?"

I climb the stairs, slowly. Light bleeds into the hall from one of the second-story bedrooms—the one with the wallpaper birds where Kate nursed me when I first arrived. I push the door all the way open. Kate sits there, next to the bed, dressed in one of Varina's gowns, working on a hoop of embroidery. She smiles at me, too wide. "Hello, sweetling," she says, tilting her head. "I was wondering when you would come home."

Something hits the back of my head, hard. Pain explodes inside my skull. I crumple to the floor. As my consciousness fades, I hear Kate's voice: "There, I've done my part."

When I come to, I'm tied to the bed, my wrists bound with scraps of fabric. I panic, crying out. A stinging slap lands across my face. Kate grasps my jaw, her thumb pressing against my pulse. Her eyes are cold. Vacant. Even though she's wearing Varina's clothes, she's become Winthrop again. Heartless, reptilian Winthrop.

Rebecca's voice rings in my ears. *Do you trust her?*

I strain against my bonds. Try to rise. My head spins, sickening me. "You'd better not struggle," Kate scolds, pushing me back down. "You've taken a nasty blow to the head. Best to rest."

"Why are you doing this?" I ask, my voice tight as a bowstring.

"Money, sweetling. That's the short answer. Although you've been a pleasant plaything. I'm going to miss you." She drags her finger down my neck, scratching my skin with her fingernail. Goose bumps rise along my arms.

"You're going to kill me, aren't you?"

She sighs. "We have to, I'm afraid."

"We?" I become conscious of another presence in the room, lurking beyond my line of sight. I smell the faint scent of tobacco. "It's him, isn't it? Broadbent."

"Hello, Miss Carmichael." Broadbent emerges from the shadowed corner of the room and comes to my bedside, where he greets Kate with a lingering kiss. "I take it that this is a bit of a surprise to you," he says, smiling down at me.

"Some of it," I say. "But not all. Kate's a liar, and I knew *you* were a snake."

"You've always been a clever one. That's the problem. You know too much. That's why we're at this unfortunate impasse."

"Yes, I *do* know. I knew you were carrying on with my mother, and abusing my sister, even on her deathbed. You let Mama slowly poison Rebecca. But it was so easy to blame me for that, wasn't it? You are foul. A charlatan."

Broadbent's lips thin. He pushes two fingers against the skin to the left of my sternum. "Here. Here's where Katherine was supposed to place the stake, that night. But she lacked the courage. So now we've been forced to resort to other means."

He withdraws a knife from his pocket and flicks it open, its point gleaming in the candlelight. With his other hand, he raises the hem of my thin shift, exposing me. Cold air hits my bare skin. "It won't hurt, not very much at all, Miss Carmichael. The femoral artery bleeds out quickly."

I clamp my legs together tightly. I can't do much to protect myself, or my modesty, bound as I am, but I will not submit easily. "You killed them all, didn't you?"

"No. I didn't. Not all of them, in the literal sense of the word. It became too messy after Marjorie, so I hired a lackey. One of my patients with a predilection for such things and a need for money. You saw him that night, with Arabella. I was mostly concerned with obtaining their blood. The rest was for theatrics. And a bit of fun."

"It made for great theater, my love," Kate says, her voice syrupy sweet. I shoot daggers at her with my eyes. My desire for her has swiftly transformed to loathing. I want to destroy her for betraying me. For manipulating me into trusting her.

"Why did you kill them?" I ask, turning to Broadbent.

"For science. I saw an opportunity to create something new. A drug to treat my asthmatic patients and also excite the senses. Your dear sister was the key to my discovery. I noticed when I placed her in a state of heightened arousal, her asthma symptoms diminished. I drew her blood after her hysteria treatments and made an exciting discovery. An excess of epinephrine—an attribute unique to those with red hair. I've begun the process of isolating the substance. Once I've successfully synthesized it, I'm going to be a very wealthy man." He smiles. "When you escaped your grave, I saw an opportunity to capitalize on your resurrection. Casting you as my vampire enabled me to collect more samples to experiment with. Katherine and I have both read Dr. Polidori's work. It was easy enough to make you our vampire."

"Indeed," Kate chimes. "It was a brilliant idea, husband."

He shrugs, as if humbled.

"You knew," I said, my eyes accusing Kate. "You knew he was the killer and you *helped* him."

I see it then, that flicker of pain, of hurt in her eyes. The slight shake of her head as she falls out of character and Kate, *my* Kate, returns. Her eyes slide to Broadbent, then back to me.

"Open your legs, Miss Carmichael." He approaches the bed, the knife glinting in his hands. He leans over me, grasping me by the throat. I gasp, bucking my hips. "You know, I rather enjoyed bringing Rebecca to paroxysm like this. I'd take her to the brink of unconsciousness as she met her crisis. She was so lovely when she was afraid."

Beauty is a curse . . . I just want it to be over.

How long? How many years had he abused Rebecca, tortured her, without our knowing?

Just as my vision begins to darken, he releases my throat, and I gulp in a breath of air, my heart hammering in my chest.

"Open your legs, Miss Carmichael. I don't want to force you. It's a painless death, I assure you."

But it wasn't for Arabella. I saw the pain, the fear in her eyes. I lock my legs together, twisting onto my side.

"Very well . . ." he says. "I can see you aren't going to make this easy." He crouches over me, rolling me onto my back. "Katherine, if I could have you—"

A loud crack shatters the air. Broadbent yelps, falls to his knees. Blood pours from his shoulder, staining his shirtsleeve crimson.

Kate stands there, a pistol in her trembling hands, her eyes wide and frightened.

"You double-crossing bitch," he roars, clawing at her legs.

She kicks him off, then rushes to the head of the bed, her fingers working at the fabric binding my wrists. "I missed."

"Me, or him?"

"Heavens, Lil! *Him.* His heart."

"Forgive me if I don't trust you."

"We'll talk about everything later. But I only had one bullet in that gun, and I never was a crack shot. He won't stay down for long. We must hurry."

Broadbent groans, still writhing on the floor.

She frees my wrists, and I whip one hand out, slapping her. "I hate you."

"No you don't." She grins. "You're a terrible liar. Now, make haste and follow me."

"Why should I trust you?"

"Because I've saved your life three times now, sweetling. This is the fourth. You have no reason not to trust me."

"No reason? You can't be serious."

Broadbent is up on his knees now, and as I watch in horror, he pulls himself to his feet with an angry roar.

"Told you he wouldn't stay down for long," Kate says. "Come on."

Suddenly, an idea breaks through the fog of my panic. A brilliant one. I follow her out of the room, then grasp her by the arm, turning her. "I have an idea, too. But you must listen to *me*, for once."

She looks at me, one eyebrow arcing. "What is it?"

"The widow's walk. We'll lure him up."

She gestures to the stairwell. "But there are weapons in the kitchen house. Knives. I thought . . ."

"It's too risky, Kate. He's stronger than us, even injured. We can't fight this one out. We have to trick him."

"This had better work," she says. "If not, we're stuck on a roof with a madman who wants both of us dead. I don't like our odds. Not one bit."

"They're better odds than yours. He's like a rabid bear."

"Fine." She shakes her head and leads the way to the attic stairs. My legs are weak as jam as we begin to climb, my head cloudy with dizziness.

"I lied to you, Lil," Kate says over her shoulder.

I bark a laugh. "Imagine that."

"You asked why I did it. It wasn't about money. It was about revenge. He recognized me at the party. At Barbara's. Then he discovered that you and I were lovers. That we were living together. He's been following us ever since. But I didn't know he was the killer. Not until last week. I put things together when I saw the vials of blood in his armoire. Lionel always had a cruel streak. A curiosity around morbid things. But I never imagined it would go so far."

I look up at her as we make the final three steps into the attic. Darkness surrounds us, but I can see the gleam of her eyes in the shadows. She reaches for my hand. "I'm sorry it came to this. But he asked me to kill you. He paid me a great deal of money to do so because he was afraid. The last victim—the young woman from Florida, Sophie, I believe—she didn't die right away. She remained conscious long enough to tell a guardsman that Broadbent accompanied her into the gardens at the ball on Daniel Island, then simply watched as another man—his hired man—attacked her. She described the event in detail before she expired. Sophie was the first of his victims who didn't know him. Most of the victims were his patients. They trusted him. He'd lure them somewhere alone, or send them out to meet a friend, and then set his man on them like a dog."

We know about the six women who have died by his machinations. Seven, including my sister. How many more have died in secret, of so-called natural causes, over the years? He's had access. Time. Medications. The thought sickens me.

"I had my reasons for continuing the deception," Kate says. "I let him believe I regretted leaving him. That I wanted to reconcile. I can play the submissive damsel when it suits me. His ardor for me . . . was undiminished." She sighs in the darkness. "I knew he was here, in Charleston, looking for me, just as my father warned me. I managed to avoid him for all these years. But I no longer want to hide in the shadows, Lil. I want him dead so we can be together, without fear. So I lured him here with the intention to kill him. And I'm sorry I failed." Her hand tightens around mine.

"And my public execution? Our act? Was that your idea, or his?"

"Mine. I swear I came up with the idea myself, to make all of this stop. When I told him our plan, he paid me to follow through. To actually kill you. I never would have done that, Lillian. I was going to use the money to start our new life together. And no matter what happens next, how this all ends, please know that I love you. Only you. And I never meant to bring harm to you. Ever."

While I don't believe her, and will never trust her again, for the moment, I acquiesce. "I believe you," I say.

"Katherine!" Broadbent's voice is strained. Angry. A loud clatter rumbles up from the base of the stairs. Then a thump. And another. Slow and deliberate.

"He's coming," I say. "To the roof."

We climb the rickety staircase and push through the trapdoor, onto the widow's walk. There's a storm brewing in the distance. The scent of rain-charged air surrounds us as the wind rustles my thin shift around my knees. I beckon Kate to the railing, praying the metal is as weak and brittle there as the section I leaned against just yesterday.

A few moments later, Broadbent emerges through the trapdoor. He's wrapped a tourniquet around his arm, and while his sleeve is soaked with blood, he seems little worse for the wear.

"Stupid whores," he growls as we huddle together near the railing. I can feel Kate trembling. She's frightened. Consummate actress that she is, I can't fathom what it took for her to summon the courage to allow him to touch her again. Though I can't forgive her for her betrayal, I understand why she did what she did. We're two of a kind, in many ways. I've been acting my entire life as well. The dutiful daughter. The loyal older sister. I've always known that no one was coming to save me. Not then, and not now. It's up to me to save myself.

Broadbent walks slowly toward us, leering.

"When I say so, move away from me," I whisper to Kate.

"I won't, Lil. I won't leave you."

I sigh in frustration. "For once, will you listen to me?"

"Katherine . . ." Broadbent says. "Come here. I'm not angry with you. All is forgiven. We'll leave here, put all of this behind us."

I grasp Kate's arm, holding her in place next to me. We need to keep him talking. Disarm him with guile. "Why?" I ask. "Why did you have to kill those women? You said you did it for science. But couldn't you have taken their blood without murdering them?"

"I suppose so," he says, shrugging. "But the component of fear is vital. Your sister was special to me, in that respect. After her death, my studies suffered."

I stiffen, regarding him coldly.

"Rebecca was the genesis. The inspiration for my research. When her asthma showed a marked improvement with manual stimulation, along with her hysteria, I increased her sessions. With your mother's permission, I began seeing her three times a week. I would do bloodletting after each session, to see the cause and effect of my treatments—that's how I discovered her blood had special properties. When I injected myself with Rebecca's blood, it enhanced my energy. My arousal. Made me sexually insatiable. I knew I'd discovered something remarkable. I began letting the blood of my other female patients after stimulating them, to test my hypothesis, and observed the same phenomenon—but it was markedly pronounced with redheads."

Bile rises in my throat, knowing that this man violated my sister's trust and her body. Used her. Used my mother. Used me, for a scapegoat, so that he might continue his disturbing experiments after Rebecca's death unchecked.

"Do you know what the French call the paroxysmal crisis? *La petite mort.* The little death. So *I* thought, if Rebecca's levels of arousal peaked after reaching crisis, how much more might they rise if she believed her life was in peril?" He grins wickedly. "So I entered the second phase of my experiment. I began choking her to the point of unconsciousness during stimulation. Her blood sang with elevated humors!" This man was no doctor, driven by goodwill. He was a sadist who reveled in inflicting pain and fear. And we'd never known. Not until the week of her death, when I witnessed his abuse of Rebecca myself. Why did she never tell us? Was she afraid we wouldn't believe her? Did she truly feel he was helping her, until the point it became unendurable?

Looking back now, there were signs. The high-necked gowns she favored in the last year of her life, probably to hide the bruises he left on her skin. The nightmares. Her insistence on my presence when he came for house calls.

I hold back a sob, doing my best to harness my fear. My anger. Kate squeezes my hand and I glance at her. Tears glisten in her eyes, too.

"I was going to test your blood, too, my dear. That night, at the Kincaid party, you almost fooled me with your auburn wig and Scottish accent. You were going to be my next conquest, after Arabella. And then I recognized those violet eyes. Just like your mother's."

I push aside my guilt over Rebecca and face him full-on, my rage a cold fire. "Well, now you have me. Do whatever you like."

"Oh, you're of no use to me medically. But I do have to kill you. You know too much. And then I'll go elsewhere, with Katherine at my side. Set up a new practice in another town. I have everything I need to continue my work."

Anger floods through me. "You bastard."

"You're right about that," he says, laughing. "I was a whore's son. But I lifted myself quite well, I'd say."

"Our father would be ashamed of what you've become, Lionel," Kate says, her voice shaking. "You've used the skills he taught you for evil. Broken your oath. I won't go with you. I won't leave Lillian."

"You're a fool, Katherine. My discoveries will change the world. Men will praise me as a god of medicine. If you won't come with me, I'll have to kill you. Is that really what you want?"

I slide my foot toward Kate, cueing her to step away from me. I glance behind me. The rusted railing is just beyond my fingertips. Inches from my back. The wind picks up and hard rain begins to fall, pelting my face with cold droplets. "They won't praise you, Broadbent," I taunt. "You'll be reviled as the murderer you are. You're a monster. A predator. My mother knows what you did. I put it all together, sitting in her parlor this afternoon. She's going to the authorities." It's a lie, but I need to inflame his rage. Need to make him charge me, like a maddened bull.

He laughs. "She won't betray me. She's destitute. A pariah. And if she does go to the authorities?" He shrugs. "She'll be easily disposed of as well."

The rain is falling in sheets now, half obscuring him from view. But I don't need to see him to fire my final poisoned arrow. My heart gallops, but I will my voice to steady.

"I don't think there was anything special or different about my sister's blood. Or any of the others. I think it was only an excuse for your violence. So, tell me, Doctor, why it is that you must inject the blood of a frightened woman in order to become aroused? Do you lack the will and ability on your own?"

"You sharp-tongued little cunt," he snarls.

I laugh, knowing it will agitate him further. "So, it's true, then! You're impotent."

He lunges, hurtling toward me. At the last possible second, I shift to the left. Broadbent slips on the wet tar roof, stumbling forward. Just as I hoped, he puts out his hands to catch himself on the railing. But it's too late. His height, his weight, and the slippery roof all conspire to send him careening forward. With a screeching groan, the rusted railing gives way, and Broadbent plummets with a scream. Kate rushes to my side, and together, we peer over the edge of the roof. Broadbent lies crumpled on the ground, four stories below, his leg twisted, his eyes open to the weeping sky as a pool of blood slowly spreads beneath his head.

Kate leans into me, sobbing. I close my eyes, my whole body shaking. I've just killed a man. Yes, it was in defense. Yes, he deserved his fate. He murdered and abused and violated countless women. But I'm sobered all the same. My innocence is gone. I'm now the murderer I was always accused of being.

❧

The rain continues all night and well into the next day. Kate and I hole up inside the house until the storm passes, and then together, after nightfall, we drag Broadbent's body into the marsh at high tide. The swollen waters and the alligators will do the rest. If anything remains of him to be discovered, by that time, we'll be long gone.

But as we resume our preparations to leave, and go together to purchase new tickets for our departure, my resentment builds instead of diminishing. Though Kate claims she didn't know Broadbent was the killer until recently, I can't be sure whether she's lying. And she definitely knew he was the killer before we performed our act. I remember the nights she went out as Varina, supposedly to private parties. Was she meeting Broadbent instead? She endangered my life by luring him here. If I hadn't gone to town, and had been here when she came home with him, how differently would things have played out? As it was, they both waited in ambush for me. Kate's plans could have gone wrong at any point. Despite her claims of revenge, it doesn't add up. Not completely. And while I understand why she wanted him dead, why she wanted vengeance, she still took his money and agreed to murder me.

Did she *ever* love me, or was our affair merely another one of her acts? She ravished me, made me soft with her tears, her pronouncements of love. Then she used my submissive nature and my eagerness to please to her advantage. On the night of our performance, her unearthly coldness was almost demonic. Was she tempted to see it through, as Broadbent had asked her to? Would she have killed me? Had her dominance over me been a prerequisite to murder, a way to lower my defenses?

I'll always wonder, but I'll never ask her these questions. She's a phenomenal actress and a practiced liar who will only tell me what I want to hear. But everything that's happened has reframed my memories of our love. Her deception has destroyed my ardor, and I'm grateful we've been too occupied with our travel preparations for her to make any intimate overtures. Still, I pretend that everything is fine. I indulge Kate's excitement over our journey. We don't talk about Broadbent, or what happened, but I'm afraid. Afraid that someone will notice he's gone missing and start asking questions. There's no doubt that it's time to leave Angel's Rest, and Charleston. But as the hours grow nearer to our departure, I'm filled with apprehension.

The next morning, I dress and sit on the foot of our bed, watching Kate tie her cravat. She sees me in the mirror and turns to me, smiling serenely. "When we get to London, we'll marry as soon as we can find a magistrate. I've had all the paperwork drawn up, declaring that I'm Alexander Mayhew. Baptism certificates and the lot. No one will ever know I was once Katherine O'Malley. But first, we'll need to find a place to live. With Broadbent's money, we can afford a nice flat."

The money he gave you for agreeing to kill me.

I only smile. "That sounds lovely."

She crosses the room, cradling my face in her hands. "We're finally going to live the life we've always wanted. Together."

As we row away from Angel's Rest, I watch it grow smaller and smaller, until I can only glimpse the widow's walk over the tops of the trees. Leaving is bittersweet, but overdue. I think of Papa. Mother. Rebecca. My childhood years. I'll have to leave all of it behind. Construct a new past, a new future. One bigger than myself. One with true purpose, even if I'll have to tell a few lies along the way and carry my scars with me forever. Kate strokes the oars steadily and evenly as we cut through the marsh. I close my eyes and listen to the sounds of birdsong. I inhale the scent of jasmine hanging in the briny air. I hold out my hand and let it brush through the green, tender spartina. I savor every moment I have left here. I think of Ruby, and Noah, and the first time I ever saw Kate. This place is magical and generous. It saved me. It showed me freedom and who I truly was.

Freedom. Something everyone deserves.

When we reach Haddrell's Point, Kate moors our rowboat and offers her hand to help me out. We walk to the steamer office, where Kate gives the porter our bags. I didn't pack everything in mine. I've kept my pouch of jewelry, money, and the remaining fishing hook, twine, and matches Ruby gave me in my pockets instead.

As we make our way to the pier, Kate is animated, invigorated by her London ambitions.

"Just think, Lil, I'll perform on the same boards Shakespeare once trod upon!" she exclaims. She insists we buy ices and sit on the pier to watch the ships come into port. I keep my face well hidden within my poke bonnet, and no one spares us a look, even when the quay fills with waiting passengers. We're any normal couple. A man and his wife preparing to go on holiday.

A cheerful toot comes from the harbor. "There she is, sweetling," Kate says giddily. She stands, pulling me up with her as the double-wheel steamer chugs into port, her masts high. The flag of Great Britain and Ireland flies proudly from her rigging.

Kate is beaming. Beautiful. This is her dream. What she's always wanted.

My heartbeat thunders in my ears. The air is suddenly too thin, my corset too tight. Kate pulls me close, chattering on about the ship and how handsome it is. My head begins to spin.

"I should visit the privy before we go," I say, pulling free of her arms. "I'll be right back."

"I'll come with you," she says.

"Really, I'll only be a moment, my love. Stay here and hold our place in line."

I push through the crowd, my heart a wild drum behind my ribs. When I get to the boardwalk, I turn and look behind me, where Kate stands on the pier, a tall figure in a tailored suit, her face tilted toward the sun.

EPILOGUE

Thirty years later

I broke both of our hearts that day. I couldn't destroy Kate's dreams, nor demand she stay with me. But I could no longer sacrifice my purpose, or betray my conscience, for the sake of her happiness. I am my father's daughter. I always have been.

After I left Kate at the dock, I hid until her ship departed, then booked a ticket for New Orleans. On the steamer that took me south along the coast, I stole from every finely dressed man or woman I could. Then I took another riverboat and went north to Baton Rouge, where I stole some more. I stole from the rich all along the Mississippi, until I got to Saint Louis, where I found a wealthy widow, just like Kate had, and asked for a job at her boardinghouse. She died two years later. And that's when my real work began.

I don't know how many souls I hid in the basement of that boardinghouse over the years. How many I helped ferry across the river to Illinois. To freedom. It doesn't matter. I saw the work that needed to be done, and I did it without fanfare, just like every other agent on the Underground Railroad. I hid the enslaved belowstairs, and on the upper two stories, I boarded only women. Those in desperate situations. Unwed mothers. Ill-used wives. Women like me and Kate. As Mary Jones, the former governess from Charleston, I taught those who wished to learn: reading, writing, and basic arithmetic. Gave them the skills they'd need to survive.

I took a few lovers over the years. The body has its needs, after all. All of them looked like Kate. Rangy and confident, with dark hair and blue eyes. Though I shared my body, I never again trusted another with my heart. As for my mother, I sent her letters by way of Aunt Tillie, with no return address. Sometimes I sent her money, when I could afford to. Forgiveness is a complicated thing. There will always be a part of me that will remain angry. Bitter. But despite all her shortcomings, I know my mother loved me, in her broken and flawed way. I learned of her death at the end of 1860, mere months before Fort Sumter fell. I had no regrets after her passing. Only peace.

During the long, bloody years that followed, as war ravaged the country and tested my fortitude, I considered how much easier my life might have been if I'd boarded that ship bound for London. I often thought of Kate and followed her successes in the papers. Her roles at Covent Garden: Cherubino. Orlando. Count Orlafsky. But even though I longed for easier times, the war showed me how resilient I was. How brave I could be. I thought of our family motto often: *Tout Jour Prest*. Always ready. When the war ended and slavery was abolished, I left the boardinghouse to one of the young women in my employ and booked a ticket to London to see Kate's final performance as Orpheus. It was time to begin again, once more.

I'd love to tell you that Kate and I reunited, that we fell into one another again like waves fall upon the shore. We didn't. I only watched her on that stage—beautiful, majestic as ever, her mane of dark hair now silver. I worshipped her from the front row, her every word a ravishment. Her eyes met mine, once, and held them for a moment, a look of incredulity washing over her features. After the curtain fell, I waited outside the theater, hope in my heart. It was snowing, fluffy, fat flakes the size of dimes falling onto my shoulders. As I was about to give up and walk to my hotel, I saw her exit the rear doors, but she wasn't alone.

She had a young woman on her arm. Pretty, petite, with a heart-shaped face and rapturous eyes that gazed up at my first love—my only love—with complete adoration. Hidden as I was inside my cloak, they strode past me with nary a glance. I heard Kate's laughter as they walked away. That young woman might have been me, in another life, had I not made my fateful choice that summer day long ago. But some things are best left to memory. Kate's love was of a kind I dared not keep.

The next day, I boarded a train bound for Scotland. It was easy enough to find Papa's family. To this day, there's still a pub on the high street with our name, owned for generations by my Carmichael kin. When I arrived, I went inside and greeted the barkeep—and learned he was my second cousin twice removed. Before long, the whole of the Lanarkshire Carmichaels and Douglases welcomed me into their fold, with eager questions about America, our terrible war between the states, and Papa. I regaled them with stories, embellishing things along the way, as copper-haired children played at my feet and doddering aunties served me cups of mead and cider. Finally, I'd found home. Finally, I'd found somewhere I belonged.

With my savings, I bought a stone cottage tucked into a green hillside, then a cow, and a dog that reminded me very much of Walter. And I began to write down this tale, so that you might know that my two deaths weren't the end. They were only the beginning . . . of everything.

AUTHOR'S NOTE

The idea for this novel came to me one rainy winter night during my research for *The Devil and Mrs. Davenport*, when I encountered the story of Mercy Brown, a young woman in late-nineteenth-century Exeter, Rhode Island, who was suspected of being a vampire. After several members of the Brown family succumbed to tuberculosis—known as consumption in those days—their bodies were exhumed for postmortem examination. Unlike the rest of her family, Mercy's corpse bore no signs of decomposition, and her skin still held a marked lividity. The superstitious townspeople made the conjecture that Mercy was undead, and responsible for the deaths of her kinfolk. Her body was desecrated, her liver and heart burned, and the ashes used to make a decoction for her ailing little brother, in a futile attempt to save his life. He also, unsurprisingly, succumbed to tuberculosis.

But Mercy wasn't the first victim of this vampire panic. Another young woman in Exeter was suspected of being a vampire almost a century before—Sarah Tillinghast, who was treated much the same way as Mercy. The Great New England Vampire Panic ultimately spread to many states along the Eastern Seaboard, although I could find no evidence of it extending all the way south to Charleston. The myths and superstitions around these events persisted for decades, and bodies of those under suspicion of being vampires were still being exhumed and desecrated in rural areas of America as late as the early twentieth century.

While it may be difficult to believe that such a thing could happen, until knowledge of germ theory was more widespread at the end of the Victorian era, modern medicine as we know it today was in its nascent form. The causes of many contagious diseases and infections were unknown, and doctors still performed surgeries in bloodstained frock coats, often operating in open theaters where sterilization and standards of hygiene were negligible.

I chose to set *The Two Deaths of Lillian Carmichael* in 1853 because, at that point in time, early stethoscopes weren't widely available, nor sensitive enough to detect a shallow heartbeat, and premature burial was an unfortunate possibility—enough so that graves sometimes had coffin bells attached, with a cord leading into the decedent's coffin, so that if they woke, they might ring the bell to alert the undertaker, and have a chance at surviving their early interment. The fear of being buried alive was so prevalent in the era that "safety coffins" and other elaborate mechanisms were invented to prevent premature burial, although there's no proof that any of these methods were successful. Premature burial has been used as a plot device by authors of gothic fiction and horror countless times, most notably by Edgar Allan Poe. It's so compelling because being buried alive is something universally feared.

Lillian's premature burial due to catalepsy was based on a real event—that of Rufina Cambaceres, a young Argentinian socialite who was buried alive after a cataleptic seizure in 1902. Catalepsy is a neurological condition like epilepsy, another condition that wasn't widely understood in the nineteenth century and often led to mystical suspicions of demonic possession or witchcraft. During a cataleptic episode, the victim often falls unconscious, with shallow breathing and a barely discernible pulse, and a marked rigidity that mimics rigor mortis. Extreme psychological stress and trauma are known triggers for these episodes, as with many neurological conditions. Being led to one's own execution would certainly be traumatic enough to induce such an event.

The medical and sexual abuse that Lillian's sister Rebecca endures in this novel was unfortunately not unusual. The Victorian era was rife with medical malpractice and quackery. Snake oil salesmen and doctors of negligible educational background abounded. Women were especially prone to being victimized by charlatans and were often unwitting test subjects for their doctors. For thousands of years, "hysteria" was a blanket term used to explain any disorder afflicting women that the medical establishment could not readily define, and the treatments for hysteria were brutal, and often sexualized. Cold baths, bloodletting, and manual stimulation of the sex organs were all utilized to treat "hysterics." While some of these treatments led to more understanding of gynecological anatomy—as well as the eventual realization that women could experience orgasm—the catalyst for these treatments initially had little to do with a woman's sexual pleasure. Male doctors, usually at the bidding of frustrated husbands and fathers, would treat their female patients at their homes, or in-office, and sometimes these treatments took hours. If the woman's condition proved intractable, she was often institutionalized. Conditions such as migraine, seizure disorders, depression and anxiety, what we now know to be PTSD, asthma, dysmenorrhea, and infertility were often treated as manifestations of hysteria. In my research on hysteria, I consulted two works by Andrew Scull: *Desperate Remedies: Psychiatry's Turbulent Quest to Cure Mental Illness*, and *Hysteria: The Disturbing History*. For general research on quackery in the Victorian era, I read Lydia Kang and Nate Pederson's excellent and highly entertaining *Quackery: A Brief History of the Worst Ways to Cure Everything*, and *The Quack Doctor: Historical Remedies for All Your Ills* by Caroline Rance.

Dr. Broadbent's fascination with redheads and red hair has a basis in medical fact. Redheads are genetically different. Surgeons, dentists, and anesthesiologists have long held anecdotal evidence that redheaded patients often require more anesthesia and have a unique response to pain. In a study published in 2021, led by a team of doctors funded by the NIH, these anecdotal observations were finally confirmed. The physicians conducted their studies on red-haired mice who carried the MC1R gene variant, the gene responsible for creating the redhead's distinctive pigmentation. The mice showed a higher tolerance to pain, but an increased sensitivity to opioid painkillers. While my own natural hair color is more on the dull auburn side of the spectrum, I have a markedly high tolerance for pain, it takes a greater amount of lidocaine to numb me, and certain conditions like eczema and allergies/asthma have been a lifelong struggle. I'm also Rh-negative—which tends to be more common with redheaded people.

Research has also shown that redheads excrete more adrenaline when their nervous systems are excited. The existence and physiological effects of "nervous excitement" were just beginning to be observed and studied during the time period in which this novel takes place, though adrenaline—or epinephrine—was not clinically isolated and identified until 1901, when a Japanese chemist named Takamine Jōkichi was able to effectively isolate and purify the hormone, leading to lifesaving advancements in the treatment of asthma and, eventually, anaphylactic shock. We have Dr. Takamine to thank for our modern asthma inhalers and our EpiPens. I took advantage of artistic license to have my fictional Dr. Broadbent discover the effects of adrenaline well before actual science caught up. In many ways, Dr. Broadbent was ahead of his time. But genius during the early decades of modern medicine was often a hairbreadth away from obsession.

Redheads were very much in vogue during the mid-nineteenth century, thanks in part to the Pre-Raphaelite Brotherhood and their elevation of the red-haired "stunner" in their paintings. Plagued by stereotypes, the redhead has been considered both Madonna (Queen Elizabeth I is an example) and harlot (Mary Magdalene is often depicted as a redhead). But no matter the circumstance, the redhead is always symbolic of the uncommon. *Red: A Natural History of the Redhead* by Jacky Colliss Harvey is a fun and informative exploration of redheads' unique characteristics and their place in cultural history and helped aid my research and give background to my antagonist's unhinged fixation.

Writing a novel set in the pre–Civil War South requires sensitivity, honesty, and a respect for history and the people who lived it. In my research, I focused on the decade leading up to the Civil War, and the rumblings of unrest that were stirring in Charleston, South Carolina, and other major Southern cities. Charleston was a thriving port city in the mid-nineteenth century, driven by its heavily agricultural economy. Sea Island cotton, rice, and indigo were all major exports, and the plantations that provided these crops were plentiful throughout the Carolinas. But these thriving plantations could not run without the unpaid labor of the enslaved people who were forced to toil relentlessly for the benefit of wealthy landowners, under brutal conditions. Charleston was a major hub in the transatlantic slave trade, with an estimated 40 percent of enslaved Africans coming through its ports. It is impossible to talk about the history of Charleston without acknowledging the hard truths of slavery in a city where almost every brick bears the fingerprints of enslaved people.

The propaganda around slavery was rife in the South, and slavery apologists were consistent with preaching about the "benefits" of slavery for the enslaved. All anyone has to do is read a newspaper or magazine from the era to see the evidence of this collective gaslighting. The planter aristocracy, known as the chivalry, were so entrenched in their world of vanities and social graces that they imagined themselves a kind of American nobility, and their priorities reflected their grandiose fantasies. Elaborate balls and evening promenades on the city's Battery—the elevated seawall protecting the city peninsula—were an opportunity to see and be seen, and an obsession with the works of Sir Walter Scott and the chivalric code prevailed. All the while, the gap between the rich and the poor increased, and inequities abounded.

It was for this reason that I chose to set the novel in the 1850s, at the cusp of the Civil War, in an era where an abolitionist's daughter would have undoubtedly witnessed the injustices at hand. While white abolitionists living in the South like Lillian and her father were a rarity, due to the inherent danger of such a role, there were examples, such as Angelina and Sarah Grimké, daughters of a wealthy Charleston slaveholding family whose strong sense of justice transformed them into ardent abolitionists, and James Birney, a former slave owner from Kentucky who became one of the most influential members of the abolitionist movement. There were also several undercover agents who were able to accurately convey the atrocities of slavery they witnessed firsthand to sympathetic lawmakers and the abolitionist presses. Lillian's father in this novel is one of those undercover agents.

Several books informed my research on the social and political landscape of pre–Civil War South Carolina. *A Short History of Charleston* by Robert N. Rosen provided an excellent overview of Charleston's history, and Erik Larson's *The Demon of Unrest*, while mostly focusing on the events leading up to the fall of Fort Sumter, also provided abundant information about Charleston's cultural and class distinctions during the antebellum period. *Mary Chesnut's Civil War*, written by diarist Mary Chesnut, was a vital primary resource for what life was like for a white, upper-class woman living in Charleston during that era.

For my research on slavery, the Underground Railroad, and the abolitionist movement, I reread Frederick Douglass's *My Bondage and my Freedom* and *How the Word Is Passed: A Reckoning with the History of Slavery Across America* by Clint Smith, a wide-reaching exploration of the history of slavery and its impacts into the modern day. *On Slavery and Abolitionism: Essays and Letters* by Sarah and Angelina Grimké was an invaluable firsthand resource. Documentaries such as *American Experience: The Abolitionists* and *The Underground Railroad: The Paths & Places of Refuge* provided a wealth of information. For my research on the rich culture of the Gullah Geechee people of the Lowcountry, I consulted *The Gullah: People Blessed by God* by Llaila Olela Afrika as well as *Gullah Geechee Heritage in the Golden Isles* by Amy Lotson Roberts and Patrick J. Holladay, PhD.

Finally, the most pleasant and educational aspect of my research for this novel was journeying to Charleston, South Carolina, to walk the same streets as my characters and learn as much as I could about the Lowcountry marshes where Lillian took refuge. Several local tour guides, librarians, and historians provided vital information to help support my research. Special thanks to Dave M. with Bulldog Tours, a fellow history buff who led my tour of the Old City Jail and told me where the gallows and the potter's field were located during the era of Lillian's imprisonment. My inclusion of Lavinia Fisher, Charleston's most famous ghost, and the first woman to ever be hanged in South Carolina history, was inspired in part by Dave's fantastic storytelling during my tour. Thanks as well to Lisa, also with Bulldog Tours, who led a wonderful historical walking tour of the Charleston Peninsula and answered my questions concerning government, agriculture, sex work in historical Charleston, and the social lives of Charleston's elite. The story about Lillian's grandmother having met George Washington during his visit to the city was inspired by Lisa's tour. She also provided invaluable information about many of the historical homes and buildings on the Peninsula, and if you ever get the opportunity to visit Charleston, I highly recommend Bulldog Tours.

The librarians and archivists at the Charleston County Main Library were incredibly helpful with sourcing historical maps of the Peninsula, Hog Island (now Patriot's Point), and Mount Pleasant. I spent an entire morning inside the South Carolina Room with a magnifying glass, snapping pictures of street names, the locations of artesian wells in the historic district, and the names of the wharves along the waterfront. Many thanks to the staff for their willingness to aid in my research. *The Charleston Time Machine*, a podcast by Dr. Nic Butler sponsored by the Charleston County Public Library, was also an invaluable source of detailed information about historic Charleston. Dr. Butler provides a wealth of knowledge for anyone looking to learn more about Charleston's history. I highly recommend his podcast.

The true highlight of my trip, and the most vital to my research, was the ecotour I took of the Carolina salt marshes with Carolina Outdoor Adventures. Although it was an unseasonably frigid day, Captain Josh gamely navigated us through bracing winds and imparted priceless information about the Lowcountry ecosystem, its flora and fauna, and the importance of pluff mud. From Josh, I learned almost everything I needed to know to fully immerse Lillian in her chosen place of refuge. Many, many thanks for his patience and commitment to giving us the full experience of the marshes in less-than-ideal conditions.

Even with the breadth and depth of my research for this novel, there are undoubtedly things I got wrong. My apologies for any errors or historical inaccuracies, which are fully the responsibility of this author.

It's always my hope that my novels will spark conversation and cause my readers to consider how the past parallels our modern world. We are currently living in a time of great division. Much like the Charleston of the 1850s, the gap between the wealthy and the poor, the privileged and the marginalized, is widening. These inequities have resulted in the violent, illegal detainment of immigrants, suspicion and paranoia directed toward members of the LGBTQ+ community, inflation and unemployment, ableist policies that impact the disabled and elderly, and whispers of revolution. Right now, as I write this, the National Guard is occupying downtown Los Angeles in an unnecessary show of force meant to incite panic and civil unrest. I challenge you, as readers, to consider the ways in which our world reflects the past, and what we might do, in whatever capacity we can, to affect change in our communities—to lead with empathy, curiosity, and compassion, and to remember our humanity. Because at the end of the day, it won't be vampires or any other monster of myth that will destroy us. We're perfectly capable of doing that ourselves.

Paulette Kennedy
June 10, 2025
Simi Valley, California

ACKNOWLEDGMENTS

As always, so many people helped make this book a reality and supported my efforts as its author. Thank you to my steadfast agent, Jill Marr, for her career guidance and advocacy, as well as Andrea Cavallaro, Jennifer Kim, and Nick Van Orden and the rest of the SDLA family.

Bouquets of gratitude to my editors: Danielle Marshall, Chantelle Aimée Osman, Nancy Taylor Holmes, and developmental editor Jodi Warshaw, who has been my constant at Lake Union. I can't believe this is our fifth book together! I hope for many more. Many thanks also to copyeditor Kellie Osborne, proofreader Jill Schoenhaut, production managers Angela Elson and Jen Bentham, and cover designer Kimberly Glyder.

Many, many thanks to my publicist, Rachel Tarlow Gul, who is the most organized person I know and an amazing champion for my work. All my thanks and admiration to Lauren Ezzo, Shannon McManus, and Connor Brannigan, who bring my books to life with their voices and acting talents.

As ever, special thanks to my beloved critique partner and dear friend Thuy M. Nguyen, who is always the first to read my words, and has been my guiding light and loyal anchor for years. We are family at this point, and I cannot wait for our Vegas celebration. I'm manifesting it with all my heart!

Thank you, Mansi Shah, for your encouragement and enthusiasm when you read the first few chapters of this novel and told me it was my best yet. You gave me the confidence to pitch it to my editor, and I am always grateful for your support and friendship in all things, not just writing.

Maria Tureaud, you are a star, and we both know I wouldn't be here without you. I'll never stop telling you that, so get used to it! Kris Waldherr, you are a gothic goddess, and I am so grateful for your encouragement, friendship, and intuitive guidance ever since my debut year. Hester Fox, we are soul friends, and I just know that when we finally get the chance to meet in person, there are going to be so many tears. I admire you for your bravery, your heart, your talent. To Heather Levy, who is such a light in my life. Your sweet voice messages have cheered me up so many times! Alex Gotay, thanks for all the ways you show that you care. Jess Armstrong, you are such a beacon, and I'm so glad we are agent siblings. And a special thank-you to Christine Nolfi, who graciously welcomed me to Charleston, showed me Shem Creek, and introduced me to Mount Pleasant. Your hospitality was so appreciated.

Thanks to my author community—my gratitude list keeps growing, and there are so many of you at this point that I know I will forget someone. I don't want to hurt anyone's feelings, so suffice it to say you know who you are. I love and admire you all beyond measure! Special thanks to the authors of Blue Sky Book Chat, Business Hat, Writer in Motion, RevPit, and Write Hive.

Special thanks to podcast hosts Agatha Andrews of *She Wore Black*, Trevor Williamson of *Sley House Presents*, Tammy Takaishi of *Creative Peacemeal*, and so many others who have shared their platform with me. Your talents and work are so appreciated!

Thank you so much to every BookTok and Bookstagram influencer who takes the time to read and post about my books. I appreciate you all—whether you have five followers or hundreds of thousands.

Many thanks to my family—to Lula, my sister, who came with me to Charleston and patiently accompanied me as I checked off every item on my research to-do list. Thanks to my husband, Ryan, who is always understanding when I disappear for long hours at a time to work on my books. And thanks to Avery, who helped me brainstorm the early outline for this book. You have a gift for storytelling. You could do this thing, kid, if you wanted to. And please, for the love of God, stop calling yourself a *nepo baby*!

Thanks as always, to my Sa'dia—the Kirk to my Spock.

And finally, to my readers: Thank you. You've made my childhood dream a reality.

DISCUSSION QUESTIONS

1. Throughout the novel, Lillian's guilt over her sister's death is a recurring theme. Did you ever question her innocence in Rebecca's murder or suspect her to be an unreliable narrator? Does her inaction make her culpable in Rebecca's death?
2. When Lillian escapes her premature burial, she goes back to her childhood home but does not let her parents know she survived. What do you think you would do in a similar situation?
3. Lillian's and Rebecca's relationships with their mother are a major thematic element running through the novel. The golden child / scapegoat dynamic is common in families with a narcissistic parent. How do you think this dynamic affected Lillian and Rebecca's relationship? Do you think Lillian's relationship with her father was healthier in comparison?
4. Did you have a clear impression of what was at stake for Lillian and why she made the choices she made? Why or why not?
5. How did you feel about Lillian and Kate's relationship? Did their relationship mirror Lillian's relationship with anyone else? Do you think Lillian would have been happier if she made a different choice at the end? Discuss your feelings about the ending of the novel.

6. Nineteenth-century Charleston was rife with inequities and polarizing class distinctions. Discuss the ways in which the setting and events in the novel parallel current events.
7. Did you ever believe a real vampire was responsible for the murders in the novel? Were you surprised by the reveal? Why or why not?

About the Author

Photo © 2021 Paulette Kennedy

Paulette Kennedy is the bestselling author of *The Artist of Blackberry Grange* (2025), *The Devil and Mrs. Davenport* (2024), *The Witch of Tin Mountain* (2023), and *Parting the Veil* (2021), which received the HNS Review Editor's Choice Award. Her work has been featured in *People* magazine, The Mary Sue, *Paste Magazine*, and BookBub. Originally from the Missouri Ozarks, she now lives with her family and a menagerie of rescue pets in sunny Southern California, where sometimes, on the very best days, the mountains are wreathed in gothic fog. For more information, visit www.paulettekennedy.com.